She always had the feeling that it was very, very
dangerous to live even one day.

Virginia Woolf, *Mrs. Dalloway*

PRAISE FOR *STILL HERE*
NATIONAL BESTSELLER

"A powerful, atmospheric, perfectly plotted thriller . . . An outstanding read."

**Samantha M. Bailey, #1 bestselling
author of *Watch Out for Her***

ripping . . . Readers will cheer Clare all the way to the satisfactory res-
tion. Those new to the series will want to go back and read the first
o books."

Publishers Weekly

'The reigning queen of Canadian thrillerdom . . . [A] stay-up-past-your-
bedtime page-turner."

Reader's Digest Canada

PRAISE FOR *STILL WATER*
NATIONAL BESTSELLER

"Instantly captivating, mysterious, and relevant—Amy Stuart has done it again!"

**Marissa Stapley, *New York Times* bestselling
author of Reese's Book Club Pick *Lucky***

"Brings back the same characters in a new setting and proves that Stuart is no one-book author . . . Even better than her debut."

The Globe and Mail

"Riveting, twisty, and full of tangled secrets . . . A stay-up-all-night read. Impossible to put down!"

**Karma Brown, bestselling author
of *A Recipe for a Perfect Wife***

"Complex characters with gut-wrenching backstories propel this twisty mystery toward its shocking conclusion. I was engrossed!"

**Robyn Harding, bestselling
author of *The Perfect Family***

"Utterly compelling and intriguing, *Still Water* is a very clever whodunit with a most appealingly vulnerable protagonist . . . Warn your families before you pick up this book."

"Her prose is rich and descriptive, building suspense and creating a moody atmosphere."

PRAISE FOR *STILL MINE*
#1 NATIONAL BESTSELLER

"A gripping page-turner, with a plot that takes hold of you and drags you through the story at breakneck speed. The characters are compelling, the setting chilling, and the suspense ever-present. Add to that, Stuart has an ability to tap into the dark psychology behind addiction and abuse, and to bring these complex struggles to life in a way that stays with you for days."

"Stuart is a sensitive writer who has given Clare a painful past and just enough backbone to bear it."

"Twisty and swift . . . A darkly entertaining mystery machine."

"An impressive debut, rooted in character rather than trope, in fundamental understanding rather than rote puzzle-solving."

"Both haunting and compelling."

"Utterly compelling and intriguing, *Still Water* is a very clever whodunit with a most appealingly vulnerable protagonist . . . Warn your families before you pick up this book."

Liz Nugent, internationally bestselling author of
Strange Sally Diamond* and *Little Cruelties

"Her prose is rich and descriptive, building suspense and creating a moody atmosphere."

Quill & Quire

PRAISE FOR *STILL MINE*
#1 NATIONAL BESTSELLER

"A gripping page-turner, with a plot that takes hold of you and drags you through the story at breakneck speed. The characters are compelling, the setting chilling, and the suspense ever-present. Add to that, Stuart has an ability to tap into the dark psychology behind addiction and abuse, and to bring these complex struggles to life in a way that stays with you for days."

Toronto Star

"Stuart is a sensitive writer who has given Clare a painful past and just enough backbone to bear it."

The New York Times

"Twisty and swift . . . A darkly entertaining mystery machine."

Andrew Pyper, bestselling
author of *The Residence*

"An impressive debut, rooted in character rather than trope, in fundamental understanding rather than rote puzzle-solving."

The Globe and Mail

"Both haunting and compelling."

The Vancouver Sun

4 Oct

PRAISE FOR *STILL HERE*
NATIONAL BESTSELLER

"A powerful, atmospheric, perfectly plotted thriller . . . An outstanding read."

**Samantha M. Bailey, #1 bestselling
author of *Watch Out for Her***

"Gripping . . . Readers will cheer Clare all the way to the satisfactory resolution. Those new to the series will want to go back and read the first two books."

Publishers Weekly

"The reigning queen of Canadian thrillerdom . . . [A] stay-up-past-your-bedtime page-turner."

Reader's Digest Canada

PRAISE FOR *STILL WATER*
NATIONAL BESTSELLER

"Instantly captivating, mysterious, and relevant—Amy Stuart has done it again!"

**Marissa Stapley, *New York Times* bestselling
author of Reese's Book Club Pick *Lucky***

"Brings back the same characters in a new setting and proves that Stuart is no one-book author . . . Even better than her debut."

The Globe and Mail

"Riveting, twisty, and full of tangled secrets . . . A stay-up-all-night read. Impossible to put down!"

**Karma Brown, bestselling author
of *A Recipe for a Perfect Wife***

"Complex characters with gut-wrenching backstories propel this twisty mystery toward its shocking conclusion. I was engrossed!"

**Robyn Harding, bestselling
author of *The Perfect Family***

Also by
AMY STUART

Still Here
Still Water
Still Mine

A DEATH AT THE PARTY

a novel

AMY STUART

PUBLISHED BY SIMON & SCHUSTER
New York London Toronto Sydney New Delhi

Simon & Schuster Canada
A Division of Simon & Schuster, Inc.
166 King Street East, Suite 300
Toronto, Ontario M5A 1J3

This Simon & Schuster Canada edition March 2023

SIMON & SCHUSTER CANADA and colophon
are trademarks of Simon & Schuster, Inc.

For information about special discounts for bulk purchases,
please contact Simon & Schuster Special Sales at
1-800-268-3216 or CustomerService@simonandschuster.ca.

Interior design by Lewelin Polanco

Manufactured in the United States of America

1 3 5 7 9 10 8 6 4 2

Library and Archives Canada Cataloguing in Publication Data

Title: A death at the party / Amy Stuart.
Names: Stuart, Amy, 1975– author.
Description: Simon & Schuster Canada edition.
Identifiers: Canadiana (print) 20220410054 | Canadiana (ebook) 20220410070 |
ISBN 9781668009109 (softcover) | ISBN 9781668009123 (EPUB)
Classification: LCC PS8637.T8525 D43 2023 | DDC C813/.6—dc23

ISBN 978-1-6680-0910-9
ISBN 978-1-6680-0912-3 (ebook)

For the brothers,
Flynn, Joey, and Leo,
with all my heart

T TAKES SOME DIGGING TO LOCATE a pulse. I catch a sudden sob in my throat then press two fingers into his jugular notch. It's faint, fluttery. He breathes, long gaps between sharp inhales. One of his hands clenches into a fist then relaxes. I pull my phone from the pocket of my silk jumpsuit and unlock it. My thumb twitches, hovering over the numbers.

I won't dial. I won't call for help.

This bathroom is hot. I focus on noise. On noises. The party upstairs. His labored breathing. I'm leaning over his body.

"You did this," I say to him, my voice quivering. In my next breath, I contradict myself. "What have I done?"

My mouth burns with bile. I grip the edges of the sink and lean into the mirror. My hair is a little out of place, but I'm otherwise unscathed. I use an old comb from the medicine cabinet to regain some semblance of order. My lipstick is perfect. Never mind that my heart beats wild in my chest. That I'm dizzy. I bend to check his pulse again. Nothing. I unlock my phone. Again, I don't dial.

One hundred guests mingle upstairs. Their footsteps are muffled overhead, the music an indistinct hum. A party in full swing. No one would think to come down here, right? The door at the top of the basement stairs is closed. Unless someone comes looking for him. Or, more likely, comes looking for *me*; a hostess can only disappear from her own party for so long.

A hand grips my leg. I barely stifle the scream. His eyes shoot open. He looks right at me, frantic, pale, gasping. No! I kick my leg loose and stumble backward into the towel rack. At once, my fear is replaced by rage. Why isn't he dead yet? He *needs* to die.

"Bitch," he says, choking, garbled. "Bitch."

Then, fainter: "Nadine."

I say nothing. I back up until I am against the wall, out of his reach. Finally, his head drops to the tiled floor with a heavy thud. And I see it: the last breath leaves him in a long sigh. His fingers uncurl. His gaze falls vacant, his mouth drooping open. I smooth my jumpsuit out with my hands then count backward from twenty, bracing against the nausea, trying not to sway. Trying to hold steady. Then I approach and crouch next to him one more time.

Already his skin feels cooler. There is no pulse. He is dead. I press the toe of my sandal into his hip and give him a nudge. Or, I give his body a nudge. There is no *him* anymore.

One more time I unlock my phone. I could call 911. I could run upstairs, land among the guests, breathless, wide-eyed. I could scream: *Help!* But I don't. I won't.

Somehow, it came to this: a dead body on my bathroom floor.

One last look in the mirror. Go.

I peer into the empty hallway then close the bathroom door behind me without turning off the light. Our basement is dark and gloomy, the ceilings low enough to touch without straightening your

2

arm. I climb the stairs to the main floor and pause at the top, statue still. My skull throbs. The sounds of the party are clearer, the din of the guests and the band tuning their instruments between songs. For two decades I've railed against the labyrinthine nature of this old house, but now I am grateful for its nooks and pathways, its many exits. I squeeze through the door at the top of the basement stairs then stride the short hall and pop out in the kitchen. I expect all eyes to turn my way. But the caterers are too busy to notice me spring from this corner. I'm mercifully absorbed into their fold.

'And where were *you* at midnight?' someone might eventually ask, after he's found.

'In the garden,' I'll say. 'Or maybe the kitchen. Ask the guests, or the caterers. A hostess can't well leave her own party.'

I pluck a champagne glass from a server's tray and smile at him.

"You've been such a help tonight, young man," I say. He beams at me. I turn to Gregory, the head caterer, who dries his hands at the sink. "It's been good, hasn't it? This party?"

"It has." Gregory smiles warmly. "A lovely night."

God. Gregory returns to organizing a platter of hors d'oeuvres. I pass through the open French doors to our patio. The night is warm, and most of our guests are here in the garden. It feels almost dream-like, the string lights crisscrossed overhead, laughter spurting from the cliques gathered throughout the lawn. I survey from the door, careful not to frown, my body overheated.

Look at all these revelers, flushed and happy, colorful drinks in hand. No one seems fussed by the messy confessional that unfolded an hour ago. A young colleague of my husband's is the first person to lock eyes with me. In my fog I can't remember his name. His wife sidles up to him, her glass lifted to her lips.

"Quite the birthday party, Nadine," the wife says, her smile shrewd. "You've outdone yourself. We'll be gossiping about it for years!"

When I open my mouth to respond, a roaring sound escapes me. A cry? A laugh? A scream? I lift a fist to stifle it.

"Oh my," our guest proclaims. "Glad to see our hostess is enjoying the cocktails too."

Again, I part my lips to speak, but no words emerge.

"Well." She raises her glass and clinks it against mine. "To Nadine Walsh, our incomparable hostess. To an unforgettable party. What a night!"

"Yes," I say, gulping the champagne before anyone spots the wild tremor in my hand. "What a night, indeed."

MORNING

I T COMES DOWN TO THE LITTLE things. The fine details. Picking flowers from the garden, buying the last of the cheeses, saying a prayer to the weather gods that the rain holds off. And, of course, the hope that the day unfolds without a hitch.

My mother's birthday party is tonight, the first grand event at our house in years, weeks and weeks in the making. Months, really. It's taken me ages to convince my mother, the famed writer Marilyn Millay, that she's worthy of a celebration, that her friends and family want nothing more than to gather in her honor. And what better occasion than for her sixtieth birthday? When she finally conceded, we wrote up a guest list of more than a hundred people and sent the invitations properly, by mail. A garden party in July.

And now, here we are. The party begins at eight. In thirteen hours. The last-minute preparations await.

It rained just before dawn, but the clouds have since split open to a stark blue sky. The front lawn out the kitchen window glows moist. All signs now point to a glorious July day. I'm standing at the sink drinking

7

a glass of warm lemon water. I berate myself daily for not sitting down for an actual breakfast. How many online articles have I read that say one must sit to enjoy their food and drink? I was terrible at it in the best of times, but since the accident, since my fall, my appetite has all but disappeared. Even drinking this lemon water requires my focus.

Next to the sink, my notebook is opened to my list. I make a list every day, but today's is longer than usual. As I said: last-minute preparations.

I lift my pen and strike a line through: *Water the lawn.*

Tasks written down, crossed off.

My cheeks are warm. I didn't sleep well last night, and the few hours I did get were beset by sweaty nightmares. At one point my husband, Paul, shook me awake.

'You're talking in your sleep again,' he said.

'About what?' I asked.

'You keep saying *no.*'

'Oh,' I said.

'Your arms were flailing. Like you were breaking a fall.'

He looked worried.

'Sorry,' I said, kissing his forehead. 'I'm fine. Go back to sleep.'

More fitfulness followed. At six a.m. I gave up and came downstairs. An ungodly hour on a Saturday, and now that I'm alone in the kitchen, the quiet of the house unnerves me. I'll do my tour. That's what Paul affectionately calls it—my *tour*—the rounds I make every morning to check on my family who always sleep in later than I do. It's a habit I developed after my eldest, Isobel, was born, a balm against the many anxieties that came with new motherhood. I'm just forty now, and Isobel is seventeen. I should be long past the need to check on her as she sleeps but, well. I'm not.

I climb the stairs. They creak less than they once did; they're less slippery too. Paul insisted we add a carpeted runner after I fell down the stairs and broke my hip six months ago. Still, I tiptoe to the second floor. Old habits die hard.

The master bedroom is at the top of the stairs. I left its door ajar when I got up. I peer in to see Paul sound asleep, splayed on his back, not a care in the world. He must be alert to me on some level, because though his eyes never open, he lifts his head off the pillow as if straining to hear a distant sound. For a lawyer, Paul maintains a remarkably low level of stress. I'm tempted to crawl back in bed with him, to insert myself into the warm nook formed by his bent arm. To seduce him, even. Since the affair ended—my affair—things have been good between Paul and me. There's a renewed vigor. But I can't. Not now. There's no time.

I hover in the quiet of the hallway for a moment. For the past six months, every time I stand here, I relive it. The moment of midair suspension at the top of the stairs. That pause in time, that *oh!* I felt, more surprised than helpless or afraid.

Next to the master is Isobel's room. I know the perfect sequence to follow so that her door doesn't squeal when I press it open. I lean a hand into the doorframe before gripping and turning the knob. Her room is entirely devoid of light thanks to the expensive blackout curtains I bought Isobel this spring when sleep was eluding her. I can only make out her shadowy outline on the bed, but I do hear her breaths. It sounds morbid, but fundamentally, that's what I'm checking for on these morning tours—signs of life. Isobel's gone through hell these past few months, and it's made me fear for her. My darling girl, one year left in high school and already too well versed in how cruel life can be. I blow her a silent kiss then pull the door closed.

Damien's room is next. My son. I could blast a trumpet in his face and he wouldn't wake, so I take less care in opening his door. His room is stuffy and smells of a fifteen-year-old boy; cheap pharmacy cologne and sweat. You could set a metronome to the steadiness of his breathing. He is shirtless, his blood-sugar detector glowing white on his bicep. He's been through a lot too, my boy. A diagnosis of diabetes at ten, all the tests and processes and adjustments that came with it, not to mention two stressed and overprotective parents hovering constantly. But he's endured. He's resilient. He was a gorgeous, rosy-cheeked toddler, and now he's a gorgeous, rosy-cheeked teen. Paul often jokes that his baby face helps extract him from the trouble he stirs up. That's what worries me. Lately, Damien's been secretive, quiet. His bedroom door is always closed. There's been girl trouble. Normal teen boy things, Paul always reassures me, but my tendency is to imagine the worst-case scenario. I worry about my two kids equally. Most parents do. But if I had to delineate it crudely across gender lines, the truth is that I worry about the things that might happen to Isobel, and with Damien, I worry about the things he might *do*. I fixate on how the reckless abandon that made him such a happy boy will translate as his hormones take hold. Who was it who said: You can do your best to teach your children right from wrong, but you can't fundamentally override who they are?

I yank Damien's duvet straight and kiss him. He barely stirs. Time to go.

The final room down this hall overlooks the garden. This is where my niece, Margot, has slept for the past six months. I was in the hospital for a long time with a series of complications after the accident and transferred to rehab from there. Paul needed help at home. After I was discharged, I required support to get back on my feet. So, Margot moved in to help.

Margot is twenty-four, poised and tall, kind, and clever. I press my ear to the door and hear nothing, but I won't open it. That would be an invasion of her privacy. Margot and I have an understanding. We respect each other's time and space. I'd even say we are the keeper of each other's secrets.

It's past seven now. I need to shower and get moving. Back in the kitchen, I pick up my notebook with today's list in it. I feel a little steadier now, calmed by my tour and by the sight of my beloveds cozy in their rooms. When the kids were little, they'd routinely climb into our bed too early in the morning. Paul would pretend our mattress was a boat on choppy seas, rolling them each over and back as if they were swaying on the waves. After the game was over, we'd lie the four of us in a row, and I'd reach across the span of the bed to pull all of them into my embrace at once. Paul, Isobel, Damien, and me. My purest bliss was all of us huddled like that. The four Walshes, safe, together forever.

Back to my list. Ever since the accident, my mind has this tendency to wander, to follow memory-soaked tangents until I'm all but lost. I can't afford that today. Focus, Nadine. Collect the list, check the garden, shower, head out.

This morning is set aside for small errands. Our local commercial strip is laid out so that all can be accomplished on a simple there-and-back route along the quaint main street. Even the shop owners know me and my to-do lists, my claim to fame. I started writing them when I was a kid, a tic I inherited from my mother, and I can openly admit to how thoroughly they've governed my life. There's a box full of colorful notebooks in our crawl space that's filled with nothing but lists, my days commemorated by tasks both menial and meaningful. My lists have kept me sane through the turbulence of life as the only child to a poor single mother turned rich-and-famous writer, through my early college years and the accompanying shenanigans and heartbreak, my marriage to Paul, through my on-and-off master's degree, the births of Isobel and Damien. They've grounded me through loss, through illness, friendships, betrayal. Through it all, really.

Of course, there are some things I can only include in code. Private things, womanly things. And the affair. I've seen Paul or Isobel or Damien peek inside the pages now and then. They're curious.

'Why do you carry that notebook with you everywhere?' Isobel often asks. 'You're not a writer!'

And so, in my notebook, I write *supplies** when I need to buy feminine products, or *doctor appt** when I'd arranged to meet Lionel at the hotel. Vile, vile Lionel. To think he'll be at the party tonight.

Midway down the list is a single letter flanked by two asterisks. *C*. Colleen.

Today is not just my mother's birthday, it marks another anniversary too. Thirty years ago, my grandparents threw a birthday party for my mother on their farm. I was ten, my mother turning thirty, and Colleen, my mother's much younger sister, only fifteen. We keep a picture of Colleen on the hutch in our dining room, a portrait of her taken at sunset with the farm field behind her, frozen forever in youth. There's a story to it all, a reason my mother has long been steadfast in refusing any kind of birthday celebration. This day has always felt tainted, sad. Why? Because decades ago, the morning after my mother's thirtieth birthday, young Colleen was found dead in the barn.

Anyway.

On a fresh page of my notebook, I've written PARTY in block letters at the top. It's time to start anew, to reset the tenor of this day with an overdue celebration of my mother. And I'm ready, aren't I? I've hosted parties before, if not quite on this scale. Everything is in order.

The weather is perfect. So why I am wobbly? I've been disoriented for weeks. Anxious, fixated. For years I've been exceptionally well practiced at feigning normalcy. Since the accident, not so much.

I set down my glass and run the tap to rinse it. A cardinal has landed on the thin lower branches of the maple tree on our lawn. Only when it flies away do I realize I've been staring at it in a trance.

Behind the tree a man appears on the sidewalk in front of our home. Elderly, a newspaper tucked under his arm. Do I know him? I don't think so. But this is always the issue. We live in a neighborhood called Winngrove, an affluent-but-liberal village within a city, a contained enclave inhabited by types my mother calls *champagne socialists*—university professors, doctors, artists with trust funds. The streets are lined with century-old oaks and maples, brick houses, parks, and grocers, but the core of the city is only a short subway ride away. Upurban, Paul calls it with pride.

Paul and I moved to this house when I was twenty-three, he twenty-eight, my belly swollen with late pregnancy. In those early years, Winngrove was working class. We bought our semidetached house from the estate of an elderly woman who lived next door to her sister for close to fifty years. I loved that story, sisters with a lifetime of proximity, so much so that when we found an old photograph of them in the floorboards during a renovation—the two of them on the street facing their newly purchased semis, backs to the camera—I had it enlarged and framed to hang in the kitchen.

In those early years, Winngrove felt almost like a hiding spot, most of our friends still living with roommates in small apartments downtown. Many of our neighbors worked at the nearby chocolate factory. But we—Paul, a young lawyer, and me, recently graduated, pregnant, my rich mother willing to buy us this wide semidetached in cash—we were the harbingers of the gentrification to come. The chocolate factory closed and its building was converted into lofts. More young families began snatching up houses. A business improvement group was formed. The neighborhood took the name of its local park: Winngrove. It's a moniker meant to be both whimsical and exclusive, a village within a city, an enclave that feels set apart from urbanity while still being in it. When the second sister died in a nursing home, we bought the house next door as an income property. A few of our old friends bought on our very street. So much for a hiding spot. When you know your neighbors well, it often feels like you're under watchful eyes the moment you step out the front door.

My chest tightens when the old man out the window locks his gaze on me and waves. I don't wave back. Instead, I turn the tap again and lean forward to splash cold water to my cheeks. When I right myself, he's gone.

"Okay," I say to the empty kitchen, willing myself to move. "The party."

The party. The email RSVPs arrived in quick succession within days of mailing the invites. My mother has been gracious about the fact that most of the attendees are *my* friends. Paul's friends. In just over twelve hours, they'll land on our doorstep, thrilled to be invited to a night honoring a famous writer, carefully selected gifts tucked under their arms, each guest dressed to the nines.

I close my notebook. The cardinal has looped back to the tree. It's still early, but I'll get moving anyway. Get started. I can't slow down. I'll need momentum. To everyone else, to Paul and the kids and my mother, tonight will be about the food and the mingling and dancing, an open bar with its flowing drinks, old friends catching up on gossip, the newly divorced mixing with the married and the always-single;

our children, teenagers now, gathered in the garden's nooks with their friends, their own social hierarchies, their own troubles and petty grievances, just forming.

Tonight, we will celebrate the venerable Marilyn Millay's sixtieth birthday in truly magnificent style. What fun will the night bring? It's a party, after all. It should be *fun*.

So why, then, does the day already feel so heavy?

I DESCEND OUR PORCH STEPS AND bend in the garden to pluck any rogue weeds. A few summers ago, we replaced our front patch of grass with an array of native perennials, and they've taken hold enough to bloom in full splendor every July. Perfectly timed for the party.

The sunlight slants through the trees on a sharp angle. I shouldn't be out here in my track pants and tank top, braless, hair a mess. But it's early Saturday and our street is empty. I'll risk it.

Our block is made up of tall and wide Victorian houses, the trees mature and leafy. Years ago, Paul's law partner and lifelong friend, Seymour Dunphy, bought the house directly across from us. Then another old friend, Lionel—yes, *that* Lionel—lives half a block down with his new wife, Daphne. When the kids were younger, Paul prodded me to consider upgrading to a larger detached home on one of Winngrove's more affluent streets.

'Is four bedrooms not enough?' I asked him.

These disagreements were a function of how we each grew up. Paul's life was comfortable from the start: two professional parents, two cars, a nice home, a rambunctious older brother, a hobby farm on which to pass the long summers, lots of sports and clubs and friends within the same social sphere. Meanwhile, I was a latchkey kid, raised in a basement by a single mother who had me at twenty then struck it filthy rich when she published her first runaway bestseller the month before my fourteenth birthday. A bigger house than our already sizeable one felt like a ridiculous extravagance to me. To Paul, you stepped up simply because you could.

'It never leaves you,' I used to tell Paul when he chided me for balking at the price of furniture or the notion of lavish vacations, for insisting this home was good enough. Being poor, I meant. It never leaves you. Paul knows nothing about that.

The paperboy has again dumped the weekend edition at the threshold of our walkway instead of tossing it to the stoop. I scamper to collect it, the stone rough against my bare feet.

"Nadine!"

Fuck.

Across the street, Seymour Dunphy, already showered and dressed by seven, is also collecting his newspaper. He waves. When Seymour announced his separation from his wife, Sherry, this past Christmas and dispatched to a condo nearby, I was thrilled to have him gone. Yes, he's my neighbor. Or was. Yes, he's Paul's business partner and childhood friend. Seymour's bachelor condo is one of the new builds on Winngrove's main strip, but he's been back in the family home since his seventeen-year-old daughter, River, overdosed six weeks ago, which means I'm back to running into him too often.

I detest Seymour Dunphy. I find him spineless, insensitive. His enduring presence in our lives is a strike against my own husband. I hug the newspaper to my braless chest.

"Beautiful day for a party," he calls out.

Shouldn't you be at the hospital? I want to scream. Instead, I look to the sky.

"I hope the weather holds. Please don't feel obligated to come to-night."

"I'll be there, Nadine. You know I will."

Never has my empathy been purer than it is for Seymour's ex-wife, Sherry Dunphy, divorcée to a man in the throes of a pitiful midlife cri-sis and mother to River, an only child who, for reasons still unknown, chewed and swallowed an entire bottle of prescription pills. Beauti-ful River Dunphy, my Isobel's classmate since kindergarten. Her best friend. I can't even think of it, not now, not today. And here is her father, making small talk about a party as though he hasn't a care in the world.

Please no. He's crossing the street.

"Lazy morning?" he asks, gesturing at my clothes.

What a prick. I could punch him.

"Just getting some things done around the house before I head out."

"Right. No such thing as a lazy morning, busy bee that you are."

I swallow hard, my teeth clenched. "How is Sherry doing?"

"She never leaves the hospital. Showers and sleeps there."

As any reasonable parent would, I think.

"I'll send some food with you," I say. "I have lots in the fridge."

"I'm actually not planning to visit until this afternoon." He waves me off. "Her sister is on food duty anyway. Leftover casseroles galore."

"Good. I'm glad she has support."

A lump has formed in my throat. Whether it's sadness over River or rage at Seymour, I can't be sure. The worst of all is this: my darling daughter, Isobel, was the one who found River on her bedroom floor six weeks ago. They were supposed to walk to school together to write a biology test, but River wasn't answering any messages. Sherry often left early for work. So Isobel let herself in the house with a spare key Sherry gave me years ago. Poor Isobel, ever dutiful, called an ambulance first then called me. Paul and I rushed over. I'd just stopped using a cane after my surgery and could barely keep up with him. I called Sherry. Paul called Seymour. A chain of May morning events that tie a knot in my gut even now.

When I think about that morning, limping across the street behind Paul and struggling up the stairs to River's bedroom, seeing my own daughter lying beside her friend in bed, clutching her, begging River to wake up; when I think of it, it doesn't make me sad. It makes me angry, enraged. I brought Isobel to the police station later that day for questioning, the baby-faced detective assigned to the case asking her about River, about the state of her bedroom when Isobel found her, about her drug use or drinking, her social circle. The detective was detached. Worse, so was Isobel.

In all the late-night talks with her that followed, the trauma and resulting anxiety denying her sleep, it nagged at me that Isobel was leaving something out of the story. Her answers to the police detective's questions offered little insight. Yes, River drank now and then. Maybe she'd tried drugs. No, she didn't have a boyfriend. No, nothing out of the ordinary had happened to provoke the overdose.

I didn't believe it. I'm Isobel's mother; I can sniff out her lies. There's still something my daughter isn't telling me, something I still need to figure out.

You can't fix everything, my mother often tells me. She reminds me frequently that I shouldn't involve myself in other people's problems. Of course you can't fix everything. But shouldn't you at least try?

"Any change with River?" I ask Seymour.

"Not really. The doctor told Sherry there's evidence of things going on. In her brain, I mean. They see waves. Activity." He frowns. "But six weeks is a long time to be in a coma."

"Well. Your daughter's always been one to defy the odds."

"I suppose. She's not waking up, but the switch hasn't been turned off."

"That's reason for hope, isn't it?"

"I want to believe it is," Seymour says. "I drop in when I can."

Any time I'm able to muster so much as a ping of empathy for Seymour, he manages to snuff it out with some callously inept comment. *I drop in when I can?* Jesus. Even Isobel visits River in the hospital almost every day. Last Saturday, I accompanied her. Isobel asked Sherry if she could comb River's hair and trim and paint her nails. I watched as she did just that, doting on River with a tenderness that stabbed at my heart. Most might feel buoyed by evidence that they've raised good and caring people. But not me. I worry about my Isobel. Sometimes I even find myself questioning whether her effusive displays are feigned. She's either very benevolent or very cunning, and I'm not sure which is worse.

The entire hospital visit, Sherry sat in a corner chair with her hands folded neatly on her lap, focused only on her daughter who lay in a coma five feet away. Sherry was dressed for a winter day, the hospital air-conditioning notched so high that my teeth began to chatter. She never even met my gaze. We aren't exactly best friends, but we are neighbors. After Seymour left her, I openly took her side, much to

Paul's chagrin. We text sometimes, share stories and jokes about our beautiful girls, coordinate their schedules—or rather, we did. Over the past few months, as River started staying out late, when Isobel complained her friend was changed, distant, her grades slipping, I tried to support Sherry even as I recovered from my fall, even if she seemed in denial over the shift in her daughter. I prodded Isobel for details on River's behaviors that I might dutifully pass on to Sherry, but Isobel was tight-lipped.

Ah, well. I knew I was wrong to expect more of Sherry in that hospital room, a greeting or perhaps an update on her daughter's status, a 'Thank you for coming.' But Sherry just sat there, slumped. She appeared not sad but completely vacant, almost lifeless, her eyes like glass. After a few minutes I excused myself and walked the hall to the vending machines.

The only clear thought I could muster was: *Thank God that's not me in that chair, not my daughter unresponsive in a hospital bed. Thank God Isobel is okay.*

Now Seymour watches me.

"I'll give Sherry a call later," I say. "Maybe she can be convinced to step away from the hospital for a few hours. Drop into the party."

Seymour laughs. "If I'm at the party, she won't be."

"Right," I say. "Tell Sherry we're here if she needs anything."

He salutes me. "Will do. If I actually see her, that is."

What a relief when Seymour finally crosses the street and enters his house. How many times have Paul and I argued over this man? In my eyes Seymour has always been repugnant, often dismissive or too jokey with his underlings at work, subtly disrespectful of his wife, eventually cheating on her with only a trace of effort to hide it. Five years ago, when Paul and Seymour announced plans to leave their corporate gigs and open a boutique law firm together in Winngrove, I was still able to tolerate Seymour. These days, I can't.

'What does it say about you that *this* is your oldest friend?' I yelled at Paul in the days following River's overdose.

'He's missing a sensitivity chip,' Paul argued. 'But he's a really good lawyer.'

'It doesn't bother you that he's a bad man?'

'I don't think he's a bad man,' Paul rebutted. 'You're not right about everyone, Nadine.'

'I'm right about him.'

Paul's fundamental argument is that we should avoid sloughing off our oldest friends. They are a link to our younger selves. Keepers of our memories. Paul and I are different that way too; my friendships have never really evolved beyond the eras that formed them. When I graduated high school, I mostly moved on from my friend group there, aside from the odd reunion dinner or likes and comments on our respective social media feeds. These days, I socialize with other mothers from the kids' school or sports teams. Book clubs, dinners out, daytime coffees. Unlike Paul, I don't need anyone to keep my oldest secrets. I'm not one for unconditional loyalty. And certainly not to a man like Seymour Dunphy.

Enough. There are so many things to do. I won't let this sadness touch me today. I should get something for Sherry, add it to my list. A little gesture of kindness. But I cannot take that on right now. I need to shower and get moving.

Chin up, Nadine. No looking back. Carry on.

DUCK UNDER THE STREAM. THE WATER pelts my shower cap. I'm in the basement bathroom, my clothes draped over the towel rack. A shower in our master bathroom would wake Paul, and I don't want him awake. Not yet. The truth is, this early morning will be easier to navigate without his joviality, the inevitable logistical questions about the party to which he should already know the answers.

It's a family joke that as the earliest riser, I'm relegated to performing my morning routines in this basement washroom. To think of all that's unfolded here. Seventeen years ago, pregnant with Isobel, my water broke all over the green tile floor. And then, a few trysts with Lionel. He crept over a few times after Paul left for work, and this hidden-away bathroom felt like the one place in the house where we were safe. Later, I came down here to get through my fits of crying after the affair ended. It's not just this washroom that relegates me; my office was relocated to the basement when Margot moved in.

'What do you need an office for?' Isobel will sometimes ask, poking my sore spot. 'You don't have an actual job.'

She's right, and wrong. I *do* work. Sometimes. For ten years I've taught a general interest class in crime studies at the local college. I've even toyed with writing a true crime book, taking a few courses at the same college where I teach. I have a different last name from my mother and can evade the *Did you know that she's the daughter of that bestselling writer, Marilyn Millay?* questions easily enough. It's not so much the fear of my mother's shadow as an absence of ideas to write about. The best true crime stories have already been told.

So what? I may not work in the traditional sense, but I'm always busy. '*You're* my biggest job,' I often tell the kids. If they, or anyone else, snubs their nose at this, then what can I do?

But I do have an office. When Margot moved in, she offered to sleep down here, but I saw an opening. Paul thought I was crazy to give up my upstairs den with its south light and view of our lovely yard. It played out as a sacrifice on my part, but I prefer the dungeon feel. If I drop the blinds, my office is pitch dark even in the middle of the day. I can hear everyone overhead or descending the stairs. There is no sneaking up on me.

The strangest part of this basement, and perhaps my favorite, is the door on the wall shared with our attached tenant. Story has it, the two sisters who lived here before us had an opening punched through their basement walls as a way to flit between each other's homes. They were practical about it, installing a locking door on each side much as you'd find in adjoining hotel rooms. Paul thought it baffling and wanted to seal over the strange passageway. But I refused. I loved its quirkiness. Young Isobel christened them the Sister Doors, and that's what I've called them ever since. The door is now on the far wall of my office.

Before showering I puttered in said office for a while, forcing focus despite my fluttering heart, as if someone was watching, recording my actions for later scrutiny. I've always been a worrier, but since the accident, my brain all but malfunctions when that worry gets the best of me. I get dizzy. Sweaty. Anxious. Paranoid, even. The hardest part is hiding it from Paul and the kids. There's no point in worrying them too. I'll heal eventually.

To distract myself, I printed the final guest list in alphabetical order by last name. One long page with two columns. One hundred and ten people, including some plus ones, some older children. I even laminated it with the machine Paul bought me last Christmas. He meant it as a gag gift, an affectionate repudiation of my overly methodical ways. But the joke's on him because I use it all the time. What is better than a document encased in plastic? It's a list-maker's dream.

That laminated master guest list now sits on the bathroom counter. I exit the shower and stand naked in front of the partly fogged mirror. I'm in good shape for forty-ish. I've always worked at it. My body, I mean. Regular cardio, lots of walks, strength and yoga classes, an ugly watch on my wrist that warns me when I've been sitting too long. Indeed, the doctors told me it was my good physical shape that sped my recovery from the trauma of shattering a hip. The still-tender scar runs the length from my waist to my thigh, not yet faded from its flaming purple. A crushed bone. Surgery. An infection that kept me in the hospital for weeks. Rehab. The doctors all marveled at my luck. It could have been my head, or my spine. Paul marveled too.

Margot's arrival here absolved him in terms of helping my recovery or managing the house. She cooks and cleans, pressures me to keep up with my rehab exercises. Keeps me company. Margot is the one who circles me, looking for signs of affliction, registering the small deviations in disposition that I think I hide pretty well.

I pick up the guest list and scan it. Friends, neighbors, coworkers. Most of Paul's firm and their spouses. Some of the kids' friends too, and their parents. My mother, the guest of honor. And near the bottom, Lionel and Daphne Robinson. Shit. I figured they would back out. I can't believe they're actually coming.

Lionel. God. I've known him for twenty years. He too, like Seymour Dunphy, has long been part of Paul's cabal. He's a moderately successful journalist and has been a Winngrove neighbor for ten years. I always saw him as sort of hapless, a bachelor to be pitied in his evasive approach to love or commitment. Did I find him good-looking? Sure, in a detached sort of way. Then, one summer evening two years ago, we were alone in the garden at the tail end of a dinner party and he drunkenly professed an attraction to me that he claimed was always there. I brushed him off, ignored his advances for six months. Then what? Paul and I hit a rough patch. He traveled too much, spent too many evenings in the den. I found myself returning Lionel's gazes. What can I say? That it just happened from there? That I can't delineate what exactly led me to break my marriage vows with the worst possible choice of suitor?

The affair is over. And now, there's Daphne to contend with. His new wife, mother to his new baby. Since Lionel's elopement with Daphne, Paul and I don't hear directly from him anymore, no matter that he lives just down the block, no matter that we screwed in this very bathroom how many times? Five? Ten? In short order, he's gone from being Paul's sturdy bachelor friend, to my secret lover, to the pliant husband of a woman a decade younger than us all.

Hope you don't mind we bring the wee baby! Daphne wrote in her RSVP, her PhD signature filled with titles and pronouns and accolades that make my jaw clench. Tonight will mark my first time meeting said *wee baby*, a daughter that I'm ashamed to say I felt a little smug to hear suffered from colic at birth.

I toss the list and watch it land in the sink—laminated!—then towel off and dress. Screw you, Lionel. I can't believe he has the nerve to come tonight. What a gift it would be to never have to see him again. It's not just Lionel, though, is it? Over the years I've gathered a handful of people who've crossed us or let us down or betrayed us in ways big and small. That's what happens with age, I guess. With successes or failures, with memories of events, betrayals, and tragedies that shift with time and perspective, with new information. The list of people no longer worth your energy grows longer. People with whom the pretense of friendship, or even just cordiality, erodes me every time I'm forced to play along. People I'd just rather have gone.

Wait. Footsteps overhead. Is someone awake? I ascend the stairs and am startled to see Margot leaning into the island in the kitchen, her face in her phone. The espresso machine churns behind her.

"You scared me," I say.

Margot leaps back, hand to her chest. "Jeez!" she says. "*You* scared me. Coming up from your weirdo lair."

I laugh. "It's not a lair. What gives? You're never up before nine on the weekends."

"I couldn't sleep. I have a coffee date in a few hours."

"A date?"

"Not that kind of date. Don't worry, I know you need me around today. I'll only be gone an hour."

"No worries. I have errands to run this morning anyway."

It takes effort to squelch my curiosity about Margot's personal life. She's not my daughter, and she's twenty-four. I'm grateful that my urge to pry is somewhat satiated by Margot's liberal use of social media.

"Since I'm up at the crack of dawn," she says. "Might as well be useful. Is that okay?"

"Certainly," I say. "My God. Yes. Thank you."

There's no official title for Margot around here. She's our only niece, the only child to Paul's older brother, Eric, who lives four hours away with his wife. I don't like Eric much, but I've always loved Margot. Much to her parents' chagrin, Margot opted out of college to travel, which she did, around and around the world for nearly five years, picking up strange jobs in strange countries, forming then abandoning faraway friendships, the rest of us living vicariously through her social media posts. Her return from abroad just before Christmas coincided with my accident. She visited me at the hospital once, then regularly, and soon it was agreed she'd move in with us to help. I'd like to think this is an easy enough job for a young woman plotting her next life move. I can admit that in a few short months, she's become indispensable to me. After our kids were too old for a nanny, a hole formed in our household rituals. I like having another person around, one who doesn't constantly ask things of me. Margot has been such a blessing that I've joked rather insensitively to Paul that I'd suffer more if she left than if he did.

Margot sets about making us both our coffees. I watch her rote motions, my jittery hands pressed flat on the counter. She customizes mine with the perfect ratio of milk, then slides my favorite mug to me and returns to her post at the far end of the island.

"I'm a bit shaky," I say. "I should water this down."

"Everything's under control," Margot says. "So let's get ahold of that shakiness, okay? No need for it."

"A walk will help. I'll walk my errands."

"Where's my list?" Margot asks. "I *know* you made me a list."

"I did. It's on the bulletin board."

Margot lifts a finger, remembering something. She disappears briefly, heading toward the foyer and returning with a large gift basket.

"There was a knock on the door a few minutes ago," she says. "Look at this! Gourmet chocolates. High-end sea salt type stuff."

"Who's it from?"

"I didn't check." She rips off the card and Frisbee tosses it to me. I catch it then pry it open with a finger.

"And?" Margot asks.

"It's from the birthday girl. My mother."

"I love your mom."

"So do I," I say.

It's funny. Margot's mother, my sister-in-law, never comes up in conversation, and I see no evidence of regular contact between them. I like to think I've become a bit of a mother figure to Margot, my smugness at this offset by my fear that one day the same could happen with Isobel and me. We are close now, but who says we always will be? Some other mother-figure could easily appear in Isobel's life. The thought makes me even more jittery. God. When I look up, Margot has her phone pointed at me. I raise a hand to shield my face.

"Don't take my picture! No posts. Not today."

"Not for social, Nadine. Just to say thank you to your mom."

Margot studies me. Bless her heart, my tone has surprised her. I try, albeit not very successfully, to appear as the sort of person whose moods are steady. But lately, I can't even fake it. A few months ago, Margot offered to start a few social media accounts on my mother's behalf, a little side gig. I was fine with it, but for one caveat: no pictures of me.

Marilyn Millay, a famous writer adept at all things in life except for anything related to the internet. She's hardly even aware that a two-bit journalist, Julian Simone, tried to land an unauthorized biography book deal by selling sneak peeks into my mother's inner world to a rag newspaper. The first articles came out at the same time as her most recent novel.

"Are you feeling okay?" Margot asks me.

"I didn't mean to snap at you. I'm sorry."

"You really are on edge."

"Yes. I suppose I am."

"We'll work on that. You could take something, maybe? Don't you have some leftover pills from the hospital?"

I do. In my purse. A full bottle given to me by the nurse who discharged me. I keep them in the lining pocket of my tote bag, a security blanket. But I'd never actually take one. I can't; I know they might unhinge me.

"I don't need to take a pill, Margot. Deep breaths will do."

"Okay. Do I have your formal consent to text this photo? Only to your mom?"

"Sure. Sorry. Of course."

Her fingers fly furiously on the screen. "Should I stick the basket in the pantry for now?"

"Yes. Please."

Margot collects it and wanders away. The pantry. Jesus. Yet another room in my home soiled by memories of the affair. Most days I count myself deeply lucky that no one of any consequence—not Paul, not my kids, not my mother, not Margot—knows about my short and deeply regrettable tryst with Lionel Robinson.

The pantry was the first crime scene, if you will. A winter dinner party, eighteen months ago, six months after his first declaration. The electricity between us felt painfully obvious that night, yet Paul detected nothing. When the meal was done everyone adjourned to the living room, but Lionel followed me into the kitchen and pulled me boldly into the pantry, sliding its pocket door closed behind us. He pressed me into the shelving then one-hand caught the can of lentils that toppled and rolled off my shoulder. How easily I can remember every detail of that scene. It's embarrassing, to be honest. The clarity of it. The way I'd protested mildly at first—*They'll hear us!*—but then I'd arched and moaned so involuntarily at his touch that I was certain everyone in the other room had heard *me*. Lionel placed his hand over my mouth, his other hand up my skirt to press my panties aside. I felt the jolt of his first kiss travel down to my toes. Then he pulled away and opened the pantry door to rejoin the group before anyone found us. I couldn't breathe. I had to go upstairs and regroup in my bedroom. How flushed my cheeks were, how bright my eyes. It was the first time Lionel touched me like that, but it certainly wasn't the last.

There were a few dozen encounters between us—some at a hotel, a few in my marital bed one weekend when the kids joined Paul on a business trip, a series of daytime trysts in the downstairs bathroom, and then the pantry. I recall the nuances of every single encounter, whereas I bet Lionel wouldn't even remember which hotel he'd selected for our midday hookups.

It all lasted about three months. I felt guilty, of course I did. But my guilt was overridden by the pleasure of it. The intensity. The logistics of conducting an affair felt almost like a job. But how unceremonious men can be! Just before Easter, Lionel texted me through our secret messaging app.

I'm sorry, N. I can't do this anymore. I can't do this to Paul.

I sat in our master bathroom for six hours—yes, six—composing, then deleting, my response. **YOU can't do this to Paul???** I was smart enough to write my reply in notes outside of the app so that Lionel wouldn't see the ellipses marking my various attempts at composition. It was Margot who taught me that rule: *Never let them see your ellipses.* Also from Margot: *Never respond right away to a text message that's made you emotional. Wait at least an hour, preferably longer.* Why? Because 90 percent of the time, according to Margot, you'll come to see that no response is the best response. The cruelest, even. The most powerful.

Margot, young but still the sage of the house, the most worldly, happy to teach life lessons to her hapless, doddering aunt. And so, despite hours spent coming up with the perfect dagger words in response to Lionel's declaration, in the end I never did reply. At least not until recently, when I started hearing from him again.

"Nadine?"

I jump. Margot stands only a few feet away, clutching the list I made her. How did she sneak up on me? Were my eyes closed?

"Wow," she says. "Your jaw was literally pulsing."

"I've got a lot on my mind," I say, rubbing my forehead.

"Maybe you should lie down."

"No, no." The words come out a little too forcefully. "My mom's birthday has always been complicated. Did you know that her young sister, my aunt Colleen, died on her birthday? Thirty years ago today."

Margot frowns. "I did know that. I'm sorry. That's tough."

Naturally she knows about Colleen. I've told her the story before. Margot and I are about fifteen years apart, just like Colleen and my mother were. I probably shouldn't confide in Margot the way I do, but the truth is, she's become the person I talk to most. On the other hand, it always seemed that my mother and her much younger sister, Colleen, were not close at all. Even as a young girl, I'd notice the sharp tone of their interactions and question whether Marilyn even *liked* her sister.

"It's fine," I say, straightening up. "I'll shake it off as the day gets going."

"You always do," Margot says.

"Yes." I pause, worried that my voice might waver. "I appreciate you a lot, Margot. I think you know that."

She gives me a funny look. "Nadine. Seriously. Are you all right?"

Shit. I need to do a better job of keeping it together. I cannot crack, not this morning. But something in the way Margot asks me how I am threatens to break me open. I've often felt judged by Paul's family and friends, by almost anyone who crosses our threshold. But never by her. Normally I'm grateful for the interest Margot shows in me, in my life. But today, I need her to back off.

A long, torturous silence passes between us. Margot and I are never awkward. I muster the biggest smile I can.

"I'm fine," I say. "I'll head out now."

"Where to?"

"Paul left Damien's insulin at his office. And I need to see Zachary at the cheese shop. A few other quick stops. I won't be out long."

"Sounds good."

"Text me if you need anything," I add, my voice a trill. "Maybe we can set up the tables around lunchtime? Will you be back by then?"

"Yes," Margot says. "I'll order us salads from the café. I know you'll skip lunch if I don't feed you."

"Imagine," I say. "Me being mothered by you."

Margot circles the island, giving my shoulder a quick squeeze as she passes to head back upstairs. I finger the card that came with the gift basket before tossing it into the recycling bin behind me without reading the message.

T HE SIDEWALK STEAMS WITH REMNANTS OF the early-morning rain. Winngrove is laid out as one large residential block parceled up by a network of one-way streets. There are no big box stores or franchise chains here; only a quaint commercial strip with organic grocers and cafés, a fruit and flower stand, a few clothing boutiques, and a small and heavily curated bookshop.

I'm on that strip now, but it's still early and some of the shops aren't open. The corner store is, naturally. It opens at seven, seven days a week. I've been coming here daily for years, so much so that the owner, Marvin, and I have formed a sort of friendship. It feels almost galling that things have been tense between Marvin and me lately. He seems frosty, and until recently I couldn't pinpoint why. When I mentioned this to my mother in passing, she fell into a fit of laughter.

'Wow, Nadine,' she said. 'Only you could stir up drama with the guy who sells you cigarettes.'

The bell jingles as I enter. A portable air conditioner whirs loudly in the transom above the door. It's not Marvin behind the counter, but his daughter, Lacey. She notices me then pauses the movie she's watching on her laptop. I'm relieved actually. To not have to face Marvin.

"Hi, Nadine," she says. "You're up early."

"So are you, Lacey. A fourteen-year-old up and working before nine on a weekend? That might be a world record."

She smiles politely and shrugs. "I'm up at six every day for swim team."

"Right."

"Plus, I'm grounded."

"For what?"

She shoots me a look. I wonder if this means she's not coming to the party tonight. I regret inviting Marvin and Lacey. I'd been so excited to hand deliver an invitation to Marvin a month ago. He's a huge fan of my mother's work, and I figured he'd be thrilled to come to her birthday party. But when he opened the envelope in front of me, he made a joke about my willingness to fraternize with the unwashed.

'Unwashed?' I declared. 'I consider you a friend. People invite their friends to their parties. Are we not friends?'

He laughed as a means not to answer the question. When Lacey was small, he bought this building and opted to run the corner store it housed instead of shuttering it. They live in the apartment upstairs. For years, he's manned this store all week, then all day Saturday and Sunday while Lacey lay on the floor behind the counter, entertained by tablets and coloring books.

There was once mention of a writing career that sputtered, but Google offered me nothing to that end. I've gleaned that Marvin's wife took off when Lacey was four and started a new family on the other side of the country. I once tried to set him up with a divorcée mom of one of Damien's friends, but there was no second date, and when I pressed that mom in the schoolyard, she claimed Marvin barely said a word the entire meal.

'He's just shy,' I insisted.

'He came off as hostile,' she replied.

Marvin and I never spoke of it, and I never dared set him up again. So, yes, I regret inviting him. Too much tension. Lately I've felt the weight of Marvin's judgment. Certainly he's noticed that I'm smoking more, that I'm less put together. He's even joked about it on days I've arrived here a little out of sorts—*Did you tie one on last night?*—which irks me. Not to mention that on New Year's Eve, I caught Lacey with my own son curled under the covers in Damien's bedroom, her shirt off, bra unclasped. Every time I've encountered Lacey in the store since, I've been amazed by her lack of discomfort around me. She looks me right in the eye and smiles as if nothing ever happened.

Anyway, Marvin found out about the two of them somehow, and while he never brought it up with me directly, Damien claims I'm to blame for Lacey's new frostiness with him. I'm to blame for everything, apparently.

I know that Marvin and I aren't really friends. He's never been to my house, and I've never been upstairs to his apartment. But we've always been friendly. He asks me questions about my day, as I do about his. He's a person I'd miss a lot if he were no longer in my life. A person I trust despite no real evidence that I should.

Look at me, meandering the short aisles of the store to avoid interacting with a teenager. I don't actually want to buy anything. Even the sight of chips or chocolate makes me nauseous. I return to the counter.

"Where's your dad?" I ask Lacey.

"He's still in bed," she says. "Can you believe it? It only took about two decades to get him to sleep in."

"He deserves it."

"He really does."

Okay. Here it comes, my confession.

"I'm a little ashamed," I say. "But I'm here to buy cigarettes."

She turns to the wall behind her, unfazed. "You smoke?"

"I don't smoke anymore," I say. "Not really, anyway. Quit before the kids were born. I might smoke a few a week. Four? You know. To celebrate. Or to avoid stressing out. Ha!" I pause, swallowing. "I invited you and your dad to our party tonight, you know. It's my mom's birthday today."

"Yeah." She isn't even looking at me. "What brand do you want?"

"Oh." I'm flustered. "Camel Filters, please. The smaller pack."

She lifts onto her tiptoes to collect the package from the higher shelf then turns and places them on the counter. Is it even legal for a child to sell me cigarettes? God. Why did Marvin choose today of all days to sleep in?

"Do you need matches?"

"No."

"Okay, great," she says. "We'll see you tonight, then."

So she is coming. I thought Lacey and Damien were broken up. Are they not? Lately Damien has moped around the house, barking one-word answers at Paul and me, constantly checking his phone, frowning into his text messages in the way a boy with a broken heart might do. And now here is Lacey, suggesting she's going to show up with her father.

"Hey," Lacey says, pointing to the magazine display. "Your mom's new book came out last week."

"Yes, it did," I say. "Straight to the top of the bestseller list."

"The *Times* review was good."

I smile. "You read it? They haven't always been kind."

"Nice birthday present for her."

"Indeed," I say.

Marvin carries a collection of my mother's books on his magazine rack, an entire row in homage. What's funny is that he'd done so even before he knew she was my mother. I see her name now in bold yellow—Marilyn Millay—her most recent thriller the large hardcover at the center of the shelf. It's become a game every time I enter the store, my efforts to unload whatever supplies I've collected onto the counter without looking up and spotting her name staring back at me. One day, years ago, I waltzed in to find Marvin stocking her books for the first time.

'Do you read Marilyn Millay?' he asked me. 'I'm her biggest fan. I finally found a distributor who'll let me put in my dinky order.'

'I do read her, actually. I knew her long before she was famous.'

'That's impossible,' Marvin said. 'She was instantly famous. Her first novel sold like, ten million copies in a few months.'

'Not true. The book was released a year before it hit the bestseller list.'

At that point, Marvin grabbed his phone to verify my claim.

'I'm a reliable source,' I said, enjoying myself. 'She's my mother."

'Shut up,' he said.

'Google it. Her daughter, Nadine.'

'No way! You would have already told me that.'

'You've never told me about *your* mother,' I said, laughing.

He did not believe me. So one day, I brought my mother in to meet him, armed with a Sharpie pen to sign his inventory. When he realized it was indeed her, he began to sweat so profusely, knocking over a display of lollipops in his scramble to circle the counter and shake her hand. He was so heartfelt that my mother grew bashful, which is no easy feat. It was a wonderful scene. Thinking of it now nearly brings tears to my eyes. God, Nadine. I bite my lip and drop a quarter in the send-a-kid-to-camp donation jar next to the register.

"Thank you for supporting my terrible habit," I say to Lacey. "See you tonight, then?"

My tone is ever careful, cool. Lacey offers only a hollow smile. Her poise is certainly far beyond anything I could have mustered at her age. She returns to her perch and resumes the movie on her laptop.

Just as I turn to leave, my tote vibrates. My phone. I step outside and dig for it frantically, my heart racing. Why must my heart always be racing? Dammit. The screen lights up MM. Marilyn Millay. My Mother. I swipe to take the call.

"Are you spying on me?" I ask without a hello. "I was just talking about you."

"Are you buying cigarettes?"

"You *are* spying on me." I lift a hand to shield my eyes and search up and down the sidewalk. "Where are you?"

"In the bathtub," she says. "Relax. You sound nervous, like you're doing something you shouldn't be. I took a wild guess. Either I'm good at wild guesses or you're very predictable. Are you smoking like a little brat?"

"I'm out running errands. Everyone at home is still asleep."

"Did you get any sleep last night?"

"Not really." I look to my smart watch. "I'm headed to Paul's office, the cheese shop."

"Okay. What are you doing after that?"

"I don't know. Hosting a party for a hundred or so people?"

"Yeah, yeah. Why don't we meet at the bench? I'll bring a snack."

"Now?"

"Come on. You have a few minutes to spare. We can share a cigarette. Calm you down."

"Okay," I say. "I'll see you in ten."

"Good," she says.

We hang up. I agree, only because she's right. Winngrove Park is not out of my way. But also, seeing my mother *will* calm me. It always has. All those early years in our little underground apartment, the two of us were an unbreakable orb. We lived hand to mouth in those days, every decent meal a victory, no safety net but each other. Everything has gotten better since then, hasn't it? My mother is rich, successful. We live well, we travel, we buy fruit and cheese and meat and wine and clothes without tallying the cost. So why do I often long for the days when it was just my mom and me in our damp basement? How is it possible that that was the time in my life where I felt most safe?

T HERE'S NO WIND BUT I CURL my hand to guard the flame as I light my cigarette anyway. I'm on the park bench at the foot of the man-made hill in Winngrove Park. Any time a jogger passes I make a point to aim the smoke upward, smiling sheepishly at them, as if they give a damn about my transgression. A neighbor could walk by. Or any of Paul's colleagues. Their families. Their petty whispers. Have you seen Nadine Walsh since she took that fall? She's so thin. *And* she's started smoking.

*Re*started smoking, I'd correct them. A habit I abandoned after the kids were born and took up again after my release from the hospital. But honestly? I don't care. I'll take my chances today.

Marilyn was in the bathtub when she called, but I won't be waiting for long. My mother has never been fussy about getting ready, and her house is even closer to Winngrove Park than mine. This bench has long been our midway meeting point.

We often convene here, at this specific bench, no matter the season or the weather, a neutral zone where we are returned to our original iteration: the two of us. Sometimes I think the reason she stopped going on months-long book tours was because her absences unsettled me, especially when the kids were younger and Paul's workdays were longer. Too much time with my own thoughts. Marilyn and I are only twenty years apart, her pregnancy with me an accident at nineteen. Our age difference feels more and more narrow the older we get.

Coming! she texts. **Shoes are ON.**

No rush, I text back.

And I mean it. I feel almost relaxed sitting here, smoking on this bench like a delinquent. I pull a long drag from the cigarette and hold it until my lungs burn. I used to bring Damien to the field across from me to play soccer two nights a week. How I loved spreading my blanket on the sidelines and watching those little bodies chase a ball with the chaos of birds fighting over breadcrumbs. My mother would come too, even in the days when it required a commute from her old apartment. She and Damien have a connection that's remarkably tender. She spoils him rotten. When he was diagnosed with diabetes, her spoiling reached epidemic levels. He got whatever he asked for, got away with whatever he wanted. Isobel benefits from her soft spot as well, if more incidentally, if only because my mother's innate sense of fairness would never allow her to openly favor Damien.

My mother spoils me too. Years ago, she set up an arrangement that gives me a cut of her royalties. After I married Paul, she gave us enough cash to buy our home outright while she was still living in a rented apartment. I had to insist that if we lived mortgage-free on her dime, she should at least own a home as well. I was the one who found the listing for her, a bungalow on a dead-end street off this park. Quite possibly the smallest house in Winngrove.

'Two-car parking,' I marveled to her and Paul when she finally agreed to tour the place.

'I only have one car,' my mother said, frowning.

'You know you can afford that mansion on the other side of the park, right?' Paul joked. 'The one with the indoor swimming pool?'

'I'd rather die,' my mother responded.

Paul found my mother baffling, but I knew the bungalow was a good step for her. To this day, she is aghast at the notion of living richly. It doesn't matter how many books she sells, how much money she amasses. She spends it easily enough—the best college for me, the nicest clothes to wear to that college, a cute red car to zip around in at college, and the week after we eloped, a house of my choosing. She would have bought me that mansion if I'd asked. And she spoils her grandkids. Her friends. Her once-a-month house cleaner is the best paid in the city. But she struggles to splurge on herself.

'She's not frugal,' I often insist to Paul. 'She was poor for a long time. She just wants comfort. A rich person's life doesn't necessarily offer that.'

'Well,' he'll reply, 'she's a rich person whether she flaunts her money or not.'

One Saturday morning before she bought her house, tabloid paparazzi accosted my mother in front of her old apartment building. "World's Richest Author Lives a Pauper's Life," the headline read. A story that might have humiliated others only grounded my mother's resolve. When she finally caved on the bungalow, she settled in nicely, gutting and renovating it with the help of an architect she met in her weekly yoga class. It was nice to see her upgrade her living quarters. The locals are proud to have her as their famous neighbor and respect her privacy for the most part. I want to believe that she's happy.

"Your lips are moving."

I startle. My mother stands only a few feet away. My chest tightens at the sight of her. She wears white shorts and a fitted golf shirt, her grandma uniform as she calls it. She's so beautiful, still so youthful at sixty. I edge over and she sits close, outstretching her arm to rest on the bench behind me. I nudge against her affectionately.

"Happy birthday, old lady."

"Sixty!" she says. "At least I'm not senile. You were sitting here talking to yourself."

"I was not. It's normal to get lost in thought."

"Whatever normal means," she says. "Give it."

I hand her my cigarette. Marilyn draws a graceful inhale.

"You don't have to throw me this fucking party. You know that, right?"

That's another thing about my mother. She swears. A lot.

"I want to, Mom. I've wanted to for a long time. I've told you that."

"And I gave in. So why the frown?"

"Just can't shake the other anniversary. Colleen. Thirty years."

"God, Nadine." She gives my leg a light swat. I've irritated her. "Can we please not focus on that right now?"

"I'm just pointing it—"

"You wanted to throw this party, and you knew it fell on this day. Today of all days. My dumb birthday. You can't focus on these two things at once. I thought that was the whole point of a party. To finally let it go. We can't let it haunt us."

"Yeah."

She means Colleen. Let the pain of Colleen's death go. But I can't. I won't say it out loud, but I can't. These days, I'm focused on the past more than ever. On Colleen. She's a ghost, haunting me. She's become a fixation. I find myself replaying the small and fleeting memories I have of her. And then there's a new obsession with digging for more, with finding out everything I can about Colleen.

I watch my mother inhale the cigarette. She doesn't like to talk about her younger sister, so mostly, with her, I leave it alone. But after my fall, as I lay convalescing in the hospital, I had too much time on my hands for the first time in my adult life, and a new and strange disquiet overcame me. Always a good sleeper, I was awake at night. A buzzing anxiety kept my brain churning. Colleen appeared in my thoughts, in my dreams. She would not leave me alone.

To the local news outlets thirty years ago, the tragedy was simple: *Girl, 15, Found Dead in Barn.* The news reports all left out the fact that I, a young girl, was the one who found her.

"Your lips are moving again."

"Give me back the smoke," I say.

"This one's done," Marilyn says, dropping it and stubbing it out with the toe of her sandal. "Light another one."

I do as I'm instructed. We sit in silence, passing the cigarette back and forth. I don't like the chasm that seems to have formed between Marilyn and me recently. During my two months in the hospital, my six weeks at the rehab center after that, she visited every second day, coordinating with Paul and then with Margot, sitting at my bedside for hours on end. I should have been grateful, but the truth is, her insistence on pleasantries, on staying *positive* as I lay there, broken, left me lonely even when she was in the room. I knew she was worried about me. That's how she copes; the more worried Marilyn Millay gets, the sunnier her outward disposition. I didn't want to trouble her even more, so for months since the accident I've avoided mention of my roiling brain, my glitching anxiety.

"Do you miss her?"

Colleen, I mean. My mother bites her lip and shakes her head. "What a silly question."

"Sorry," I say. "I'll drop it now. I promise."

The bench is warm. I feel my thighs sticking to its paint, my hands clammy. *Silly*. Such a gentle word. My mother's composure can feel like an affront to me. It's just too strong a counter from my youngest memories of her. I grew up with an entirely different Marilyn Millay, a young single mother hunched over the stove at our basement apartment, stirring canned soup and wiping away tears she assumed I couldn't see. We traveled to my grandparents' farm most weekends, but during the week, it was just the two of us. *Making a go of it*, my mother often said. How unsettled she'd been in my early childhood years, how stressed and lonely and, I imagine, afraid. It's not that I preferred that overwhelmed and discouraged version of my mother to this one. But she was more relatable. She was more like me.

My mother shifts to face me, smiling. "Let's talk about the party. How many people, again?"

"Well over a hundred."

"Jesus. I only have, what? Ten friends? Remind me who else you invited."

I mash the cigarette out on the bench and allow the butt to fall through its slats.

"Paul insisted we include the neighbors. And most of his colleagues. Sorry. I know you don't like them."

"Even what's-his-name? Condo Man?"

"Seymour?" I say. "Yes. He'll be there."

My mother throws her head back and releases a groan. "I never understood that about you."

"Never understood what?"

"You do nothing but complain about that man. You seem incapable of cutting anyone loose."

"Cut him loose? He's Paul's business partner. What am I supposed to do?"

"Spare me. You've always been like that. Girls would be mean to you at school, catty or nasty, and yet you'd insist on going to their sleepovers."

"Maybe I'm just empathetic. Forgiving."

My mother laughs. "That's not it."

"Fine. I'm a horrible wimp. I hate conflict that much."

She pulls me into a one-armed hug. "That's not it either. You hate conflict. But you are no wimp, Nadine. You like your enemies close."

"Please." I pause, biting hard at the inside of my cheek. The pain calms me. "Jesus, Mom. I don't have time for a therapy session. He's our neighbor. Paul's colleague. Not inviting him would be scandalous. That family is going through a lot with River in the hospital. It's been a terrible month. Enemy? Please. Now's not the time to stir things up."

"I suppose," Marilyn says. "Let's drop it, shall we? I need a mint."

"Here." I reach for my tote to extract them then pry open the tin and shake a couple into my mother's palm. I'm sweating. "You were supposed to cheer me up. That's why I agreed to meet. This hasn't been cheery at all. I'm even more wound up."

"I'm sorry. You're right."

"Can we start over?"

"We certainly can," she says. "And listen. I don't like seeing you stressed. You've had a rough few months. I'll come over at noon. I'll be your bitch for the day."

"Don't use that word. You know I hate it."

She laughs. "All right, all right. You can boss me around to your heart's delight. Direct all your stress at me to avoid losing your shit on anyone else. Your birthday gift to me is allowing me to help you. For once."

A woman has stopped in her tracks across the path from us. She's staring. She clutches a book to her chest. Right. This happens a lot. Marilyn and I make brief eye contact before turning our attention to this starstruck fan.

"Is that a Marilyn Millay book you've got there?" I ask her.

"Wow!" the woman says, stepping forward sheepishly. "I'm so sorry to interrupt. I just, I recognized you right away. I'm from out of town, I'm here visiting an old friend, girls' weekend, you know? And I remember reading that you live here, I know that about you. Of course I do, I'm a huge fan. Did I say that already? I just bought your latest book, and I'm reading it. It was in my purse, and now here you are! In the flesh. Oh my God!"

I root again through my bag and extract a pen. "I think you should sign this nice lady's copy," I say.

"Most definitely I should," my mother says, calling her forward.

The woman approaches, giddy. She hands my mother the book and turns her attention to me.

"Are you her daughter? Are you Nadine?"

"I am indeed."

"Is it weird that I know your name? I'm seriously your mom's number one fan. Is that creepy? I've been reading those profile articles by that journalist, should I even admit to you? His name is escaping me."

"Julian Simone," I say.

"Right!"

"We don't talk about him," my mother quips.

No, I think. *We don't.*

"Yeah," the woman says. "It seems like he's trying to get all in your business. He writes like he knows you. Like he's your friend. But I guess I feel like I know you too, so—"

"What's your name?" my mother interrupts, wielding the pen.

"Oh!" The woman is flustered now. "It's Gillian. With a G." She leans over my mother with a gaping, breathless smile. "So what was it like growing up with a famous murder mystery writer as a mother?"

"Well," I say, waving a hand. "I was actually fourteen when her first novel became a bestseller. And I left home at eighteen. So for most of our life together, she wasn't famous at all."

"Quite the contrary," my mother says. "I was a failed writer. Bitter and alone."

"Alone aside from me, you mean," I say, rolling my eyes for effect. "Come on, Mother."

Gillian clasps her hands together, thrilled or appalled by our banter, I can't tell. We are good at this, well-practiced in this repartee. We play the parts of the frosty pair, the famous mommy dearest and her too-cool daughter. We'll play for any audience that will have us.

"Back then," I say. "I could make a mean noodles and margarine when I was barely tall enough to reach the dials on the stove."

"And then suddenly, we were rich," Marilyn adds, her eyes never lifting from the book that she's signing. Already she's written nearly a paragraph for her new friend Gillian, every fan she encounters treated as her favorite.

"Your rags-to-riches story is the stuff of legends," Gillian says. "Remember that *People* magazine spread you did when your first book came out? What was it, twenty years ago?"

"Twenty-five," my mother corrects.

"I still have it," Gillian says. "I was in high school. I kept a copy. Okay, now I sound really psychotic!"

My mother smiles, ever gracious. "Not at all, Gillian. I'm flattered. I'm quite sure even my own daughter doesn't have a copy. I'm glad someone does."

She's right. I don't. That magazine shoot marked my initiation into the realities of our new life. I stood in a dark corner of the photographer's studio chewing my nails and watching in horror as my mother lay poised in a silk robe, a clutch of diamonds in one hand and a glass of champagne held to her red lips. "Rags to Riches," the headline would read. "A Single Mom Hits the Jackpot with the Bestselling Novel of the Decade."

Aside from the deep sense of adolescent horror, what I remember most from that photo shoot was my mother sucking back tears as her newly assigned publicist and the magazine handler wrestled her into that robe. We'd only just moved out of our basement apartment where I'd grown up, and my mother, cognizant of not imposing too much change on me, fearful that even this vast amount of money could come and go, opted to upgrade only to a better apartment, a two-bedroom rental where she remained until I finally convinced her to buy the bungalow. She hands the book back to her fan.

"It was lovely to meet you, Gillian with a G," she says. "I'm so glad our paths crossed."

Thankfully Gillian understands that it's time to go. She backs away from the bench, clutching the book. I'm worried she'll trip in her effort to remain square to us as she takes her leave. It's lovely. To meet fans so besotted with my mother. So loyal to her. It gives me comfort.

For the most part, my mother has avoided the pitfalls of fame. She gets recognized regularly, sure, but the interactions are usually short and pleasant. Marilyn claims it's because people are generally less interested in writers than in actors, singers, athletes, royalty. But that's not it. She's been well protected. Most of the stories written about her have been slim on details. These recent stories that Gillian mentioned have gotten a little more personal, but just barely. My mother rails against Julian Simone as a has-been journalist looking for relevancy after being laid off by the Arts section of a major paper. If only she knew how much worse it all might have been.

Gillian with a G has now receded fully from view.

"She was lovely," my mother says. "One of the nicer ones."

"You'll have lots of fans at the party too," I say. "Bring an array of pens to sign your wares."

"I'm telling you," she says. "They can pop out of the woodwork. I had to stop getting my chin waxed because, truly, no place was safe."

I laugh. "Don't be sorry. It's nice. I love seeing them gush over you."

"Okay, then." She slaps her hands to her legs. "Let's get moving. You've got your Nadine list, I'm sure. Your notebook. Tasks at hand."

"Yes," I say, feeling pinned to the bench. "I should get moving."

"Are you okay?"

"Yes," I say, a lie.

She kisses my cheek. "I love you, darling. I'll come at noon, okay?"

"Okay. Jesus."

Before I can blink it back, I'm wiping a tear from my lash, breathing to avoid a full cry.

"Poor Nadine." My mother wraps her arm around me again. "You put too much pressure on yourself. You've only just recovered. It's a lot. You really underplay everything you just went through."

"I don't want to talk about it."

"I know you don't. And I don't want you to throw this party."

"But I *want* to throw it!"

"Yes!" She matches my fervor. "You've made that clear."

"I'm fine. I'm just feeling nostalgic." I pause, gauging. "I was think-ing about stopping in at the graves. Leaving flowers."

"Why would you do that? It's not the day for it."

"It's the anniversary of her death, Mom. It's actually *the* day to go."

I can detect my mother's posture change without turning to face her. She's erect now, clearing her throat, her hands in fists on her lap. She'll stay calm—she always does—but I've riled her.

"Nadine? You don't need that today. I should have made you promise. That if you threw this party, you had to let everything else go. I don't want to sound insensitive, because I know that you had a terrible experience when Colleen died. I know that. And I probably didn't handle it all that well. It was a mess. But you didn't really know her, Nadine. You didn't know her. Not really. You were a little girl. And I think you've created this image of her in your brain, this version of Colleen that never existed."

"What's that supposed to mean?"

My mother heaves a long sigh. "She was fifteen. You were ten. She was . . . troubled. What happened was tragic, of course it was. But it was so long ago, Nadine."

She shifts to face me, setting a warm hand on my leg. "I'll go to the cemetery with you this week, okay? We can sink into it. But it's not fair to ask this of me, or frankly, of yourself. I'm already worried about you. I only agreed to this godforsaken party because you seemed so keen on it."

"I am," I say.

"Then I need you to promise me that you'll stay focused today. On the party. Okay?"

"Okay. I promise."

Sometimes it's just easier to lie as a means to end a conversation.

"I'll be there at your front door at noon." She looks to her watch. "A few hours. Got it?"

"Yes." I pat her leg. "I'll pull myself together. I just need a minute to myself."

At that my mother hugs me and then leaves. She knows I mean it when I say I want to be alone. She's one of the few people who respects my wishes.

We can't let it haunt us, my mother said. And she's right.

I look to my watch. Nine a.m. The cemetery where Colleen's buried is only a short walk away. There's time. I'll pick up some flowers on the way. Marilyn need never know.

I stand and watch my mother walk briskly down the shaded path of Winngrove Park, back to her humble bungalow, to the half-written draft of her next novel.

People always ask what it's like to be the daughter of the world-famous writer Marilyn Millay. And I could choose to recount the Saturdays I spent in front of the television while she sat at a whirring old computer and wrote furiously, pinning her hopes on a dream that seemed ridiculously far-fetched. To be honest, I think my mother prefers it when I tell it that way. It paints her as cold and detached, so clichéd a story that it often releases us from further prying.

We spent so many years in that basement, poor but banded together. After Colleen died, our little world closed in even further. It really was just the two of us. That era built up a mutual devotion we both know will see us to the grave. We'd do anything for each other, that's how kindred we are. Her own editor once half joked that I should be the one to write her biography, not that hack journalist Julian Simone. I am, after all, the daughter enmeshed in her mother's mammoth success. I balked. Imagine the betrayal! I would never. My job is to protect Marilyn, even if that means keeping secrets from her. No one, not even her, knows the truth better than me.

S T BASIL'S CEMETERY COVERS A SMALL city block, its perimeter marked by a shoulder-high stone wall. I walk the footpath that meanders through the newer graves to the older section at the back. The trees in this cemetery form a remarkable canopy, a green ceiling so dense it feels almost indoors.

Colleen was buried at St Basil's because this is the location of my mother's family's plot; her great-grandparents were cousins with the farmer who owned the land Winngrove was built on. Sometimes I wonder if moving here all those years ago was some symbolic way for me to circle back to Colleen years after her death. If my mother has ever wondered the same, she's never brought it up. She doesn't like to talk about her family. *Our* family.

I open the wrought iron fence of the Fitzgerald family plot and beeline to their little row of gravestones. My grandmother. My grandfather. Colleen. Instantly the surge overtakes me; a sob rises in my throat before I can stem the tide. I lower to my knees and count my breaths until the tears subside.

Even breathing can feel hard these days. Overwhelming.

Most of my life has unfolded without my grandparents in it. And yet their absence still feels like an open wound. The tragedy of Colleen's death formed a rift in our family that never healed. By the time I was old enough to consider seeking them out myself, behind my mother's back, it was too late. The year I turned sixteen, my grandmother died of cancer. Three weeks later, my grandfather had a heart attack. I was ten the last time I saw them. So why this ache? Every time I come here, it's this same. This inexplicable ache.

I stopped at the flower shop on my way here and bought three peonies to place on the graves. Each of them is freshly bloomed, moist and unwilted. I lift them to my nose. They smell like citrus. Then I set each one down on the graves, flattening my palm against the cool marble of my grandparents' shared headstone.

Adam and Angelina Fitzgerald.

My grandparents were farmers. They lived on a hundred acres just outside a small hamlet called Terriville, three hours north of here. Despite the formal grandeur of this cemetery plot, any family money was long gone before their time; my grandparents lived a modest life. For years they had a full thousand acres, but after a particularly terrible harvest, my grandfather was forced to sell off parcels of his land to weekend warriors who built summer hobby farms and rented his own fields back to him to work.

I loved my grandparents, but my mother's relationship with them was delicate, fraught. When Marilyn got pregnant with me at nineteen, my grandparents kicked her out. And so my mother decamped to the city, found a basement apartment, gave birth to me alone, and finished a college degree part-time while working temp jobs to pay for rent and day care. She even dropped the name Fitzgerald and took Millay in homage to her favorite poet.

But I don't remember any of this. I can't quite comprehend the bitterness my mother has expressed in the rare moments she alludes to this period, a bitterness that never quite resolved even though my grandmother showed up in the city around my third birthday to make amends, to ask that they be allowed to play a part in my life.

Marilyn said yes. And so my early memories include my grandparents and Colleen during our visits to the farm. We'd make the drive from city to country in our rickety sedan and then, for much of the weekend, my mother would abscond to the farmhouse's attic room to write. It suited us both.

Life with my mother was casual to say the least—*bohemian*, as she called it, which was code for lacking all structure. My grandparents, on the other hand, were keen on routines, systems, accountability. I relished the predictability. Every weekend morning at six, my grandfather would collect me with a gentle knock on my bedroom door.

'Keen to help at the barn?' he'd ask.

I'd sit up and dress quickly. That pink-skied early hour alone in the barn with my grandfather was my favorite part of each day.

'You get outside much this week?' he'd ask, handing me a rake to start on the stalls.

'My class took a field trip to the park.'

He'd scratch his head, baffled. 'A field trip to the park.'

When I turned nine, my grandfather taught me how to brush the horses.

'What do we always do first?' he'd ask, seeing if I remembered.

'Tie them up. So they don't kick you or try to run away.'

'Good. And when you brush, what do you always watch for?'

'Their stress.'

That word made my grandfather smile. 'Not quite stress. Keep an eye on their reactions. If they're yanking at the ties, back up. Give them a minute to breathe.'

My grandparents were the only married couple I interacted with meaningfully as a kid. They seemed so formal compared to the couples I watched on TV sitcoms. For one, my grandmother was very strict about what she allowed him to eat. No sugar, ever. No ice cream, no chocolate, no cake.

'Why can't you have pie?' I asked him once at the dinner table.

'He's diabetic,' my mother explained.

'Never mind all that,' my grandmother said.

'It's not a family secret,' Colleen mock whispered.

I looked to my grandfather then. 'What's diabetic?' I asked him.

'Sugar's not good for me, that's all,' he said. 'My body has some trouble with it.'

My grandmother was strict with her husband, but she was strict with me too. By the time I was in the third grade, she was well versed in the workings of my life.

'Okay, miss,' she'd say once she had me settled in the kitchen after our Friday arrival. 'What happened with that math test of yours?'

'I got a C.'

'Nadine!' she scolded. 'You promised me you'd study.'

'I did study. But my teacher is mean.'

'Are you blaming your teacher for your C?' my grandmother asked.

Of course I was blaming my teacher. My mother simply nodded along whenever I complained to her about my teachers. She was happy to concur. Even though my grandmother never yelled at me, her rebukes were quiet, but cutting. When I disappointed my grandmother, I tried harder in school just to earn back her praise. After winning first place in the fourth-grade spelling bee, I brought my grandmother my ribbon to display on her fridge.

'Doesn't your mother want this for your fridge at home?'

'No one would ever see it there,' I responded.

She frowned. 'What did you have for dinner last night?' she often asked me.

'Sandwiches,' I'd answer. Or macaroni. Pizza. Frozen this or that.

'She needs her vitamins,' she'd say to my mother at dinner, sliding a plate of raw vegetables in front of me. 'Does she eat any fruit and vegetables in the city?'

'She's grown three inches this year,' my mother replied. 'She's just fine.'

Deflecting these little jabs had long been Marilyn's way; my grandmother's judgments just slid off her.

Any weekend my mother debated skipping our trip to the farm, I would beg her to go. I loved the drive northward, the open spaces. I needed my grandparents. I needed my aunt too. My beloved Colleen.

Colleen Fitzgerald. Fifteen years younger than my mother and only five years older than me, she bumped like a pinball against the relative stiffness of her parents. My grandparents were well into their forties by the time she arrived, the second child they never expected. For all the rigor they displayed in their lives, Colleen's energy, her free spirit, frightened them both. But I adored her. I spent every moment I could in her bedroom, studying the posters on her wall, the books and toys on her shelves—all artifacts at a museum built just for me.

By the time I was six, Colleen eleven, my grandparents mostly left the two of us unsupervised. On rainy days, we'd hide in the attic where they kept an old TV, laying out a spread of wool blankets and watching whatever shows the antenna picked up.

'What's it like living in the city?' Colleen would often ask.

'Boring.'

That made her laugh. 'As if! I'll move there the second I can.'

'Why? I like it better here. With you.'

On sunny days, we had the run of the rolling fields and groves.

'Come along, my little tail,' she'd say as I chased her to the frigid stream that ran the back length of the fields. 'Now strip!'

Together we'd pull off our clothes and jump in, squealing in our underwear. We'd dry off in a patch of sun, me sitting between Colleen's legs as she attempted to French braid my wet hair.

'Sit still,' she'd order. 'Your hair is so curly. Do you think your dad had curly hair?'

'I don't know my dad. Your hair is curly too.'

'Not as curly as yours.'

'Look at you two,' my mother would comment as we traipsed past her in the kitchen or on the porch. 'Two peas in a pod.'

'Can I keep her?' Colleen would joke. 'Pretty please?'

'She's not a pet,' my mother would reply.

At night, Colleen often tiptoed to my room and crawled into my bed, curling into me.

'Do you ever have nightmares?' she whispered.

'Sometimes. Not really.'

'I do,' she said. 'All the time.'

'About what?'

'Being chased. But I never know who's chasing me.'

Then she'd nuzzle into me and we'd fall asleep like that. But by the time my grandfather came to get me in the morning, Colleen was always gone.

The summer I turned nine, a plan was hatched: I would stay at the farm for two full months while my mother worked nights at a bar in the city and joined us on her days off. Colleen, fourteen and about to start high school, would make a little wage to look after me. My mother was uneasy with the plan, but as we sat in the kitchen to discuss it, I all but begged.

'Please. Please say yes!'

'It'll be good for Nadine,' my grandmother insisted. 'And Colleen as well. To have a little job.'

'You can't possibly think she's responsible enough,' my mother said.

'You think I'm not?' Colleen retorted.

'You know what? Fine,' my mother said.

Colleen and I both leapt to our feet, hugging and dancing. A whole summer at the farm with Colleen. What a dream.

And at first, it *was* a dream. Colleen took the job seriously, planning our days—swims in the spring, time in the barn with the horses. But I soon sensed that she was bored. After a few weeks, she sat me in front of the TV while she paced the attic, whispering into my grandparents' new cordless phone.

'Obviously I want to go,' I once heard her say. 'But I can't just leave. I have to look after my dumb niece.'

That hit like a bullet in my chest. I felt my eyes hot with tears. Colleen noticed and ended the call.

'I meant my favorite niece,' she said, crouching next to me, tucking a strand of hair behind my ear. 'Sorry. I didn't mean that, okay? Don't tell your mom I said that. I'm just in a bitchy mood.'

Bitchy. I hated that word.

'Where do you want to go so badly?' I asked.

'To the lake. To a picnic with some friends.'

'I could come with you.'

She smiled. 'Yeah. I don't think so. Nine-year-olds aren't really welcome.'

Again, my eyes brimmed with tears. But Colleen nudged me, then edged my chin up with her hand.

'Hey, forget about it. What if I asked my dad for twenty bucks to hit the craft aisle?'

'Okay,' I said.

So I gathered myself and followed her. After a brief exchange with my grandfather in the barn, Colleen emerged waving a twenty-dollar bill. Fifteen minutes later, we were parking our bicycles in front of the Terriville General Store.

'You pick,' she told me once we reached the craft aisle. 'Your heart's desire.'

'What about popsicle sticks and glue? We could make little cabins.'

'Sure,' she said. 'Whatever you want.'

But she was distracted, peering around me down the aisle. After a few minutes, a group of boys appeared and approached us. Clearly, Colleen had told them we'd be there.

'You coming to the lake?' one of them asked.

'I'm babysitting.' She elbowed me gently. 'This is Nadine. She goes where I go.'

'I didn't know you had a sister.'

'She's not my sister. She's my niece.'

'Yeah,' one of the boys said. 'Your sister's a slut. Had a kid at eighteen or something?' He pointed at me. '*This* kid. It was all my parents talked about for weeks.'

I felt my cheeks flare red. *Slut?* I wasn't even sure what that word meant. I wanted to bolt from the store. I tugged at Colleen's shorts, but she swatted my hand away and stepped to within inches of this boy. Was he even a boy? His face was stubbly. He was older than Colleen.

'Say sorry,' Colleen said to him. 'Right now.'

But he only smirked. Then Colleen closed all remaining space between them and cupped his crotch, squeezing, then squeezing more. I stared dumbly down at her hand, amazed. At first he almost moaned, but then he bent over and yelped. She didn't let go until the shopkeeper rounded the corner.

'He pulled my hair,' Colleen said, feigning distress.

We were all led to the door and cast outside, resuming our circle formation on the sidewalk.

'You're crazy,' one of the boys said.

'She's a bitch,' said the boy she'd grabbed.

That word again. I glared at him. Why was he smiling?

'Maybe I am a bitch,' Colleen answered. 'Maybe I'll see you at the lake.'

The boys wandered away.

What had just happened? I couldn't make sense of it. Were these her friends or enemies? My heart was racing. It wasn't until we were alone that I realized I was still holding the bag of popsicle sticks in my hand.

'We need to go pay for this,' I insisted.

Colleen laughed. 'Don't be such a prude, Nadine. Put them in your pocket.'

I understood right then that everything had changed. The Colleen who braided my hair, who snuck into my room to cuddle with me, was all but gone, replaced by this shifty, wily teenager. Our time together felt much less fun. For the rest of the summer, my reprieve was the early mornings with my grandfather.

'How's your summer going?' he asked.

'Fine. Good, I guess.'

'You and Colleen having fun?'

'Yep. A lot of fun.'

'She's behaving herself?'

'Yep.'

Lies. How I wanted to tell him the truth—that Colleen spent most of her time on the phone or dragging me to fleeting encounters with boys like the one at the general store. But I couldn't. I knew he'd just get angry at Colleen.

Regardless, he figured things out himself the day Colleen brought me to the barn. We climbed the ladders up to the highest loft. Together, we stood at its precipice and stared down through the trapdoors that opened to a mound of hay below.

'Jump,' she said.

'No way! It's too high.'

'Don't be a baby. I jumped when I was your age.'

This infuriated me. 'Then *you* jump,' I barked at her.

'Scaredy-cat.'

That did it. I jumped, right as my grandfather was entering the barn. I heard him call my name as I leapt. *'Nadine!'* I landed splayed, my wrist bending sharply against a rake hidden in the hay. He scooped me up and squeezed me against him, casting his eyes up to Colleen, still in the loft.

'Jesus Christ!' he yelled. 'What have you done?'

See? I get lost in these thoughts. These memories of Colleen.

The air in the cemetery feels cooler than the street. I crouch in front of Colleen's grave, scratching at her etched name with my fingernail. What strikes me most when I come here is what could have been, a life where Colleen is alive and part of my day-to-day, where my grandparents remained in my fold instead of dying of heartbreak.

My phone rings. Shit. I stand and swipe fast to catch the call before it goes to voicemail.

"Hello?"

"Hi. Where are you?"

It's Paul.

"I'm out," I say. "I'll be home soon. Less than an hour."

"Okay. But where are you specifically?"

This will require a lie. Paul won't want to hear that I'm at the cemetery. Like my mother, Paul can set his emotions aside in a way that can sometimes feel hard-hearted.

"I'm near the cheese boutique," I say. "Why?"

"Well, my linen suit is at the dry cleaner. I was thinking . . ."

"Are you still in bed?" I ask. "It sounds like you're still in bed."

He laughs sheepishly. I can hear the sleep in his voice.

"You caught me," Paul says. "How about I get my ass up and go pick up the suit myself?"

"I think that's a good plan," I say. "Or wake up Isobel and send her."

"A better plan!" he declares.

As we speak, I rest my hand on top of the stone cross of Colleen's grave and lean my weight into it. I never bring Paul to this cemetery. There's a reason for that. Early in our dating life, Paul and I discovered that our families had a fateful connection. His family owned a hobby farm in Terriville. So did Seymour's family. Their parents leased their acres to the farmer down the road. That farmer? My grandfather.

Anyway, I don't bring Paul here because he has a way of turning any mention of Colleen back to this coincidence, the sort of happenstance you'd toast at a wedding, as I'm sure he'd have done if we hadn't eloped. A couple who realizes a meaningful childhood connection? I can't blame Paul for framing it as our meet-cute and not as a tragedy. I never really talk to him about Colleen. He doesn't understand that she meant the world to me.

"You there?" Paul asks me now on the phone.

"Yes," I say.

"Do I have a task list?"

"Of course. It's on your bedside table."

I hear sheets rustling. "God, you're sneaky," he says. "Like a stealth cat."

"You're the only middle-aged man I know who still sleeps past ten."

"It's a superpower," he says. "I'm getting up. Come home soon."

"I will. Love you."

"Love you too," he says.

I end the call and drop my phone back into my tote.

I need to keep moving, but I'm stuck in place. I lean forward to scratch a cluster of dirt from the top of Colleen's gravestone.

That full summer I spent at the farm turned out to be my last. One day, in late August, my mother joined us midweek so my grandparents could head to the city overnight for some medical appointments. Late that night, my mother shook me awake.

'Where's Colleen?' she asked me.

'What do you mean? In bed.'

'It's three a.m. She's not in her bed.'

I saw the panic in my mother's eyes.

'Try the lake,' I said.

'The lake?' She shot up to standing. 'Get up. I'm not leaving you here.'

And so we found ourselves in the car. I was half asleep in the back-seat, but I perked up when the car slowed. There it was. The lake. A bonfire. Milling bodies. Music. I squinted into the crowd as we parked.

'I'll be right back,' my mother said, hopping out of the car.

'Please don't leave me here!' I pleaded.

'Just sit tight, baby. I'll lock the doors.'

Then my mother disappeared. I held my breath until she emerged minutes later pulling a stumbling Colleen by the arm. She unlocked the car then opened the back door.

'Get in,' she hissed at Colleen. 'Now.'

I slid across the seat to make room.

'No,' Colleen slurred. 'Fuck you, Marilyn.'

'Hi!' came a voice from behind us.

Marilyn craned slowly.

It was the boy from the store. 'Look, everyone. It's Marilyn Fitzger-ald. Terriville's favorite teen mom.'

A titter of laughter shot through the gathering crowd. My mother didn't even cast him a glance.

'Let go of my arm,' Colleen said.

'Get in the goddamn car, or I call the cops.'

Then Colleen was next to me and my mom was in the driver's seat, peeling away. Colleen smelled of sugary apples. Booze. Her eyes were glassy, makeup smeared. Her black shirt was cropped jaggedly five inches above her jeans. In the darkness of the backseat I reached for Colleen's hand, my wrist still in a cast from my fall in the barn.

'Don't touch me. You fucking tattletale.'

A strangely childish word. I recoiled from her.

When we pulled up the farm's long driveway, my mother parked, turned on the interior car light, then spun to face Colleen. 'How old were those boys?'

'Who the fuck do you think you are?'

'You're wasted.'

'What do you care?'

'I do care, Colleen. And you can bet Mom and Dad will care when I tell them.'

'Mom and Dad? Fuck you,' Colleen said, laughing bitterly. 'News flash: Family slut turns into Daughter of the Year.'

My mother barely flinched. 'You'd better watch it, Colleen. Those boys? They're seniors. You're fourteen.'

Eventually, we went inside. I couldn't sleep. I was anxious, but secretly relieved too, glad that Colleen would be punished, forced to stay home. I wanted desperately for her to revert to the girl she'd been before.

The next morning, my grandparents came home, and Marilyn and I left. For a long while, we didn't visit the farm. When we did, Colleen all but ignored me.

The next spring, I turned ten and Colleen turned fifteen. All I wanted was to make amends. I used my birthday money from my grandparents to buy her a silver-chained flower pendant I'd spotted at a vintage store. I wrapped the box and made her a small card, then mailed it to the farm. A few days later, our phone rang.

'Hello?'

'It's Colleen. Nadine, are you there?'

A voice. Behind me. In the cemetery. I spin, nearly losing my balance. An elderly man stands ten or so feet away, his hands lifted in deference.

"I'm sorry, dear," he says. "I didn't mean to sneak up on you. I'm the caretaker. Just about to water the garden. Might get a bit soggy."

"Sorry," I say. "I was lost in thought."

"Well. That happens a lot here."

I open my mouth to speak, then think better of it.

"Why don't I give you a minute," he says.

I watch him start down the path, then turn and crouch one last time to arrange the peonies into perfect formation.

She never said sorry. On that phone call. Colleen thanked me for the necklace, then paused.

'I have an idea,' she said. 'Your mom turns thirty next month, doesn't she?'

'Yeah,' I said.

'What if we threw her a party?'

OUR FAVORITE BISTRO IN WINNGROVE HAS a cheese boutique at its rear. I pass by the tables filled with the early brunch crowd and wait at the counter. The fromager's name is Zachary. When he spots me from the kitchen, he waves me in with such warmth that I'm tempted to fall into his arms for a hug.

"How are we today?" he asks once he reaches the counter.

"I'm good, Zachary. Just wanted to pop in and make sure all is well. Do you need Paul to pick anything up this afternoon?"

"No way. I'll be at your house by five. Want to sample?"

"I'd love to," I say.

Zachary owns this boutique bistro with his husband, Gordon. Saturdays he oversees the boutique, Sundays the brunch. They opened fifteen years ago, in the earliest stages of Winngrove's gentrification. For years a group of us neighbors have gathered here for Sunday brunch at regular intervals, as if we weren't already immersed enough in each other's lives. Zachary and Gordon always save us the harvest table by the window and pour us mimosas on the house. It's generally remained a joyful ritual, our babies joining when we couldn't find sitters. Zachary felt part of our group too, even if he was the one pouring our drinks.

I'm grateful to Zachary because he's a man who can keep a secret. Nothing changed between us after he ran into Lionel and me in a hotel lobby on the far side of town. He was making a delivery for the boutique on a random Tuesday morning while Lionel and I stood at reception collecting our room key. I could feel his shock when he met my gaze. Zachary had been hosting our group at the bistro long enough to know that Lionel and I were not the correct pairing, that I belonged with Paul and Lionel belonged alone. Still, Zachary smiled at me discreetly but didn't come over. Everything he did was meant to assure me: *Your secret is safe.*

Secrets are safe with no one, my mother often says. I've since wondered how the trajectory of my life might have changed if it hadn't been Zachary to catch us at the hotel, but Paul. Or one of the kids. My mother. Even someone like Seymour Dunphy, a man far less likely to be discreet than Zachary.

It's been two years since that dinner party where Lionel first processed his affection. Eighteen months since that fumbling encounter in the pantry. Last spring, a few months after Lionel ended everything via text message, I caved and agreed to our regular Sunday brunch. I could only avoid Lionel so long before someone—Paul, namely—took notice and asked why. How I'd preened in the bathroom that morning; it was crucial I look my best at my first encounter with Lionel post-affair. You can imagine my reaction when Lionel arrived late. And not alone, but with Daphne.

'Meet Daphne McKee,' he'd declared to the group. 'My great love.'

If I can thank my tendency to flush for anything, it's that Paul wouldn't have questioned my cheeks flaring a deep red as they did in that moment. I wanted to die. Daphne, elegant and gracious, a tenure track professor in clinical psychology. Watching Sherry Dunphy fawn over this new Daphne made me want to vomit into my eggs Benedict. How murderous I'd felt in that moment, my stomach roiling, my pulse too fast, my face burning hot. Daphne was nearly ten years younger than me, childless and fit, and it showed in everything from her breasts to the lack of bags under her eyes. *What could be worse than this?* I remember thinking. Nothing.

Zachary reaches over the counter and hands me a disposable spoon coated in a glob of cheese. "*Chabichou,*" he says, watching me as I taste it.

It melts on my tongue, creamy and sweet. "Delicious," I say.

"I've got a *clochette* here too. You have to try it. Let me cut you off a piece to go."

I lean against the counter, my gaze out to the restaurant. I remember Zachary coming over to check on our table that day, the way his eyes darted, spotting Lionel's arm around Daphne, doing the calculations. He placed a warm hand on my shoulder as he poured my drink, a show of sympathy that landed like a punch. Lionel, ever competent in his cruelties, ignored me the entire meal. I don't mean that he said a quick hello before settling into a distant seat. No. He did not acknowledge me at all, in any way, not *once*. I ate my brunch while plotting the interaction that would surely come at the end of the meal, settling on the icy grace my mother taught me so well. After all, I'd been the one to not text him back after he'd ended things. My silence had been the last word.

But there was no final interaction.

At the end of the meal, he paid his bill and ushered Daphne, his *great love*, out the door while I was in the washroom reapplying my lip gloss and trying not to vomit.

When Paul and I returned home, I climbed into the bath and wept for an hour before refreshing the hot water and spending another hour googling symptoms of early menopause. My looks are not terrible, I remember telling my reflection in the mirror, prying at the skin of my cheeks, the folds around my eyes. I could still squeeze out another child if need be. I had that thought, that's how bad it was. In that moment, I would have done anything to gain back the upper hand.

I take another spoon from Zachary. This time the cheese is salty. Perfect.

"You are very good at what you do, Zachary."

"Thank you, my dear."

God, I love Zachary. I do. The Monday after that brunch I stopped in here to pick up some cheese en route to my book club. Zachary shuffled back and forth to fetch me samples, commenting on my hair, the shade of my lipstick, how beautiful I looked. Despite my heart-ache I marveled at his kindness. He understood exactly what had un-folded. He'd probably curled up with Gordon and a glass of wine the night of our brunch and woven the whole sordid web for him: Nadine, married to Paul, sleeping with Lionel, Paul's best friend, until today—gasp!—when Lionel showed up with a young fawn named Daphne. You couldn't write a juicier plot. There was no doubt that I was the villain in this story. And yet, Zachary chose compassion.

"These cheeses," I say to Zachary. "Can you include them on the trays for tonight? They're both magnificent."

"I'll add them just for you."

"Thank you. I appreciate it."

"You can repay me with fancy cocktails."

"As many you can drink, Zachary. I promise."

I blow him a kiss and turn to leave. A line has formed at the door, the brunch servers zipping past me as I make my exit. Outside the sun is higher, hot. I don my sunglasses and turn the corner to head for Paul's office, my last stop before home.

It's been a little over a year since that brunch. I survived the heartbreak, despite the curveballs that followed. Daphne moved into Lionel's home up the street from us. She got pregnant. Lionel whisked her to a southern island to elope, the photographs on Facebook garnering so many likes that in a fit of self-loathing, I'd considered writing on his timeline: *Congrats to you two lovebirds—and to think that Lionel and I were fucking in my bathroom only months ago!* But I'd resisted. I'm not an animal.

But Daphne's pregnancy did serve to grant me a reprieve. Winter came, and Lionel disappeared into the novel role of dutiful husband. I muted him on social media. The distance helped. Once, I walked by their house with Paul on our way to a late dinner at this very bistro. The baby had just been born. Only their upstairs bedroom shone with light.

'I wonder if he feels trapped,' Paul said out of nowhere.

'Who?' I asked, playing ignorant.

'Lionel! Domestication must feel pretty heavy after forty-five years as a bachelor.'

'Maybe,' I said, changing the subject.

I believe Paul knows nothing of the affair, and I've since tried hard to make amends in my marriage. To be a better wife. To erase the whole seedy thing from my brain. My marriage is strong. It was just an affair, a mistake borne from the monotony of midlife. I've made peace with it, haven't I?

But Lionel, it seems, has not.

A few weeks ago, he began texting me, insistent that we speak, that it was urgent. I asked him twice to leave me alone, and then I blocked his number. I'm not willing to chance it all again, especially for Lionel Robinson. All it would take is one phone call to Paul, one admission of evidence, to destroy everything I have and love.

T HE NORTH END OF WINNGROVE'S COMMERCIAL strip is its busi-
est. The early Saturday morning quiet is gone, replaced by a bus-
tle that has me dodging joggers and young families on the sidewalk.
It's hot outside now. I'm disoriented, thirsty. My mother may well have
been right—the cemetery was not a good idea. My brain swirls with
memories. Sticky thoughts. I clutch my tote to my chest and pick up
my pace. When my phone buzzes in my pocket, I tuck into the shaded
vestibule of a closed boutique and retrieve it.

Where r u? Isobel has texted.

You're awake! I reply. **My, my. It's barely ten. An early riser today ;)**

Dad made pancakes. A pause, then she adds: **Don't worry, I'll
make sure he cleans the kitchen.**

I wasn't worried. Or was I?!

It calms me to text with my daughter. My relationships with her,
with Damien, are true constants; motherhood is the one role in my
life in which I've consistently felt capable. I watch the screen as Isobel
types her response.

He's making me pick up his dry cleaning.

Your father is incorrigibly lazy, I write. **You should charge him for your time.**

LOL, she writes. **Yeah maybe.**

Did you sleep okay?

Fine, I guess. Gonna go to the hosp this afternoon.

The hospital. To see River, as she does almost every day.

Just ask Margot if she needs any help before you go, okay?

Margot's not here.

My thumbs hover.

Right. She had something to do this morning. I add a row of heart emojis. **Love you. I'll be home in 30.**

Okayyyyyy, she writes back.

Texting isn't my favorite mode of communication, but it allows for a level of gushy emotion that Isobel, and especially Damien, would never tolerate face-to-face.

I slide my phone into my tote's pocket and continue down the block toward Paul's office. I have to pick up Damien's insulin. A thumping sound startles me. My hand flies up to my chest. Knocking. I can make out someone banging on the glass of the café window. Margot! She's in the café. Right. She said she had a coffee date. But now she's alone at a table for two, the Saturday newspaper folded open to the crossword puzzle. She waves at me to come in.

I can't! I mouth to her, pointing down the street then at my wrist. *I have to go!*

Margot fans out her hand. *Five minutes.*

Okay. I nod at her. I'm thirsty. It won't hurt to say hi, grab a lemonade to go.

It's not until I open one of the café doors and am halfway to the table that I spot her at the counter: Daphne Robinson. Lionel's Daphne. Oh no. No. She wears a loose red dress, the pink sling that bisects her chest enveloping an invisible lump that must be her newborn baby. No.

"Nadine!" Margot calls, waving me over.

Daphne hears my name, looks up and smiles brightly at me. I find myself wobbling my way through the tight tables toward Margot by the window. When I land there, she pulls up a *third* chair. It registers. Margot's coffee date is Daphne. She's calling to Daphne now to order me a lemonade, my favorite drink. No. I want to spin on my heel and sprint outside. But I can't make a scene. Instead, I slide into the seat Margot offers me. I feel like I might faint.

"You okay?"

"Dehydrated," I say.

"Lemonade is en route," Margot says. "We're stuck on a few clues. Maybe you can help us?"

We? Us? What is happening here?

"How do you know Daphne?" I ask.

Before Margot can answer, Daphne returns to the table and places a large lemonade in front of me. She leans in to double kiss my cheeks before settling into her seat. She smells of lavender and baby powder. God, she is so attractive, even this soon after childbirth. I'm dizzy. I lift the lemonade and heave a long gulp, Margot and Daphne watching me curiously.

"Slow down!" Margot says. She reaches for the lemonade and lowers it to the table on my behalf.

"I'm thirsty."

Margot pats my leg. "She's had a busy morning."

I sip the lemonade with deliberate slowness. Once in a rare while, you'll find yourself in a situation that calls for poise when poise feels utterly impossible. This is one of those times. What in all hell is Daphne doing here with Margot—*my* Margot!—the two of them sidled up like a pair of old friends? I want to puke.

"How's our lovely hostess holding up?" Daphne asks.

"Fine," I say. "Good. Mostly ready. You know. Always last-minute stuff."

"That family of yours any help?"

"Yes. Paul certainly is."

What? Margot shoots me a quizzical look: *Is he?*

"Give Nadine a clue," Daphne says to Margot, gesturing to the crossword puzzle.

"Okay. Capital of Latvia. Four letters."

"Riga," I say.

"Yep," Margot says. "I should know that."

What have I stumbled upon? What is the dynamic between these two women? I want to take Margot by the arm and drag her outside. *What are you doing with her?* But Margot knows nothing of my affair with Lionel. To her, Daphne is a neighbor. They are only a few years apart in age. Both young and well traveled. It makes sense that they somehow found each other and latched on. It's just: How did I not know?

The lump in the sling begins to squirm. Daphne opens the flap to peer inside. A perfect pink fist punches out in salute. Daphne cups a hand under the baby and rocks her until the fist retracts and the squirming subsides.

"How's she doing?" I force myself to ask.

"Okay," Daphne says. "She gave us trouble those first few months. But the colic's nearly passed."

Us. Daphne and Lionel. I smile tightly. Margot is watching me.

"I didn't realize you two were friends," I say, sipping my drink again.

"Am I cool enough to be your friend, Margot?" Daphne asks. "Ragged new mother that I am?"

They laugh. There are bags under Daphne's eyes, and she is paler than I remember her, but otherwise she remains beautiful. How I want to hate her. In theory, it should be easy. She cracks witty jokes that make Paul and even my mother laugh. She married Lionel only months after my affair with him ended. She is a nemesis as purebred as they come. Except that she is sort of lovely too. Vulnerable, in a way. Sweet with our children. Curious about my life, generous with her questions. She's a PhD fellow at a prestigious university. Meanwhile, I teach Criminology-Is-Fun introductory courses at the community college. Still, in the few times we've spoken of our work, she engages me as a peer. I want to hate her even for that.

My focus returns to the conversation. Margot and Daphne are talking about the advent of their relationship.

"We were both at a reading. At the library," Daphne says, gesturing to the baby. "About a month before this creature came along."

"I'd just moved in with you guys," Margot clarifies.

Is her tone defensive? I can't tell. She'd just moved in because I was in the hospital healing from a broken hip. But that won't come up right now. Margot and Daphne are lost in their own happy recollections. Under the table, I press my fingernails into my legs.

"My PhD thesis was the impact on media coverage in sexual assault cases," Daphne tells me. "But my focus was on the UK. I spent a lot of time there. So did Margot."

"Yes!" Margot says. "But *I* was slinging beers in a bar."

"The reading where we met was my favorite UK writer."

"Who, it turns out, is my favorite too," Margot adds.

Shut up, both of you! I want to scream. Rage burns in my stomach. I haven't eaten, and I feel sweaty, light-headed. I point to the half-finished Danish in front of Margot. She nods immediately, ever aware of my needs, pushing the plate my way.

An awkward silence passes between the three of us. I wish Daphne would leave. But then, it's not Daphne who is the third wheel here, is it?

Margot presses her pen to the crossword. "Sense of unrest. Seven letters."

"Anxiety?" Daphne suggests.

"Doesn't fit. *A* is the second letter."

"Malaise," I say, my mouth full of Danish.

"Your brain is a computer, Nadine Walsh. Sharp as ever."

"It's not," I say. "It's glitching more than usual these days. Too much on my mind."

Daphne frowns. "How is our River doing?"

Our River? My teeth clench. Daphne would know River, at least peripherally. Seymour and Lionel are old friends. But she and River have likely never met—or have they?

"She's doing better," I say. "There's still hope."

In our brief flash of eye contact, I see empathy in Margot's eyes. She knows how difficult it's been with Isobel, with River. She knows how much I have on my plate today. Yet I'm angry with her. For waving me down, for inviting me into the café, for subjecting me to this exchange with an archrival. I'm angry I didn't know about this burgeoning friendship with Daphne. What other secrets is Margot keeping from me?

"Tell her what you told me," Margot says to Daphne.

"No, no. It can wait." Daphne looks to her watch. "Besides, Lionel will be here shortly to pick us up on his way home from the gym."

Lionel? The gym? Reflexively, I touch my hair. As if this couldn't get any worse. I need to leave.

"Tell her!" Margot exclaims.

I bite the inside of my cheek. "Tell me what?"

"Fine," Daphne says. "You know that journalist, Julian Simone?"

"I do. He's been stalking my mother."

"He invited Lionel to lunch the other day. Wait. I'm telling it all wrong. Julian Simone didn't invite him. A mutual journalist friend set up a lunch date with Lionel and then Julian Simone showed up. It was more of an ambush."

"Wow," I say. "When was this?"

"A few weeks ago?" Daphne says. "Apparently he was full of questions. About your mom's past. I was totally confused when Lionel mentioned it. 'How would *you* know anything about Marilyn Millay's past?' I asked him. I had no idea that you and Lionel and Paul go way back, that your families all knew each other when you were kids."

"I . . ." I trail off, frozen.

"Anyway," she continues. "Lionel told me that he doesn't really remember meeting your mom or her family back then. He has some vague memories of neighbors or trips into the local village. Terriville? Is that it? Talk about six degrees of separation."

"Seriously," Margot says.

"But I promise you, Nadine, Lionel knows to keep his mouth shut about your mother. I've made sure of that. I've read the articles this Julian character has written about your mom. That one he wrote last month about your mom working as a hostess in a men's club to make ends meet before she sold her first book? I wanted to throw up." She pauses and looks at me. "Is that true?"

I don't answer.

"Definitely not true," Margot says.

"Right," Daphne says. "Just gossipy trash."

But they're wrong. That story *is* true. Marilyn did work as a hostess at a men's club. The summer I was nine, while she left me at the farm, she was working late nights. She told my grandparents it was at a hotel bar, but later admitted to me what she'd really been doing. Bartending at men's clubs pays a lot; she made enough money to take most of the following year off to write.

"People gobble those stories up," I say to Daphne, pasting on a smile. "I mean, *you* read it."

"Only because I feel protective."

Sure, I think. *Whatever you say.*

"Wasn't Julian Simone fired by the *Times*?" Margot asks.

"Laid off," I say, my voice quiet.

"Your mom is one of my favorite writers, did I ever tell you that?" Daphne continues. "Her novels got me through a really tough time when I was in college. So you can't even imagine my shock when Lionel told me she was *your* mom. If someone had suggested to me two years ago that I'd be going to Marilyn Millay's birthday party, I'd have called them insane. What I'm saying is that it's not just your job to protect her, Nadine. It's up to all of us. She's a treasure."

"Yes," I say. "She is."

I sip the last of the lemonade then ready my tote, signaling my intention to leave.

Here's a secret I've never told anyone: while I was in the hospital early this year, Julian Simone reached out to me. The fog of the pain meds compelled me to invite him to the hospital on a weekend I knew my mother was away. Even now, I can drum up a long list of excuses for why I engaged with him, why I threatened him, the revelations that forced me to strike the terms of the deal we ultimately struck. I was protecting my mother. I was protecting my family. And I was protecting myself.

Margot watches me too intently. I'm holding my phone, ready to go. I feel on the brink of tears. I need to leave. I absolutely need to leave before Lionel gets here. I stand.

"Do you want me to take you home?" Margot asks.

"No, no. I have to stop at Paul's office. Then home."

"I'll be home in twenty," she says. "Okay? We'll get back to business."

A small wail interrupts us. The baby is awake, the fist poking through again. Daphne extracts her from the sling. I offer my goodbyes and exit the café as quickly as I can. My pace is as fast as it can be without breaking into a run.

"Nadine!"

A man's voice. No. Please, no. It occurs to me to bolt into traffic to avoid him. But Lionel is already upon me on the sidewalk. I step back as he approaches. It bothers me that I still find Lionel handsome, that the sight of him still forces that little lurch in my chest. Freshly showered, he carries a small duffel bag over his shoulder. Saturday morning at the gym. Still keeping up appearances, despite his new baby.

"Nadine," he says again, eyes narrowed. "Are you okay?"

"Fine!" I blurt. "Daphne's in the café. She's waiting for you."

"I need to speak to you," he says. "It's not about us. I—"

"I told you. I don't want to talk."

We edge over on the sidewalk to make room for the stream of pedestrians.

"Please, Nadine."

"I really have to go," I say. "Busy day. Go see your wife and baby. I'll see you tonight."

My shoulder brushes his as I push past him. He doesn't call my name again.

After two blocks of brisk walking I reach the door to Paul's office and punch in the code to unlock its heavy door. Once inside I climb the dark stairs to the second floor.

Now that I'm alone, now that he's not in front of me, I'm desperate to know what Lionel is so keen to tell me. I'm over the affair. I'm over Lionel. I truly am. But that doesn't mean I want him to be over me.

ONLY ONCE I'M IN PAUL'S OFFICE do I register that the alarm system never beeped. Someone is here. Shit. It's not unusual for Paul's colleagues to stop in on a Saturday. When he and Seymour opened Walsh, Dunphy & Associates ten years ago as a boutique corporate litigation firm, there were five employees. Now, there are twenty, including some very ambitious junior associates, none of whom I'm keen on seeing this morning.

The space is large and airy, walls of exposed brick and glass. Paul's office takes up the southwest corner and the natural light that comes with it. I stop in my tracks when I spot Seymour through the window to his office. He is seated at his desk, pecking at the keys of his laptop, his back to me. He hasn't seen or heard me yet.

Fuck. Just my luck that Seymour is here. He never mentioned going to the office when I saw him this morning. I manage to dart to Paul's office without catching his attention.

"Hi, Mom."

Jesus! I nearly jump from my skin. Isobel is seated at Paul's desk.

She spins the chair like a villain, a devilish smile on her face. Then she stands, taller than me by two inches, her shoulders wide, her body strong and full. A woman, no longer a girl. Her dark hair is always a perfect mess, her skin flawless.

"What the hell, Isobel? What are you doing here?"

"Picking up Dad's dry cleaning."

"Here? It's not here."

She waves a small piece of paper. "The ticket is."

"Did Seymour see you come in?" I ask.

"Yeah. We were texting earlier today. I knew he'd be here."

We were texting. My jaw tightens. "Texting about what?"

"About River, you psycho," Isobel says, reading my thoughts. "You're so weird."

Isobel circles the desk and gives me a hug.

"You need to calm down, Mom. Your face is red."

I lean into her, inhaling the fruitiness of her hair. I'm grateful for this crumb of affection. In the handful of hours since I spied her sleeping peacefully in her room, she's woken, showered, dressed, eaten the pancakes Paul made, left our home, and come here. I'm both awed and worried by her capacity to hold herself together in times of stress. Her friend is in a coma. It's a crime that a girl of seventeen is forced to manage that, but she does it with unfailing calmness. She grips me by the shoulders and meets my gaze.

"How are you on the psycho-meter today? Above five?"

"A solid three," I say.

"I don't believe you," Isobel says. "Your skin is . . . blotchy. You're sweating. Your pupils are like pins. You're at a seven."

This is our mother-daughter joke. Nadine, the psycho, slightly unhinged. Even when she was a girl of nine or ten, Isobel had an almost supernatural ability to gauge my state of mind. 'What's bothering you today?' she used to ask me at the breakfast table if I looked worried, distracted, stressed. Over time this skill has only sharpened. She studies me intently now.

"Did you go to the cemetery?" she asks.

I don't answer.

"Don't lie. It was a trap. I was tracking your location on your phone."

"Cripes. So why are you asking, then?"

"Who goes to a cemetery on the day of a birthday party?" Isobel asks. "A crazy person, that's who."

"It's the thirtieth anniversary of Colleen's death, Isobel. It was a quick stop to pay my respects."

I often forget that we recently began sharing our location via our phones. I'd argue it's so I can track her, but the opposite often seems to be true. I try not to be an overbearing mother. I am in frequent touch with Isobel's teachers, her volleyball coach, her friends' parents. I don't allow sleepovers unless at our house. I check her pupils when she arrives home late, just as she now checks mine. And she tolerates it, I suppose because it benefits her if I stay even-keeled. What can I say? I am certain she is hiding something. About River? I don't know. I am afraid for her, though until that morning that we found River, Paul was convinced I had no reason to be.

"Don't parent me today, Daughter," I say now, resting my hand on her cheek. "You don't need to. I'm fine."

"What are you doing here, anyway? Tracking *me*?"

"No, actually. Damien's insulin is in the fridge. Your dad picked it up at the pharmacy yesterday and forgot to bring it home."

"Speaking of Dad." Isobel reaches for the glass door. "I'm gonna run downstairs and grab his suit. Can you bring it home to him? Seymour's offered to drive me to the hospital."

I hate the idea of Isobel alone with Seymour. I can't even pinpoint why.

"Sure," I say.

"Excellent."

And then she's gone. Seymour looks up from his desk as Isobel skips by his office with a wave. He smiles at her. Is it friendly, innocuous? Fatherly? I don't know. Everything about him rubs me the wrong way. I sit in Paul's chair, still warm from Isobel, and watch Seymour. I lift a pencil from the desk and snap it in two. The cracking sound doesn't rouse him. He appears to be talking to himself. His hair is thinning and he's out of shape.

I'm sure that Seymour Dunphy thought divorce would be more freeing than it's turned out to be—a life of first dates and restaurants and perhaps a personal trainer. Paul mentioned that Seymour has been on the town here and there with some other bachelors. But my impression is that he spends most of his time alone in his condo, eating takeout, swiping on his various dating apps to no avail. He isn't a confident man. Does he ever wish he hadn't left?

'You spend the first half of your life making mistakes,' my mother likes to say. 'And, if you're not careful, the second half of your life regretting them.'

I'll always wonder if Paul regrets hanging on to Seymour. I watch him now, and he must feel my gaze, because he finally looks up. We lock eyes. He stands and wanders along the glass corridor until he's at the threshold of Paul's office. Is he smirking at me?

"Nadine Walsh," he says. "Twice in one morning. You didn't say hello on your way in."

"You looked busy," I say. "What are you doing here on a weekend?"

"I left my wallet in my desk drawer," he says. "Can't do without a wallet all weekend, can I?"

I don't answer.

"Figured I'd catch up on a few emails while I'm here."

"Well done," I say, my jaw twitching.

"How about you, Nadine? Running Paul's errands again?"

"Always."

"You two amaze me. The true modern couple." He laughs. "I'd be aghast at my wife sitting at my desk. But then, I have no wife, do I?"

Idiot. But somehow he's been the powerhouse of the firm since it opened, the one luring in the most lucrative corporate clients. I'm not sure Paul would ever say anything to Seymour about leaving his wife and daughter. I'm not sure he's spoken to Seymour at all about River, about the overdose. Their capacity for compartmentalization some-times feels downright sinister.

"You look lovely today, Nadine," Seymour says. "Very party-ready."

Is he being sarcastic?

"Isobel says you're headed to the hospital," I say. "You said this morning you weren't sure whether you'd go."

"I'll drop Isobel there at least. Listen, I've been meaning to say that I've been grateful for your patience as we've navigated the past few months. With River, I mean. But also with the divorce. Life is a quagmire to navigate these days, don't you find?"

Is there a trace of sadness in his voice? No, I decide. "I'm not the patient one, Seymour," I say. "Paul is. You'd be wise to direct your grat-itude his way."

"I always do."

A thick silence sits between us.

"Well," I say. "I should get a move on. Lots left to do today."

"I'm sure," he replies.

"Tell my Isobel I'll be tracking her. Home by three."

"Right."

He meanders back to his office, hands in his pockets. I consider lifting the paperweight from Paul's desk and launching it at him. But I need to focus. Focus. There is a task at hand. What was it again? Ah. Damien's insulin. I crouch at the bar fridge and collect the prescription tucked in its rear corner. I close my hand around the paper bag, feeling for its contents, a glass vial smaller than my thumb.

I tuck it into my tote and ready myself for home. But before I even reach the door of Paul's office, Isobel appears again at the stairs, Paul's dry cleaning slung over her shoulder. She offers Seymour a big grin and wave, then taps her wrist as if to tell him: *We have to go!*

My tender, beautiful Isobel. The lengths I'd go to protect you.

Isobel sets the dry cleaning down on the reception desk and points at it, mouthing to me through the glass: *Don't forget!* Seymour collects his wallet and phone then swoops out into the hallway, resting a hand on Isobel's back in greeting. It's a harmless gesture, but I trust no one with Isobel. No one.

Once they're gone, I close my eyes and take precisely ten deep breaths. I exit Paul's office then stop at the door to Seymour's. The painting over his desk is a romanticism knockoff of a woman in repose, a hint of her creamy breast on display.

A few weeks ago, shortly after River's overdose, we invited Seymour over for dinner. Not my idea. After the meal was cleared, he cried in discussing River. For a moment, I felt true sympathy for him. What I never told Paul, or anyone else, was what I came upon when I went upstairs to check on the kids. Damien was sound asleep in his room, splayed on his back with his cell phone rested on his belly. Isobel was in our room, asleep on our king bed. In the days after finding River, she often fell asleep in there while watching our TV.

I don't know why I stopped at Isobel's room, having already accounted for her. Maybe I heard a sound. But there I found Seymour, standing at the window, gazing down to the street below.

'What the hell are you doing?' I barked at him.

'Oh,' he said, turning to me, his eyes teary. Or glassy. 'I took a wrong turn. Where's the washroom?"

'You're in my child's room.'

'What child?' He looked around. Then he shook his head, drunk, lost, peering around the room as if he'd just arrived there. 'Do you think River will be okay?' he asked me. 'What if she isn't?'

'She will be,' I replied. 'I think she will be.'

'Right,' he said, his gaze off into space. 'Right.'

He stumbled toward me, out of Isobel's room and into the hallway. I turned off the light and closed the door, then pointed him to the bathroom down the hall.

As I tell it now, Seymour likely *did* mindlessly wander into Isobel's room. Perhaps it was a fit of longing, of pain surrounding his own daughter's overdose. But what if it wasn't? What if I'm wrong?

I do this. I assume the worst. Paul often chides me for it. He argues that I'm a catastrophist. 'Why is everything suspicious to you?'

Why? Because ever since I found Colleen dead in that barn all those years ago, I've doubted my own memories. The morning I found her, when the police questioned me, I kept certain details to myself because I wasn't sure what I remembered. What I should keep to myself to avoid getting Colleen in trouble. Everything was fuzzy. Have I been certain of any memory since? No. I have not.

I edge open the door to Seymour's office and step inside. Before I can stop myself, I've spit on the floor.

I straighten, catching a ghostly glimpse of myself in the glass.

Jesus, Nadine.

Then I descend the stairs, punch in the alarm code, and step outside into the hot air of this Saturday morning.

T HE PLANTER BOXES LINING THIS SIDEWALK are filled in with bright annuals. I reach down and pick an impatiens, lifting it to my nose. It carries no scent. I'm walking at a snail's pace, my tote and Paul's dry cleaning slung over my shoulder. My eyes burn behind my sunglasses. I drop the flower in the next planter.

It's time to go home and begin the last preparations for the party. But my feet are heavy as I walk. In my haze I almost don't see Damien up ahead. When I do, the sight of him takes me aback. I duck into a store vestibule before he spots me. He stands like a statue. He's wearing his soccer uniform, typing a message into his phone, oblivious to the stream of Saturday-morning neighbors weaving around him on the sidewalk. Who is he texting? Lacey?

Don't, I want to yell to him. *Whatever you do, do not give her the upper hand.*

My beautiful boy wears his sandy-blond hair long. His eyes are a piercing hazel. He doesn't look like either Paul or me. My mother often says that he got the best of all of us, a prototype drawn from our least flawed parts. We don't discuss how much he looks like Colleen.

'Maybe I look like your father,' Damien said to me once.

'Maybe you do,' I responded.

Marilyn rarely speaks of my birth father. I know only the basics: He was married and scandalously older than her on the one-night stand that conceived me. He died shortly after I was born, without ever knowing I existed, when his car slid off an icy road not far from the farm. He and his wife had no children. I've never felt terribly curious about him, and neither have my own children, aside from the odd question. Damien has always been more interested in my grandfather because of the diabetes connection.

When Damien was first diagnosed at age ten, Paul was bereft, sick with fear. But I assured him and Damien both that all would be okay. I began telling Damien stories about my grandfather Adam Fitzgerald, painting him as a near-superhero despite his diabetes.

'Did he hate needles?' Damien asked.

'He got used to them,' I said.

Needles. Once, I entered the barn uninvited and found my grandfather on a metal stool, a tourniquet around his bicep, a needle pressed to his inner arm.

'What are you doing?' I asked him.

He was pale, sweating.

'It's medicine,' he said. 'Helps my body process sugar.'

I leaned in closer to observe as he broke skin then depressed the syringe.

'Why don't you just take pills?' I asked.

'This is faster,' he said. 'Gets the medicine straight to my blood.'

'Why are you doing this in *here*?'

My grandfather released a genuine laugh.

'Your grandmother hates my needles. So does your mother. So I hide in here.'

I reached to swipe away the tiny bulb of blood that appeared where the needle had pricked his arm.

'Can you die from diabetes?' I asked him.

'Not if you look after yourself. It's not a disease. It's a condition.'

'What's a condition?' I asked.

My grandfather had a slow way of answering questions. He glanced upward and frowned, as if formulating each response in his head before uttering it.

'A disease makes you sick,' he said. 'A condition, you just have to manage.'

I nodded, solemn.

'Can we keep this between us? Your grandmother won't like me discussing this with you. She doesn't like people to know. Thinks people will judge.'

'Okay,' I said, standing tall, glad for our little secret. 'For sure.'

A few years ago, I found a photo of my grandfather in the barn in a box in my mother's basement. How my heart lurched to see him again, this hardworking, quiet-but-funny man, the closest I ever came to a father, however briefly I had him in my life. I showed the picture Damien.

'See?' I said. 'He had diabetes. And look at him. No man was stronger than him.'

'But didn't he die young?' Damien asks.

'Yes, at sixty. But not of diabetes.'

'Of what, then?'

'A heart attack.'

Yes, a heart attack. A broken heart. Damien asked if he could keep the photo. Despite the teenage angst we get at home, out in the world, Damien is a charming and reliable boy. He even wears his diabetes like a badge of honor, giving speeches to his classes and raising money for insulin funds by hitting up parents on his soccer team. But he can be careless about it too, enough to leave me with a constant low hum of worry.

I stay tucked in the vestibule where I can spy without him noticing me. He's just turned fifteen. When Damien was a small boy, I'd time my midday walks to pass the school at his recess. I loved nothing more than catching a glimpse of him in the yard when he didn't know I was there. Isobel spent her recesses tucked in a corner with her friends, but Damien was always gregariously out in the open, easy to spot. He was the boy running and laughing wildly, chasing the ball, wrapping his friends in bear hugs. Tumbling around. You could hear Damien Walsh before you saw him. But something has changed in him these recent months. The sullenness is difficult to take. He won't talk to Paul or to me about anything to do with his life, but a mother can sense their child's broken heart as if it beats alongside her own.

When did this independence happen? If someone pointed out to me, in the hours following their births, that one day my children would be fully formed humans with lives mostly detached from mine, I would not have believed it. I know how it works, but doesn't every mother experience her children like she is the only person in history to have borne them? And what a marvel mine are. Isobel a wonder because she is so like me in looks, and yet my foil in disposition. And then sweet Damien, a child so earnest and hopeful, tall and messy. I miss the days when my children climbed all over us. These days, we are like planets, the four of us, Paul, Isobel, Damien, and me, all in our own orbits.

Damien holds his phone to his ear, waiting. And then he is talking, his features animated. There's a pleading to it, a vehemence. *Don't*, I want to yell at him. *Don't!*

To my horror he begins walking and stops in front of the store. Lacey emerges, and the two of them face each other, a standoff. I step out from the vestibule. Do I intervene? From my distance I can hear the sharpness of their exchange, but not the words. *Stop it*, I think Lacey says before spinning on her heel and reentering the store. Damien stands alone. Pulsing. Angry. Oh no. I tuck back out of view.

Just then, two of his teammates approach from behind, calling to him and slapping him on the back. Damien exchanges a series of affectionate handshakes with his friends, regrouping with unnerving speed. The trio sets off on their way to practice, opting for a side street route to Winngrove Park that avoids any possible run-ins with me.

Damien. My darling boy. He turns the corner, gone.

When our kids were younger, women assured me all the time that things would feel easier with Damien. Second kids are just less work. And there's generally less to worry about with boys. Has it panned out that way? I don't think so. I don't think Damien has spared me much worry over the years. Certainly not now.

The truth is things have been different between Damien and me since I fell. The New Year's Eve party itself is hazy, but the fall isn't. I remember the moment in perfect detail. After I caught him with Lacey, Damien scrambled to follow me to the top of the stairs. In my rush to escape such a horrifically embarrassing moment, I tripped. Was Damien close enough to reach out and catch my arm? That's the question I can't answer. What I can recall perfectly is the sensation of lightness when there is nothing behind you to break your fall. It feels like flying.

After that, my memory is blank. Paul and my mother both claim I tried to sit up right away, waving them off despite the obvious and unnatural twist of my body. Apparently, I was belligerent in the ambulance. My memory holds nothing until I woke up after the surgery. The last thing I remember is my son's expression as my arms whipped in circles, flailing for something to grab. I remember the exact look on Damien's face.

I dig through my tote for the pack and light another cigarette, crossing the street to a sidewalk bench under a tree. This morning I woke up with an unwavering sense of dread. I'm good at channeling that dread into purpose, my lists always at hand, my tasks simple enough. My phone reads 11:27. I'm barely half a mile from home, but the prospect of retracing my morning journey overwhelms me.

Get up, Nadine. Get up and go home.

All this nostalgia is unwelcome, but I can't shake it. All I want is to be ready for the party.

The party. Thirty years ago, the party for my mother was Colleen's idea. I remember showing up with my mother at the farm a week or so before the big day. I was overjoyed to encounter Colleen in the kitchen wearing the necklace I'd sent her for her birthday.

'Hi, bear,' she said, wrapping me in a hug. 'Look at you. Ten. All grown up.'

All was forgiven, it seemed.

'You don't have to do this, you know,' my mother said to my grandmother. 'Throw me a party? You really don't.'

'Yes, we do,' Colleen said. 'You deserve a party.'

'I don't mind,' my grandmother said.

'She's actually enjoying it,' Colleen said.

My mother smiled at Colleen, unconvinced. The cease-fire felt devious, insincere. But in the days that followed, I was surprised to see that my grandmother *did* seem to enjoy the planning with Colleen.

'Who's invited?' I asked them at the kitchen table.

'Neighbors, mostly,' my grandmother said. 'I'm not sure where we'll fit everyone.'

'We can use the folding tables,' Colleen suggested. 'With table-cloths. Rows of pies.'

'*Rows* of pies?'

But my grandmother was laughing. Colleen squeezed my shoulders. What profound relief to have her back. I was equally thrilled to be in the barn again every morning with my grandfather. And a party to look forward to! What fun we would have.

A few days before the party, my grandparents again traveled to the city for an appointment with my grandfather's specialist and opted to stay overnight when a summer storm blew in. That night, I woke to the howl of rain and the barn doors flapping in the wind. My mother was a sound sleeper, so I got up and debated going outside to close them myself. The clattering doors was surely upsetting the horses. I debated waking Colleen, but when I went to her room, she wasn't in her bed.

Only once I got to the porch did I notice the light at the rear of the barn. I found my raincoat and boots and sprinted through the lashing rain across the lawn. I reached the barn doors and flicked on the stall lights.

Voices. I heard voices.

'Hello?' I called. 'Mom? Colleen?'

The horses watched me, eyes wide and sidelong. Scared, like me. The youngest steed lifted his muzzle over the stall door so I could scratch the gap between his eyes. Then came the sounds of an engine.

I watched through the doors as a car appeared then receded down the driveway. It was one of those Jeeps with no doors. Black.

I left the steed and walked the length of the stalls. How my heart pounded.

'Colleen?'

There she was. The barn floor was swept clean but for a few square bales of hay. She sat on one of them, her shirt half-unbuttoned. Even from afar I could see her eyes weren't just glassy. They looked dull. Vacant.

'Colleen? Who just left?'

She waved a single finger at me. 'You nosy little thing,' she said.

'Are you okay?'

'I'm fine,' she said.

Her eyes were closed, her head swaying. I approached and sat beside her on the bale.

'Who was that?' I asked again.

'City boy. He's taking me places.'

'Taking you where?'

Colleen seemed to finally take note of me then. She angled to face me, then swept her thumb across my lips. 'You're really pretty. You know that?' Over and over, she cleared her throat.

'You won't tell anyone, will you?' she finally asked. 'I hate getting in trouble.'

You fucking tattletale.

'I won't tell anyone,' I said. 'I promise.'

She smiled and hugged me. 'I love you, Nadine.'

How my heart soared. 'I love you too. We should go back to the house.'

'Yes,' she said. 'To bed.'

I turned off the barn lights and fastened the doors closed. I helped Colleen up, and we held hands as I guided her back to the house and into her bed.

Once I was finally in my own room, I lay awake in the quiet, the wind gone. My stomach turned. I had a terrible feeling something bad was about to happen. Whether I knew it or not, I sensed what was coming next.

The party.

Three days later, I would again wake to the sound of the barn doors and again chart that same path down the stairs. It was almost morning, my mother's birthday having ended only hours earlier. Out the window, the east sky held its first trace of light. The oven clock read 4:30 a.m. Again, I climbed the stairs to Colleen's room. Again, I found her bed empty. I could have woken someone else. My grandfather, my mother. But what if we found Colleen with a boy? I didn't want to get her in trouble. So I went downstairs, put on my boots, and slid through the back door as quietly as I could.

The air felt fresh and cool. I stepped inside the barn, approached my favorite horse, and listened. I must have stood there for two minutes until I heard a sound. Later, the police officers who interviewed me would ask me to describe it.

'What did you hear?'

And I couldn't. I couldn't make sense of the sound—was there even a sound at all?—so I told them I'd heard a voice.

When I close my eyes now, I can picture the deep brown eyes of the horse in its stall, the whinny when I turned away to follow whatever sound had caught my attention. I walked the length of the stables until the barn opened up to the field at its far end. And there she was, my darling Colleen, lying on a bale of hay, one arm over her face, her legs bent oddly at the knees. Even at ten years old, I knew the color of her skin was wrong, unnatural.

'Colleen?' I called.

A sleeping body will flicker with small signs of life, a rise and fall of the chest or a twitch of a lip or finger. And I so kept my eyes fixed on Colleen as I repeated her name. I stood at some distance, searching for the tiniest tremor. But there was none. It was her stillness that gave it away. A stillness that comes only with death.

AFTERNOON

NINETEEN YEARS AGO, IN THE FIRST month of my sophomore year, the handsome and charming Paul Walsh waltzed into my life. He was a law student five years older than me, a teaching assistant in my political science seminar. He belonged on the pages of a fashion magazine: tall and lean, his jaw angular, his hair wavy but not too long. Two dimples even formed on his cheeks when he smiled, which he often did. When his eyes landed on you, your instinct was to shift in your seat.

Funnily enough, I wasn't even attracted to him at first. The other girls in the seminar would blush when he entered the classroom. But not me. Objectively, I could acknowledge his good looks and his wit, but he seemed so far out of my league that my body responded by muting any chemical reaction to his presence. I was studying criminology, one of only four girls in my program and a GPA at the top of my class. I refused to be distracted from my studies by something as unoriginal as a good-looking TA.

One afternoon, Paul and I ran into each other in line at an off-campus coffee shop. I was surprised he even knew my name. He suggested I join him that afternoon at a documentary screening. I did. There I met his two closest friends: Seymour Dunphy and Lionel Robinson, one a law student and the other a fledgling journalist. Neither of them was pleased by this sophomore tagalong, but Paul was. He walked me home and we talked and talked. It felt like a revelation to have someone engaged by my ideas. To think of me as smart. To look at me the way Paul did.

Soon enough, I was exactly what I swore I'd never be: distracted. Paul began showing up at my dorm to take me for walks. We'd sit shoulder to shoulder on the couch at his off-campus bachelor apartment, watching police procedurals and pretending our intention was to remain friends. At parties, he'd crack jokes about the impropriety of a TA forming a crush on a student. He'd wrap a protective arm around me and warn his friends that I was off-limits. In class our eyes would sometimes lock and my heart would flutter. Suddenly, I was a hopeless romantic, no better than my tittering classmates. I'd never been a sucker for love, but the barrier formed by our initial teacher/student dynamic built up so much tension between us that by the end of term, I'd arrive at class ready to burst.

Now, seventeen years of marriage later, I stand at the bottom of the basement stairs and listen to Paul's laugh echo through our kitchen. He's ribbing Margot about her sneakers. His voice is still gravelly with sleep.

I love him. I do. It was a risk marrying as young as we did, an elopement to city hall on account of my pregnancy. We settled down and had a baby, then another baby, while the rest of our cohort was busy sowing their wild oats. Our marriage has weathered its share of storms over the years, but Paul is a great father, a devoted if sometimes oblivious husband. For months after my affair with Lionel ended, I'd lie in bed and wonder what Paul would do if I confessed to the entire sordid thing. Divorce me? Lobby for custody of the kids? My guilt forced me to ponder the messiest outcomes I believed I deserved, but the truth is, he'd probably forgive me, move on. He's much more pragmatic than I am.

I take one last deep breath and ascend the basement stairs. Paul spots me and approaches with opens arms. I enter the hug gratefully. His smell hasn't changed in decades, the musky deodorant giving off a scent both familiar and sexy. I pinch the loose cotton of his T-shirt.

"Your dry cleaning is in the hall closet."

Paul and Margot exchange a glance.

"I can't believe you made Nadine pick it up," Margot says.

"I didn't!" Paul says. "I sent Isobel."

"You're a terrible man," I say.

He laughs and we hug again. Margot hovers on the far side of the island. Her list rests on the counter, over half its tasks already crossed off. God, I couldn't live without Margot. I should be hugging *her*.

The kettle on the stove begins to whistle, startling me yet again. Margot lifts it and sets about making us tea. She is the only person in my life, my mother and Paul included, capable of calibrating the milk and tea at the exact ratio to my liking. I accept the mug from her and sip the warmth. It burns down my throat. When I arrived home from my errands, I entered the house via the side door and took a good twenty minutes in the basement to gather myself, changing my shirt and running a dryer sheet through my hair to mask the smell of cigarette smoke.

The tension between Paul and me is palpable. Margot must detect it because she clears her throat and moves toward the front hall.

"I promised Isobel I'd help her pick out an outfit," Margot says.

"Why don't I go upstairs and lay her out some options before she gets home from the hospital? Give you two a minute to drink your tea and get reacquainted?"

"Or bicker," I say.

Paul's eyes land on me the instant we are alone. For years I've been able to predict our encounters before they happened, the energy between us gathering like clouds before a storm. I step closer to him.

"Ready for a fun party?" he asks.

"Mostly."

He kisses my cheek. "I promise to be diligent with my task list. A devoted foot soldier. No more delegating."

"That's right," I say. "I'm the only delegator in this family."

"You are. And I love it when you order me around."

There it is. I take his hand and lead him down the stairs to my basement. Paul would surely assume we'd go upstairs as we usually do. Lock our bedroom door. Even once we are inside the downstairs bathroom he seems not to understand what's happening, looking around at the sink and toilet as though I'm about to present him with a chore. I shake myself out of my capris and panties and reach for his belt buckle, pulling him into a deep kiss and lifting a leg to wrap it around him.

"Jesus, Nadine," he says, breathless.

We fumble. His breath smells like morning and coffee but I don't care. I am riled up today. This will be good for me, a sure way to shake off some of the energy. Not to mention it'll put Paul at ease, send him into a bit of a spell that will allow me more leeway to move about the rest of the day unencumbered. He leans into me. We're both sweating. When I close my eyes, Lionel's face appears. What was I thinking bringing Paul down here? This should fill me with guilt—*you are a bad person, Nadine*—but it doesn't. It only riles me up more.

"You smell like cigarettes," Paul whispers.

"I've been bad," I say.

Lately, I've been reminiscing more about our early days. By the time my seminar ended at Christmas, and he was no longer my TA, Paul and I were locked in a duel of sorts. Who would relent first, admit their feelings? One day Paul drove me out of the city for a winter picnic on a lake, an outing between two young people still pretending to be friends. When we stood to pack up and leave, Paul wrapped me in his peacoat and kissed me with the gusto of a romantic film hero. I remember feeling something in me snap open. His lips pressed into mine, his ungloved hands freezing against my cheeks.

After that kiss, things progressed quickly. Paul was fumbling but enthusiastic in bed, a *body scholar* he jokingly called himself, so we did well as lovers from the start. He made me laugh. He was ambitious and high achieving. Incredibly handsome. His life seemed uncomplicated. His friends, namely Seymour and Lionel, were snobby but devoted to him. He was impressed but not thunderstruck by my mom's fame. It all felt lovely, easy, happy.

One Saturday morning, a month or so into our dating life, Paul arrived breathlessly to my dorm room while I studied with a friend. He'd casually mentioned my mother to his family, the famous writer Marilyn Millay, and his aunt made the connection for him: Paul's parents used to own the hobby farm next to my grandparents' in Terriville. And guess what? Seymour's family had a place nearby too! Lionel even used to spend time there. It's where their early trio of friendship formed. They all used to run wild there in the summers, driving dirt bikes along the edges of the wheat fields. Paul recounted these memories to me with a glaze of wistful wonder.

'We've been connected all this time!' he declared.

'So you knew my grandparents?' I asked.

'Well, no,' Paul answered. 'Kind of. My parents knew them. Your grandfather rented our fields. Farmed them. I think I remember their farm. The Fitzgeralds?'

'That's them.'

Paul frowned. 'I think your grandfather might have even boarded my horse.'

My horse. I remember thinking: Paul had the kind of childhood where he owned a horse.

'Yes,' I said quietly. 'He probably did. He had a stable.'

'Do you think *we* ever met?' Paul asked, breathless. 'I'd go there to see my horse. I was at a party there once. The one where that girl was found dead in the barn.'

That girl. Perhaps Paul noticed my features twist then, a grimace I tried to mask. His own face shifted with the realization.

'Hang on,' he continued. 'Holy shit. You were related to her.'

'She was my aunt,' I said. 'My mom's younger sister.'

Now, in the basement bathroom, Paul shudders against me at the same time as I come. We are terribly efficient that way, a well-oiled machine. He stands and wipes my brow with a tender thumb.

"Sexy thing," he says.

I pull him in for a last, long kiss.

"I am," I say. "Now go away."

We tug our clothes back into place. Paul kicks the bathroom door open and strides down the hall and up the stairs to the kitchen. We'll exchange glances for the rest of the day, this encounter our dirty little secret.

In the early stages of our dating life, I kept Paul a bit of a secret too, from my friends and even from my mother. When I finally did tell her about him, I led with the detail I suspected would disconcert her most.

'His family had a farm in Terriville. What a small world. They sold it a few years ago. The Walshes?'

'I don't remember that name,' she replied. 'Walsh, you said?'

By then my mother had been famous for years; she'd endured enough prying interviews on TV and onstage and was exceptionally well practiced at maintaining her composure.

'Paul says that Grandpa was the one who farmed their fields for them. Even boarded their horse for a while. Their family was at your birthday party. The night Colleen . . .'

'A lot of people were at that party,' my mother said. 'Small world, indeed. I'll have to meet this Paul.'

'Maybe you've already met him.'

'I don't think so.'

I dropped it. And so here's my confession: In the darker moments of our marriage, I've sometimes wondered whether this extraordinary link between our families kept me drawn to Paul after the sheen of our early romance began to wear off. Once, at dinner with the Walshes, I attempted to press for details, about my grandparents, even about Colleen. I did the same with Paul's friends who'd been in Terriville too— Seymour, and even Lionel. I asked them about a Jeep with no doors I'd seen on the farm in the days before Colleen died, city boys who might have been around. But no one seemed to remember much about the Fitzgeralds or their farm. Seymour was the only one with any real sense of nostalgia. He used to visit my grandparents' farm with his father to talk about farming the land. He remembered Colleen, but claimed he never saw much of her. Farmers, he said, didn't mix with the rich weekend warriors.

One night, as we lay in bed on a visit with his parents, Paul turned the tables and started to press me.

'You're always bringing up the farm,' he said. 'You seem kind of fixated on it.'

'Maybe I am.'

'Why?'

And so I told him. About my beloved grandparents and my years of visits. About finding Colleen dead in the barn. About the chasm that formed between my mother and my grandparents after she died. How we left the farm right after her death and never returned. I told him about how my grandparents took me to the police station the morning of Colleen's death and allowed me to be interviewed alone while my mother slept off the party, oblivious to it all. But even though I was sharing the facts of the story, I chose to omit the depths of my anguish. Paul believed me to be a reasonably happy person with a reasonably happy past, and it felt too early in our relationship to shatter that illusion. As my relationship with Paul grew more serious, the omission felt both weightier and impossible to undo.

Colleen's death haunted me. Yes, I could fixate sometimes. Did I really need to admit it?

'I wish I remembered more,' I offered him. 'Or more clearly.'

'I get it,' Paul said, hugging me.

After that, he dropped it. But at the end of my sophomore year, as I was helping Paul pack to head home for the summer, I found a shoebox at the back of his dresser drawer. It was full of stories and articles about Colleen's death. The news stories I'd already read—I had my own collection, my own files tucked away. But at the bottom of the box was a photo I'd never seen before, a group shot from the party. It depicted a crowd in a long row and included Seymour, Lionel, my grandparents,

Paul's parents, and Paul, so coincidentally, standing on one side of me. Colleen was on the other.

My heart sputtered. I sat on Paul's bed and waited for him, shaking, the box resting neatly on my lap. When he sauntered back into the room and spotted me, his hands immediately flew up in defense.

'What the fuck is this?' I asked.

'Wait. Slow your horses. It's not what you think. I was trying to help.'

'Help what?'

'Help you . . . I don't know? Work through what happened . . . Find out more. My aunt gave me this photo. I looked up some articles. I was going to give it all to—'

'You realize this is fucking creepy, right?' I interjected.

And then I threw the box at him. It hit him in the chest then dropped to the floor when he failed to catch it. The contents scattered, Colleen's young face staring up from one of the clippings. Paul looked scared.

'This was all for you, I swear.' He bent down to pick up the box, turning it to show my name, NADINE, written in block letters on one side. 'See?'

'Then why'd you keep it from me?'

'It wasn't meant to be a secret, I swear,' he pleaded. 'It was meant to be a surprise.'

These memories swirl today. I still have that box of articles Paul collected for me. It's in my office, locked in a drawer. I'm tempted to retrieve it now, empty its contents on the floor of my basement office, rifle through them, immerse myself in the dark nostalgia of it. But that's a bad idea. Not now. Imagine Margot or my mother coming down here and finding me like that? More evidence for them that I'm acting crazy.

It's been five minutes since Paul left me here in the bathroom, and I'm still frozen in place, staring at my own blank reflection. Paul and me? We're okay. Even a marriage that seems steady to an outsider can be full of ups and downs. I've often thought that it's the downs that ultimately bring you closer. The losses you endure. The secrets you keep. I hope that for all our downs, Paul and I will hang on forever. Because despite my wrongdoings, the risks I've taken with our life together, I don't know what I'd do without him. I need to believe he'd forgive me for almost anything.

MARGOT AND I ARE IN THE garden on our knees, passing my fancy clippers back and forth as we select flowers for the centerpieces. She descended from upstairs shortly after I emerged from the basement. We came outside together. There's been some chatter, but the stretches of silence feel strange, heavy.

The backyard is a splendor. Its July blooms are plentiful and bright, the grass a lush and deep green. The deck space has been cleared to make way for the caterer, Gregory, and his BBQ station, and then the bar and the band. Yes, a band. It was Paul's idea, his surprise for my mother. She loves live music. Last night, Isobel and Margot zigzagged rows of white string lights over the deck then brought me outside after sundown so I could examine their handiwork. The effect was dazzling. The weather is beautiful. In a matter of hours, the yard will be packed.

If only my hands would stop shaking. Margot hands me the clippers.

"How long have you and Daphne Robinson been friends?" I ask her.

"You asked us that at the café."

"Right. Did you answer?"

"We met at a reading, remember?" Margot wipes her brow with the back of her arm. "Do you not like her, Nadine? What's the issue?"

"I don't *dislike* her." This, clearly, is a lie. "I just don't know her very well. She's quite young."

Margot laughs. "She's five years older than me."

"Young to be married to one of Paul's friends, I mean."

"Well, she likes you. Admires you. She was telling me this story about you taking on city council when they tried to sell parkland to a condo developer. Said you gave some big speech at city hall. And you won too. Swayed them. Why did I know nothing about that?"

I frown. "That was years ago."

"So? You did a really cool thing."

"Once." I yank at a weed. "How would Daphne even know about that? It was well before her time."

Margot shrugs. "Lionel probably told her? Anyway, she was impressed. You two have similar interests. I think she'd like to be your friend. If you'd let her."

Oh God. I can't parse Margot's tone. To think of Daphne and Lionel talking about me, Lionel opting to tell his new wife that condo story, casting me in a positive light. This can't be right. *She was impressed*. It all feels like a blip. Aren't we supposed to hate each other? Some part of me is tempted to confess the whole affair to Margot right now. Every last wretched detail. Just let it all spew out and take what comes. But I can't do that.

"Are you okay with me cutting some of the peonies?" Margot asks.

"Sure. Whatever you want. Speaking of which, I went to visit Colleen's grave this morning. On my errands. She's buried at St. Basil's."

"The cemetery just up the road? That's weird. I thought she lived on a farm in the country."

"She did. But there's a family plot at St. Basil's from a century ago. My grandparents are buried there too. Marilyn's parents. Anyway, I leave peonies on their graves when I go."

"Oh," Margot says.

She tugs at the flowers' stems to snip them at the right length. Margot's body language is telling; if she's keen on a topic, she'll stop what she's doing and make eye contact, square herself to you, and engage. And if she's not, she'll continue her task and offer only small interjections. *Oh.*

"Did you know that Marilyn hates peonies?"

"What?" Margot laughs. "Impossible."

It's true. My mother hates peonies. Once, years ago, she threatened to rip any evidence of them from my garden. I was aghast. Who hates a flower as beautiful as a peony?

'Their blooms die too fast,' my mother insisted, waving a hand at the shrub. 'And look at them, bent right to the dirt. What good is a flower too heavy for its own stalk?'

Now, Margot lays a selection of pink peonies in a row on the grass.

"Gorgeous!" she exclaims.

She's right. They are dewy, complex. Fragile.

"How about some lilies of the valley?" Margot suggests. "They're still in good shape."

"Good choice," I say, sipping my water. "So. Did you pick an outfit for Isobel?"

"I laid out a few options for her. I'll warn you that she might not wear a dress. She told me she doesn't care how she looks tonight. That it feels weird to put in any effort. She's stressed out."

Of course she would be. But Isobel certainly doesn't show it.

"Has Isobel spoken to you much, Margot? Has she talked to you about River?"

Margot shifts to sitting cross-legged. She doesn't meet my eye. "A bit. Not really."

"I've noticed she's not on social media anymore. Like, at all."

"Yeah," Margot says. "I noticed that too."

Something is up. Since Margot came to live with us, I've tried to encourage a rapport between her and Isobel. I've been deliberate in not prying for insider information, in not pressing Margot to play the snitch by relaying any insider details Isobel might share with her. But this? This is different.

"Margot. If you knew something about River, you'd tell me, right?"

With a sigh she sets the clippers on the grass and faces me.

"There was a video, apparently. A video of River. Isobel . . . she filmed her."

I feel the blood drain from my face. "Filmed her doing *what*?"

"Dancing, I think. Dancing drunk. It might have been some kind of striptease. I asked Isobel to show it to me, you know . . . so I could help gauge the threat. See how bad it was. But she balked and told me she'd deleted it pretty much right away."

"*Pretty much* right away? When did she film it?"

"A few weeks before the OD. She claims only a small group of people saw it. Damien might have been one of them."

"What? My son Damien? Margot!"

"I know, Nadine. I'm sorry. Isobel swears it's been wiped. Contained."

"How can she be sure of that?"

Margot shakes her head. "Listen. I feel like I have my ear to the ground around here. You know, with the kids and their friends. If this was a big thing, like a video that went viral, something a lot of people saw, if it had anything to do with . . . what followed with River? I would have heard about it. You probably would have too. Viral videos don't just go away. You can't unshoot a gun. Isobel swears it's gone and there's no evidence that she's lying. So I believe her."

"Then why did she confess to you?" I ask.

"I think she just needed to get it off her chest. She probably feels guilty. When someone you love gets hurt, you rehash everything that led up to it. You know?"

"Yes," I say. "I know."

"And, Nadine? Isobel only told me a few days ago. I swear. And now I'm telling you."

"You should have told me as soon as you found out."

"I was going to wait until after the party. I was compartmentalizing on account of your stress levels. Wrong move, I guess. I'm a traitor for telling you, and a traitor for *not* telling you. Isobel's going to kill me."

"Not if she doesn't find out," I say. I sit quietly for a moment, plucking at the grass. "She was interviewed by the police the afternoon she found River. She made no mention of a video. That could get her into trouble. It could be perjury. Or something."

"What? No way. There's no crime. A kid overdosed. No charges can be laid for that."

"No. Not for that. That's what the officer told Isobel. That any charges were unlikely."

"Your daughter did a good job of protecting River."

I consider this. She filmed River doing something scandalous then tried to bury the evidence. Is that what a friend does? I'd say Isobel has done a good job protecting herself.

As usual, Margot reads my mind. "Come on, Nadine. You know how kids are these days with their phones. They film everything. River's been depressed. She was drinking a lot. Experimenting with drugs." Margot pauses, frowning. "Fucking a lot of guys."

"Jeez," I say. I'm taken aback by her use of that word. *Fucking.*

"I promise you," Margot says. "This is not something to fixate on. It's not a big deal."

"What's not a big deal?"

This is a man's voice. Both Margot and I scramble to our feet. Our neighbor, Theodore Rosen, stands next to the cedar tree at the low part of our fence. His arms are crossed and he smiles at us, amused. Was he eavesdropping?

"Hi, Theodore," I say, flustered.

"Teddy. How many times do I have to tell you to call me Teddy?"

He's chiding me. Flirting, perhaps. I clear my throat.

"I hope I'm not interrupting," he says.

"Actually, you are," Margot says abruptly.

"Margot!" I exclaim. "She didn't mean that."

"I wasn't eavesdropping," Teddy says. "I promise."

"Right," Margot says.

Why is she being so rude? I release a flustered laugh. My only way out is to gloss it over with small talk. I show him the clippers I'm holding. "We're just cutting flowers for the centerpieces."

"Centerpieces?" Teddy says. "My goodness. This will be some party."

Theodore is on the guest list for tonight. It's always good to keep peace with your neighbors, even if Theodore—Teddy—is also our tenant. We've rented out the house attached to ours ever since we bought it, mostly to visiting faculty or doctors completing fellowships at the local hospital, our way of assuring good neighbors. Theodore is an old friend of Seymour's, a fact I try not to hold against him, a financier who moved back from London last Christmas after taking early retirement. He's spending a year renting before buying a condo or a house of his own, probably nearby. He's a bachelor, a quiet neighbor.

'Why is he single?' I asked Paul the day Theodore was set to move in.

'Who knows?' Paul responded. 'Seymour says he's had a few girl-friends and that's it. Maybe we should set him up with your mom. She could use a nice younger fellow, don't you think?'

'My mom hates money men. Besides, I don't trust a straight man who's never been married.'

Paul laughed. 'Your mom's never been married!'

'My mom isn't a man.'

'Ha. Not everyone domesticates, Nadine.'

Now, Teddy Rosen stands before Margot and me. He's in a golf shirt, tanned and fit, handsome, his salt-and-pepper hair shorn to nearly a buzz cut. He's only a few years older than Paul, but the weath-ered skin around his eyes ages him.

"I don't think we've ever been properly introduced," he says to Margot. "You're quite familiar to me, though. I've seen you around."

"This is Margot Walsh," I say. "My niece. She's staying with us."

"Right!" he says. "Eric's daughter. What a resemblance."

I cock my head at him. "Resemblance?"

"I met Paul's brother, Eric, a few times through Seymour. The fa-mous Walsh brothers! Seymour idolized them when we were young. I imagine he still does."

His words are directed at Margot. I knew about this connection. Teddy is the same age as Paul's older brother, Eric. They all ran in overlapping circles as teenagers. Teddy waits for Margot to speak, but she doesn't.

"Well, that was decades ago," he continues. "We were boys! Anyhoo. You look just like your dad did at your age. A prettier version, naturally."

"Gross," Margot says, turning away.

I smile apologetically at Teddy but he only laughs, unfazed. What is happening? I've never seen Margot act this way. I'm not sure whether to scold her or admire her nerve. She plucks her phone from the rear pocket of her shorts.

"Your mom just texted me," she says. "She's on her way."

"Well," Teddy says. "I should let you both go. You've got a busy afternoon ahead."

"We'll see you tonight?" I ask.

"Wouldn't miss it."

As Theodore walks away, Margot sidles up to me and watches him climb the porch steps and enter the house.

"Puke," she says.

"What is wrong with you? You were downright hostile."

"Give me a break. He's disgusting."

"You've never even met him before!"

"Yes, I have. When I was twelve, my dad brought me along on a business trip to London and Mr. Teddy Rosen took us out for dinner. I totally remember him. My dad became another man in his presence. I'd never seen him like that. Old-boys thing. Teddy Fuckface drank, like, five martinis and . . . touched me."

"Touched you how?"

"I don't know. He closed his hand around my bare arm and sort of rubbed my skin with his thumb. It wasn't a grope. My dad didn't even notice. But I remember the feeling. You know, girls just have that built-in sense. Like you can detect when a man is touching you like you're . . ."

"Theirs," I offer.

"Exactly. Like you're a woman. And I was just a girl."

Margot pulls her phone from the pocket of her jeans, her fingers flying over the screen in response to a message. A knot has formed in my stomach. When I was on the cusp of puberty, my mother made a few things clear to me: Sometimes, men will look at you or touch you in a way that feels foul. They might mean nothing by it, but their intentions don't matter. Always trust your own gut. Years later, I had the same talk with Isobel.

I bend over to collect the flowers we've cut. The sun is high and warm, but my arms are goose-bumped. I turn to Margot.

"I think we have enough. Shall we go inside?"

"Yes," she says. "Isobel just texted. She's almost home."

T HERE'S A CROWD IN THE KITCHEN. Paul, Isobel, my mother, and Margot are gathered around the island. I plant a kiss on Isobel's cheek, craning when she leans away to avoid my affection. She's home from her hospital visit with River much sooner than I thought she'd be. She picks apart a croissant without eating it. Paul and I make eye contact. He lifts and lowers his eyebrows, a boyish allusion to our basement bathroom tryst.

"We all have our orders, Captain," he says to me. "Unless you've got more duties to add."

"Where's my list?" my mother asks.

"It's your job to boss everyone around, Marilyn," Paul says. "You're the proxy drill sergeant."

"I'm not doing anything else," Isobel whines. "There are twenty things on my list! And you should take some of them off my hands, Dad, since you made me go fetch your suit."

"Didn't your mom promise you a phone upgrade if you pulled your weight today?" Margot asks.

"She did." Isobel plucks a grape from the bowl in front of her and pops it into her mouth. "You can be absolutely sure I haven't forgotten about that."

"One day you'll outgrow bribes," Margot says with a laugh.

"Isn't that what *working* is?" Isobel asks. "One career-long form of bribery?"

"She's kind of got a point," Paul replies.

"I'd say that I shouldn't have to pay my children to participate in the running of a household we all live in," I say.

Isobel cocks her head. "Then lower your standards, Mom."

They all laugh. This is their silver bullet. Paul, Damien, and Isobel have long unionized against me, Marilyn weighing in on their behalf. If the kitchen is clean by any normal person's standards, they argue, then it *is* clean. Should I want any further tasks completed to meet my wildly elevated expectations, then I'm welcome to make up the difference myself. Paul tows this line above all.

"All I ask is that no one makes a mess," I say, exasperated. "Practice no-trace living today, please? Me and my stress levels will thank you."

"Sure," Isobel says. "But tell *him* that."

"Tell me what?"

Damien stands in the kitchen's threshold, his face and soccer jersey both streaked with dirt. He holds his mud-caked cleats in one hand. He heads straight for his grandmother's wide-open arms. Damien is well into the march of puberty. Still, the changes feel new and shocking to me. He burrows into my mother's hug.

"Happy Birthday, Nana," he says.

"Thank you, darling. You excited about the party?"

"I guess?"

Damien elicits a collective gasp by setting his cleats down on the kitchen island.

"See?" Isobel shrieks. "You are such a pig!"

"I'm starving," Damien says, patting his belly, ignoring his sister.

"Have you checked your blood sugar?"

"Yes! Jeez, Mom."

Paul glares at me: *Stop hovering.* Here's the thing about Damien. He can be careless with his shoes and socks, his schoolbooks, his soccer equipment, his phone. But he can also be careless with his insulin. How many times have I found used syringes cast about the house? How many times have I had to chase down a supply at the last moment to ensure he has enough? I'm often walking around with a prepped syringe in my pocket just in case he's forgotten his dose. It's not hovering. It's parenting.

"Toast?" Paul says to Damien.

"Yes, please."

"If you make a mess anywhere, Mom will basically murder you," Isobel says.

Damien takes the pose of a soldier and holds it for comedic effect.

"How was practice?" I ask.

"Fine. Hot. Lots of running."

"I picked up more insulin for you. It's in the basement."

Damien sips at the tall glass of ice water Paul has placed in front of him, lifting his phone so I can read his sugar levels transmitted from a patch on his arm. I've collected his soccer bag and retrieved the small kit that houses his insulin. The group watches as I prepare the needle.

"Can't he do that himself?" Isobel says.

"Mind your own business," Damien says.

Margot stands at the fridge, using a cloth to wipe down the condiment bottles on its door. "A friend of mine from high school has diabetes. He uses a pump. It's entirely automatic."

"We tried that," Paul says. "Mr. Six Pack here didn't like wearing it. Cramped his style."

Damien presents me with his arm. I tighten the tourniquet around his bicep. I shouldn't enjoy this process, but I do. Damien is perfectly capable of managing this himself, but he still lets me, and I'll take whatever chance I get to mother him. The ritual of it reminds me of my grandfather. Damien sucks in a quick breath when it pierces.

"I like the needles better," he says to Margot. "Weirdly, the chicks seem to dig it."

"Literally no chicks dig you," Isobel says.

"Tell that to your friends," Damien quips.

Chicks. I hate that word too. I think of him in front of Marvin's store in a standoff with Lacey. The rage on his face. Did Damien come right home after soccer practice? Or did he stop at the store again?

"Is Lacey coming tonight?" Isobel asks as if cued.

Damien shrugs and retreats to his phone. His expression betrays nothing.

"Mom invited them," Isobel adds. "Marvin and Lacey. Not sure what it says about your *relationship*"—she emphasizes the word with air quotes—"if she fails to show. Don't worry. You'll get over it by the time you start college."

"Shut up," Damien says.

"Just saying. Has she officially dumped you yet?"

"Whatever. I'd ask if your boyfriend is coming, but if I recall correctly, you've never fucking had one."

"Damien!" Marilyn interjects. "Come on, now. Stop it."

My back is turned. I'm handling the small collection of dishes in the sink, biting my lip against the threatening wave of tears. I can't do this right now. Referee my kids. Navigate my mother trying to navigate me. Paul is right: now that Marilyn is here, she'll be the one giving orders. Even in my own home, I'm still the daughter.

I need everyone to leave the kitchen and go on their merry ways. I want to spin on my heels and slam my fist to the countertop, plead for them to stop bickering. I want to remind my children what friends they used to be, the hours they'd spent together digging holes in the yard or finishing puzzles in the den. Paul claims this animosity is a normal sibling phase, one that he and his brother and everyone else experiences in adolescence. Maybe he's right. What would I know? Ever the only child.

It's quiet now. They've picked up on my tension. I dry my hands on a towel and turn to face them. Damien chews the toast Paul set in front of him.

"I'm going to google some flower arrangement styles," Margot says.

"I will help you with that," Marilyn offers.

The two of them retreat to the dining room.

"How's River today?" Paul asks Isobel.

"Fine. The same."

"Seymour told me there were some encouraging signs," I say.

"Yeah. The EEG test is showing activity in her brain."

"That's really good, isn't it?" Paul offers.

"Depends on how much activity," Damien says.

"Shut the fuck up, Damien," Isobel shouts. "Are you a neurologist all of a sudden?"

He shrugs. "I'm just saying."

"Absolutely no one fucking asked you."

"Stop it!" Paul says. "Right now. The two of you, stop it."

And they do, unaccustomed to any sharpness in their father's tone.

"Go shower," he orders Damien. Our son obeys, collecting his cleats then directing a glare at his sister before heading upstairs.

"He's such a little dick," Isobel says once her brother is out of earshot.

"He can be," Paul says. "He's stressed about River too, you know. She's your friend, but she's been in his life for a long time."

"Whatever. He should focus on his own shit."

"Let's change the subject," Paul says. "Did you see Seymour at the hospital?"

"He drove me there. Dropped me at the front door."

"Didn't even go in," I say. "Not exactly Father of the Year."

Paul shakes his head. "Don't start."

"Whatever," Isobel says. "Sherry won't let him stay. He's basically not allowed in River's room if Sherry's there. And she's always there. So what do you want him to do?"

"It's all so terrible," I say. "I wish I could convince Sherry to drop in for a bit tonight. We invited her."

"Are you joking?" Isobel scoffs. "That's not the charitable gesture you think it is."

"Excuse me?"

"Sherry won't even be in the same room as Seymour, and you invited him. Plus, her daughter's in a coma at the hospital. So I don't think she wants to come mingle with her ex-husband and a bunch of people who don't give a shit about her. You can understand that, right?"

"Hey. It could be a nice distraction," Paul interjects, ever the mediator.

"Would you want to go to a party if *I* were in a coma?"

"Jesus," Paul says. "Gear down, Izzy Bear. We get it."

I swallow hard. There is no point in engaging. Isobel is right.

"I'll drop by the hospital this week to see Sherry," I say. "Find her some magazines or something. Some easy reading to distract her."

"Whatever."

With that, Isobel and Paul scatter too. I look at my watch. The caterer, Gregory, will be here soon. This day will march on. I don't blame Paul for not staying behind to comfort me, for finding somewhere else to go. On a day like today, he knows to give me a wide berth.

As for Isobel? She's entitled to her mood. It's been a terribly long six weeks for her. A lifetime. And now there's this video in the mix. A layer of guilt, or fear, added to the saga that Isobel has been carrying all on her own. A secret she's kept from me. From the police.

The day we found River, I was the one to accompany Isobel to the police station so she could give a statement. The detective left Isobel and me waiting for over an hour in the reception area. Never have I felt so protective as I did at that police station, as if I'd armed myself for that moment for years, decades even, my memories of finding Colleen bubbling to the surface.

'What's he going to ask me?' Isobel said, worried.

'The obvious questions,' I responded. 'About what you might have noticed when you found her. What you saw. River's state.'

'She was basically dead,' Isobel said.

'They might want to know what River's been up to. If she's said anything to you recently. Anything worrisome that stuck with you. Or if she's done anything worrisome.'

'I'm not going to puke out her life story,' Isobel said.

'No,' I said, cupping her face close to mine. 'Listen. You have nothing to hide, okay? When he asks you a question, just tell him the truth.'

'There's nothing to tell,' she said. 'I didn't do anything.'

In the end, the interview barely lasted ten minutes. The detective was a rookie not a day older than thirty.

'Where was she when you found her?' the detective asked.

'On the floor next to her bed,' Isobel answered. 'I tried to wake her up. But I didn't move her.'

'Did you touch anything else in the room?'

'No. I don't think so.'

'She didn't,' I interjected. 'She called me right away.'

'Do you know if River was dating anyone?'

'She didn't have a boyfriend.'

Isobel never once made eye contact with him. I knew exactly how it felt to have a detective's questions bearing down on you. Except I was only ten, and my grandparents left me alone for the length of the interrogation. When I went through it thirty years ago, my mother—Marilyn—was at the farm, hungover after a rare night of celebration, still sleeping. My grandparents never bothered to wake her. At least this time, Isobel had me.

The final question the detective asked Isobel was the very same one I was asked when the police interviewed me about Colleen.

'Is there anything else you think we should know?'

'No,' Isobel answered.

No. Nothing about a video, about River's depression, about the promiscuity Margot mentioned in the garden. Nothing about red flags. That question—*Is there anything else you think we should know?*—I understood, in watching Isobel evade it, is simply too open-ended. Too easy to dodge. Thirty years ago, I also opted to omit some details. Details about how, at the party for my mother, my grandmother briefly left me alone in the kitchen to add candles to the birthday cake when Colleen barged in, her face crazed and desperate.

'What are you doing?' I asked her.

'Looking for someone,' Colleen said.

'Who?'

But Colleen didn't answer. She was flustered. Angry. When I tried to follow her out the door to the back porch, she spun to face me.

'Nadine,' she said, angry. 'Go back inside. Got it? Don't follow me around. I don't need your mom on my back.'

I didn't tell the detective any of that. I didn't tell him about three days earlier when I'd found her in the barn in a state, how I'd seen a Jeep with no doors drive away in the storm. I also didn't mention that on the night of the party, when the last traces of dusk hung in the sky, as most of the guests were gathered in the front garden, I watched from the porch as Colleen circled behind the house to the barn. Not alone, but with a man.

Why did I leave that detail out too? Because all I cared about was avoiding Colleen's wrath. I didn't follow her into the barn because I didn't want to be a tattletale. It wasn't registering in my frightened little brain that I should tell the police everything about that night, that there was no more protecting her secrets, no more finding my way back to her good side. Colleen was gone.

Is there anything else you think we should know?

Just like Isobel, I said no.

A few weeks ago, the detective assigned to River's case called me. River's overdose had been ruled accidental, he said. She got hold of her mother's prescription tranquilizers and took too many.

'Happens way too often these days, unfortunately,' the detective said. 'No charges will be filed. It's a family matter, not a criminal one.'

Indeed. That same fact will hold here: River's OD is a family matter, and so is this video. I won't phone that detective. Of course I won't. If I'm to take up its omission from that interview with anyone, it's Isobel. My only duty is to her.

LEAN BACK AGAINST THE COOL glass of our patio doors and watch Gregory prepare the barbecue station on the patio. He unfolds a muslin cloth then lays out the tools of his trade with a surgeon's precision. All the equipment is embossed with his moniker: *Gregory's Farmhouse Catering.*

Gregory's catered some of our smaller gatherings before. I enjoy watching him work. He strikes the perfect balance between rustic and formal—BBQ mixed with gourmet fare delivered by servers in white shirts and ties.

It's hot. Gregory sweats, and so do I. I step away from the door and the kitchen's view and light another cigarette. The first tug causes my chest to ache. The kids will freak out if they catch me. Or maybe they'll rejoice at the prospect of gathering ammunition against me to bank against any future transgressions of their own.

But fuck it. Fuck it, especially today.

"Sorry," I say to Gregory. "I should have asked before lighting this. I know it's a vile habit. Do you mind?"

"I'm around smoke all day," Gregory answers. "Doesn't bother me."

"Ha. Right. Well, I usually only allow myself four a week."

"That's a very specific number."

"One for each member of my family," I say with a laugh. "This is already my third today. Or my fourth? I've lost count. I'm being bad."

Jesus, I think. *Go inside, Nadine.*

"Looks like a big crowd tonight," Gregory says. "One hundred and ten, to be exact?"

"Indeed. Thank you for getting here so early."

"Want to hear something funny?" he says. "My mother lost her mind when I told her I was working Marilyn Millay's birthday party. Wait. It's okay that I told her, right?"

"If she can be trusted. Surely she won't tip off the paparazzi."

He laughs. "Nope. She loves your mom's books."

There's something so casual about Gregory. He's easy to banter with, though that might be a function of him feeling obliged to make pleasantries. When I booked him, he warned me that he liked to arrive early to begin the slow-cook process. The smoking of the meat. I notice that he's brought his own water bottle and coffee carafe, even a bagged lunch. He doesn't wear a wedding ring and has never mentioned a wife or family. But I know that says nothing of his actual status. In my time, I've come across many a man who can small talk for hours without once bringing up his wife.

The last time Gregory was here was the night of our small New Year's Eve gathering. He prepared a magnificent celebratory dinner of roast beef and root vegetables, every bite dripping with flavor. But I don't remember when he left. Most certainly he would have packed up and snuck out just as Paul and my mother were dialing 911.

"How was your winter?" Gregory says. "You were planning a trip to Costa Rica, if I recall."

"We were! Good memory. We had to cancel, unfortunately. Turns out I spent a good chunk of winter in the hospital. I was there right into spring, in fact."

"Damn." Gregory grimaces and casts me an awkward glance. "Right. I remember the ambulance being called. I tried to get out of the way. I figured you'd broken an ankle or something."

I laugh. "I wish. It was my hip. And I shattered it."

"I'm sorry to hear that." He pauses. "Well, you seem really physically healthy now."

His back is turned. I tilt my head upward to exhale a strand of smoke. I've made him uncomfortable, but I don't care. The muscles in his arms ripple as he rotates the meat on the barbecue. *Really physically healthy*, he'd called me. How desperate would I be to take that as a compliment? Gregory is roughly my contemporary. He's attractive, with the sort of gruff, inelegant features that grow more handsome with age. He lives on a few acres outside of the city and makes a good living catering parties for lofty urbanites. The local bourgeoisie, as he likely thinks of us.

The silence between us is heavy. God. I can tell by his body language that Gregory would prefer I leave.

"It could have been much worse," I say. "Falling down the stairs, I mean. I hit my head but . . . aside from some fogginess, I've mostly been okay. Or at least I think I'm okay. My brain weathered it well enough."

Is that a lie? I can't be sure.

"Broken hip's not great," Gregory says, holding up his knife. "Any way you cut it."

"Ha. Well, I'm lucky that I'm young. Or young by broken hip standards, at least. They opened me up to put in a few screws and plates. There was a complication, an infection that got right into the bone, so I was confined to the hospital for a lot longer than expected, but I healed well." I'm rambling. I pat at my hip. "It aches a bit in the rain, but otherwise it's good as new. No limp, which my physical therapist claims is a miracle."

"Right," he says. "Well, that's good news."

He's fully frowning now. My hovering is ruining Gregory the caterer's afternoon. I take one last long drag of the cigarette and watch him return to his tasks in silence.

The confinement was the best and worst part of my long hospital stay. At first my legs were bound together to prevent any rotation of my hip. I'd wake in the middle of the night desperate to move, to stand up, so much so that the nurse once threatened to tether me to the bed if I jostled or fought the restraints. Then the infection set in, and I lost a week or two to intravenous drugs and a febrile fog.

And so I figured I was imagining it when the phone in my hospital room rang early one morning. Not my cell phone, but the landline next to my bed. I stared at it for a solid ten seconds before registering that I had the option to answer it.

'Hello?'

'Nadine Walsh?'

'Yes?'

'This is Julian Simone. The journalist.'

I recall gazing out the window, feeling as if the puzzle pieces weren't fitting together. There I was in a hospital room, thirsty and sore, my leg still swollen and hot with infection, a beige phone receiver in my hand, a man's voice speaking through it. Julian Simone. The journalist. My mother's much maligned wannabe biographer.

'How did you find this number?' I asked.

'I'm a journalist, Mrs. Walsh. It's my job to find this number.'

'Okay,' I said, rather dumbly.

'Do you have a moment?'

To this day, I know that the appropriate answer to his question was: *No, I do not have a moment.* This man was digging into my mother's life without her consent, sifting through her past in search of salacious tales to put in print. He'd long had an interest in her, having reviewed many of her books. A few years ago, an old television interview resurfaced where Julian Simone asked famed writer Marilyn Millay a deeply inane question about the intelligence of her female characters. The clip went viral because my mother—poised but ruthless—positively skewered him in her response.

When he started circling last year, I was diligent about prepping our friends and family to avoid his calls. My mother stayed above the fray, leaving her publisher to answer all questions. Maybe it was the painkillers, or the boredom of weeks and weeks tethered to a hospital bed. Maybe my brain wasn't working properly. Because I didn't say no to Julian Simone when he asked about my mother. I did the very opposite.

'What do you want?' I asked him.

'I would love a chance to speak with you,' Julian Simone said. 'Entirely on your terms.'

Gregory uses a carving knife to skim a piece of cooked skin from the roast he's placed on the spit. He holds a fork aloft and steps my way.

"The skin cooks fast," he says.

I lean in to take a bite.

"Delicious," I say, catching the juice on my chin. "Very tender."

Gregory watches me. I feel a twinge in my chest. I cross my arms, the lit cigarette still dangling between my fingers.

"We'll get Marilyn to sign a book for your mom," I say. "I have a box of them in the basement."

"That would be amazing," Gregory says. "Your mom came out a few minutes ago to say hello. She seems . . . humble." He adjusts the settings on the BBQ grill. "It must be exhausting for her. The fame aspect. Keeping people off your back."

If only he knew—if only anyone knew—the degree to which the work of keeping people off my mother's back falls to me. There's a reason the articles Julian Simone has written have been mostly benign, recycled fare. That reason is me.

Gregory gestures to the meat. "I'll start shaving it now as the outer layers cook through. We'll have lots on the go by the time the party starts."

"Thank you, Gregory. You're very reliable. That's a good quality in a man."

As soon as the words exit my mouth, I regret them. How inappropriate. Jesus. I can see the way his shoulder rise, the stiffening in his posture. Shit. I've crossed the line. I mash my cigarette into the brick wall then scratch at its the ash mark with my fingernail.

"I should get back to party prep duties," I say.

"Okay, then. It's nice to see you, Nadine. I'm glad you're back on your feet. A fall is a terrible thing."

"Indeed. Thank you, Gregory."

The smoke from the barbecue has wafted into the kitchen. I click the patio door shut and let the air-conditioning wash over me. Margot and my mother chatter quietly in the dining room. I close my eyes for a moment to regroup.

It must be exhausting, Gregory said just now. *Keeping people off your back.*

Even now, months later, I can't be sure why I invited Julian Simone to my hospital room. Before he arrived, I told my nurse that he was my lawyer and we'd need privacy. She shot me a skeptical look.

In person, Julian Simone was older and paunchier than the glossy headshot that popped up on Google, but still handsome enough in his late fifties. Who was I to be judging his looks, strapped as I was in a hospital bed? I'd asked the nurse to help me change into a shirt and sweater, comb my hair. Julian pulled up the chair beside my bed as if we were old friends. He sat so close, I could smell his cologne, his breath.

'I'm grateful for your time,' he said, opening his notebook.

'I've only invited you here to tell you face-to-face to back off,' I said, knowing that wasn't entirely true. 'I know my mother's publishers have sicced lawyers on you.'

'Lawyers can't stop you from telling the truth,' he said.

'Whatever. You're not the first washed-up journalist to take a kick at the Marilyn Millay can.'

'I prefer the term *seasoned* to washed-up.'

'My mother doesn't have some locked chest full of secrets,' I said. 'She had me at twenty. That's not a secret. We were poor and lived in a shitty apartment. Again, not a secret. I can show you pictures, but I'm sure you already know what a shitty apartment looks like. You rummaging around in her life stresses her out, and I don't like that.'

'Why would it stress her out if she doesn't have anything to hide?'

'Because it's her life. Not some tabloid fodder. She deserves her privacy, doesn't she?'

'Your mother is of the public's interest,' he said, referring to his notes. 'I will say that you and she have done an excellent job pulling up the drawbridge. No one who knows you will speak to me.'

'Come on, Mr. Simone. Surely there are more interesting people to write about than Marilyn Millay.'

'I thought so too,' Julian said. 'But last year, as I was prepping to review one of her books, I went down a bit of a rabbit hole. As I tend to do. I got more curious about her the deeper down I went.'

There is something so vulnerable about a hospital bed. You have no way of escaping. When I reached for the cup of ice water on the tray, Julian had to nudge it within my reach.

'I'm not sure if the naive daughter thing is an act,' he continued, 'because I can assure you, your mother does have a few secrets buried. All it took was a half dozen trips to a little backwater called Terriville to uncover the artifacts.'

Something shifted in me then. How my body ached, my leg throbbed. But I gathered myself. *Stay cool.* Everything hinged on my next move. I cocked my head at Julian Simone and offered him a small smile.

'Okay, then,' I said. 'Tell me what you've found.'

Now, in my own kitchen, I turn on the tap to wash my hands, dropping my cigarette butt into the water as I reach for the soap. Out the window, Gregory is focused on his tasks. I wrap the used butt in a paper towel and throw it in the compost.

"You okay in there, Nadine?" my mother calls from the dining room.

"Fine. Just getting myself some water."

"We'll take some too!" she calls. "With ice!"

Fine. I collect three glasses and fill one for myself, one for Margot, and one for my mom. My mouth tastes metallic. I sniff at my shirt then drop the cigarette pack in the sink and let the water run over it too. I can't keep smoking like this. Being forced to hide the evidence is the most degrading part of my dirty little habit. I'll need to go in search of a mint.

MARILYN AND I ARE ALONE IN the kitchen. Margot is upstairs with Isobel, Damien in his room, and Paul out running errands. The centerpieces are done. It's two o'clock. I'm at the sink, rinsing glasses. A specific kind of tension fills the air between my mother and me. It's as if she's always waiting for me to speak.

"How was the rest of your morning?" Marilyn finally asks.

"Mostly uneventful," I say.

"You picked up the cheese?"

"No. But I stopped into the shop. Zachary will deliver it later."

"We love Zachary."

I spin from the sink to face her.

"Okay," I say. "I went to Colleen's grave."

"Nadine. I thought we agreed."

"I sort of just . . . ended up there. I was passing by."

"No you weren't."

"Fine." I pause, rubbing my forehead. "Lately. I don't know. My brain can't move past it. Certain things are just stuck. I'm . . . ruminating."

Marilyn sips from her water glass, a concerned gaze trained on me. "Is there something you'd like to say to me?"

"You never visit her. You never visit them. Your parents! I don't get it."

"How do you know I never visit?"

"Because you'd invite me if you did."

"Quite the assumption given you went without me today." Marilyn sighs. "Okay, so I don't visit my parents' grave. Maybe I bury it all away. Maybe I need therapy. But it's . . ." She pauses, choosing her words. "It doesn't feel helpful to me to relive it. I'd rather move on."

"It's about honoring them."

"You're not honoring. You're fixating."

"Colleen was fifteen. She loved you!"

"Jesus!" my mother says. "Nadine."

"Throwing you that party thirty years ago was her idea. You know that, right? She wanted to make amends. For . . . all that shitty stuff."

"She wanted a party, that's all. It wasn't for me."

The doorbell rings. I jump at the sound of it.

"Saved by the bell," my mother quips. "Thank God."

"Don't."

"I'm sorry," she says. "That was insensitive. Who is that?"

"Probably a delivery. Maybe Zachary with the cheeses."

"Should I get it?"

I shake my head and wipe my hands on my pants. From the hallway I can see a head of curly blond hair through the high window on the door. No. There's no way. I stop still in my tracks until the knock comes again. I simply cannot handle two encounters with Daphne Robinson in the span of only a few hours.

"Answer it!" my mother calls.

There's no option. I take a quick glance at the foyer mirror, straighten myself out. Then I unlock the door and open it. There she stands, gorgeous Daphne, a large box at her feet.

"Hi," she says. "Nadine. I know it's ridiculous to show up at someone's house hours before a party. I was going to ask you this morning if I could stop by . . ." She laughs and waves a hand, trailing off. "I even thought about just leaving this on the stoop, but—"

"Daphne," my voice trills. "Come in."

When she bends over to collect the box, I spot a round patch of sweat on the back of her sundress. Daphne is agitated. I close the door behind her and we proceed to the kitchen. Marilyn, ever gracious, always warmer than me, circles the island to offer Daphne a hug.

"Hello, darling," my mother says. "What a lovely surprise."

"Hi, Marilyn," Daphne says. "I'm sorry to intrude."

"Not at all. What brings you to the party palace?"

"A little delivery." Daphne hoists the box onto the island. "For Nadine."

Marilyn flits about the kitchen, preparing a jug of lemonade for us, setting out glasses with ice, pouring. There's even a wedge of fresh lemon for each of us. Effortless.

"How's that sweet baby of yours?" Marilyn asks.

"Good," Daphne says. "Thank you for asking. Less colicky. The first few months were bad. Hard. On me, at least. Speaking of babies, Lionel and I ran into yours this morning after my coffee with Margot. Isobel. She was outside Paul's office, waiting for Seymour to pick her up."

"Yes," I say. "They were headed to the hospital."

"What a doll she is. So lovely and poised."

"Isn't she?" I say.

"How is she coping?"

How is she coping with River, Daphne means. The question feels like an intrusion.

"She's okay," I say.

"It's all so devastating," Daphne says. "You know, a few weeks before I had the baby, Sherry asked me if I'd have a chat with River. She was worried about her. That her grades had been slipping. She was missing curfew. Other things. I'm sure you know. She wanted me to check in."

"Well," my mother says. "You *are* a psychologist."

"I'm a researcher," Daphne says. "Not a clinician."

Sherry asked Daphne to speak to River? My shoulders stiffen.

"Did you connect with her?" I ask.

Daphne nods, solemn. "We had lunch. River was chilly with me. Barely touched her food. She was disinterested in any outreach efforts on my part. She did talk a bit."

"What did she say?" I ask.

"She said her parents felt guilty. Said they were scared they'd ruined her with the divorce. She said her teachers were jerks. That everyone had it all wrong. Anyway, I planned to follow up, figured maybe I could break through, but then the baby came, and then she . . ." Daphne trails off. "But since then, Lionel's—"

"Speaking of Lionel," Marilyn says. "Is he any help at home?"

I cast my mother a sidelong glare. What a swift change of subject.

Daphne coughs on her drink. "Well, he tries to be."

No, no, no. Daphne's eyes have welled with tears. My mother springs to action again, fetching the tissue box, sidling up to Daphne, and cooing at her as though she were a child arrived with a scraped elbow.

"I'm sorry," Daphne says. "This is *so* embarrassing."

"Listen," my mother says. "We've been there. You've got a brand-new baby at home. There is no tougher time. Are you crying a lot?"

"More than usual," Daphne says. "I'd say. For sure."

It takes effort to breathe. My skin crawls with sweat.

"I cried every day for a year after Nadine was born."

"Marilyn," I say. "I'm not sure how comforting that is."

"What? I'm commiserating! Some women have a really hard time in those early months. We do each other a great disservice by not being honest about it."

"It's true," Daphne says. "It actually is comforting to hear the un-varnished truth. It's hard not to feel, like, you know. Pathetic. Ungrate-ful. A sad sack. The only bad mother in the world."

Her eyes fall to me on these words. Why? I can't seem to fix my features properly.

"You are hardly a sack of any kind," my mother says. "And it's quite possible to be grateful and sad at the same time. Isn't that right, Na-dine?"

"Yes," I say. "We're really glad you stopped by."

I cringe at my own words, dropped as a heavy cue for her to take her leave. But Daphne detects nothing. If Marilyn does, she chooses to ignore it. Daphne sniffles then points to the wall.

"I've always noticed that photograph," she says. "The two women. I feel like there's a story to it."

"It's creepy," Marilyn says. "Those women were sisters. They used to live in this house."

"Not quite," I say. "One lived here, and one lived next door."

"Wow," Daphne says. "How remarkable. Where did you get the photo?"

"We found it in the floorboards when we were renovating the kitchen. The contractor figured it must have slipped between a crack in the planks. I had it touched up then enlarged and framed. I love it."

"I love it too," Daphne says.

"I guess I'm outnumbered," Marilyn says with a laugh.

Daphne slides the box she brought toward me. I open it and lift out a bottle of red wine. Château Biac. A Bordeaux.

"I'm not sure if you recall . . ." Daphne trails off.

"I do." I avoid her gaze, turning instead to my mother. "Do you remember New Year's Eve? The dinner party? Daphne and Lionel were there. Seymour too. Teddy, the new tenant from next door." I point outside toward the BBQ. "Your man Gregory catered."

"I remember," Marilyn says. "How could I forget, Nadine? That's the night you fell."

"Yes," I say, running a hand through my hair.

"You're doing so much better, though," Daphne says. "Aren't you? You look so good."

Her kindness lands like a grenade. I wish my mother knew when to leave something alone.

"Right," Marilyn says, turning over the bottle in her hands. "So. This wine."

"I believe Teddy brought it that night we were all here," I say. "Someone poured me a glass and I declared it was the best wine I'd ever tasted. I made a bit of a scene about it if I recall. Daphne, you obviously remembered."

"Yeah," Daphne says, bashful. "I ordered a case of it a few days later. Through a guy I know. A sommelier with connections to the vineyard itself. It took a while to arrive. But here it is. Just in time for the party."

"So generous and thoughtful." Marilyn rests a hand on Daphne's arm. "Truly."

"Very kind of you, Daphne," I say. "Thank you."

She smiles so warmly at me that I feel my chest tighten with guilt. Shit. This can't be happening. I should never have answered the door.

"I've been thinking about you a lot over the past few months, Nadine," Daphne says. "You know, with the fall that night. I feel bad. We were all there, drinking way too much. Not me, I mean. I was pregnant."

Indeed you were, I think. The roundness of Daphne's pregnant belly, the sight of Lionel rubbing it any chance he got, was one of the very things that drove me to drink so much of this gorgeous wine at that party.

"Anyway," Daphne continues. "What a shitty thing to have happen. I'm sure the recovery has been difficult for you."

"I appreciate that," I say.

I can admit that Daphne was one person who showed me thought and care. After I got home from the hospital, fresh meals began showing up at our doorstep. I figured it was Sherry, or some mother from the kids' school or my book club. But no. Paul came home one day and announced he'd encountered Daphne on our stoop, too shy to take credit for the meal deliveries. Behaving as a friend to me when all I want is to despise her.

"You know what's funny?" Daphne says. "I raged on Lionel when he offered to bring the case over here. There's no way I was going to let him take credit for my gift."

"Never!" My mother stabs the air with a finger.

"Besides," Daphne continues. "We all know he'd overstay and expect you to serve him tea."

A laugh catches in my throat. "Too true."

How many times have I daydreamed this exchange, the moment I'm finally privy to the cracks in Daphne and Lionel's veneer, finally given the opportunity to bask in their little marital woes? I knew it would happen eventually. There was zero chance Lionel would adapt so quickly to family life. But the longer you spend imagining such things, the less satisfying it is when they come to be.

"Anyway," Daphne says, dabbing at her eyes. "*He* can stay with the baby,"

"Yes, he can," my mother adds, ever the cheerleader.

"Marilyn," she says. "I'll never forget what you told us on New Year's Eve. About odds. Remember? I might just take your advice and get rid of him."

The two of them exchange a winking, conspiratorial laugh. Very few people can hold a room with the same robust and sincere charm as Marilyn Millay. At that New Year's Eve party, the subject of marriage arose in conversation. With Seymour just divorced, Lionel recently married, and my mother and Teddy forever single, the group was skewed in our stances. Someone, I think it was Teddy, asked Marilyn why she'd never married. Surely, she'd had plenty of suitors over the years. Plenty of options. Was he flirting with her? If he was, Marilyn deftly ignored it.

'Sure,' my mother replied. 'But the numbers on marriage just don't crunch. Did you know that, statistically, murdering someone is a safer bet than marrying them?'

'At least that's what my mother claims,' I quipped.

The table erupted, all eyes volleying between us, ready for our banter. Marilyn obliged by rolling her eyes theatrically.

'It's true,' she said.

'I told you never to repeat that out loud,' I said. 'You don't want to incriminate yourself, do you?'

'How could I? I'm not the married one.'

'This is making me really uncomfortable,' Paul chimed in. More laughter.

'Let's do the math on murder,' my mother continued. 'I research it all the time. It's a hazard of the job. And what are the current statistics on marriage? Forty percent end in divorce? Half? Can you believe that?' She paused for effect. 'So, yes, the math. We'd all like to think that the odds of getting away with murder are slim. They should be, but they aren't. Not at all. Less than half of all murders result in an arrest. *Half* go entirely unsolved. Half! Right there, your odds are pretty good. But it gets worse. Of the half that do lead to an arrest, the conviction rate is only two out of three. So overall, aside from a coin toss that you might spend an unpleasant stretch in jail awaiting trial, the odds of being convicted of murder are barely one in three. If you're married and a murderer, you have better odds keeping your crime a secret than keeping your marriage intact.'

A hush fell over our dining room then, each guest searching for the punch line. Finally, Daphne spoke.

'I'd get caught for sure,' she said. 'I'm careless. I'd leave a press-on nail behind or something stupid like that. So best not to murder you, dear.'

'What a relief,' Lionel replied.

The pressure valve released then, laughter returned to the table. I too, like Daphne apparently, have thought of that revelation many times since. When someone puts you in an impossible position, no rational person would invoke murder as a viable solution to a problem. No one. Right?

Now, my mother and Daphne chatter on. Daphne's mood has lifted. Marilyn is a revelation in her uncanny ability to yank people out of their darkest moods. She looks at her watch.

"Oh dear. Nadine, what time did you say the rest of the caterers would be here?"

"Any minute," I say.

"Now *I've* overstayed my welcome." Daphne stands and smooths the lines formed in the dress. "I feel so much better, though. Thank you both. I'm glad I stopped by. I needed it."

"It's good to get out," I say. "And thank you for the wine. We'll serve a bottle or two of this tonight, but I'm going to keep the rest for myself."

We leave my mother in the kitchen and walk to the door. At the threshold Daphne spins and wraps me in an earnest embrace. We are friends now, she's telling herself. I work hard not to stiffen noticeably against her touch.

I step outside and allow the door to close behind me, waving to Daphne once more as she recedes up our street. I can't bear to go back inside. Marilyn will quiz me. 'You don't seem to like Daphne much.' I don't need that line of questioning again today.

My phone vibrates in my pocket. I withdraw it. Shit. I haven't added this number as a contact into my phone, but I recognize it. Julian Simone.

H ELLO?"
   "Nadine! You answered."

Julian Simone's voice is low, gravelly. I step onto the front walkway and peer up and down our street in search of prying neighbors.

"Why are you calling me?" I hiss.

"I need to speak to you."

"No. You don't."

"I really do. Today. In person, preferably."

"Listen to me," I say. "We had a deal. And that deal included no more contact. So you really need to fuck off."

"There's no need for that kind of hostility, Nadine."

"Stop saying my name!"

Julian clears his throat. I stand in my front yard, my phone hot to my ear, waiting for him to speak.

"Something's come up. Something of interest to you, I'm sure."

I close my eyes. My body sways in small circles. Not today. Not today.

"I know you have a big night tonight," Julian continues. "A party, I hear. For Ms. Millay's sixtieth birthday."

"Julian—"

"I'm trying to help you. I promise. Can you meet me at the Winngrove library in half an hour? I won't take up much of your time."

"Fuck. Does it have to be today?"

"I'm on a plane tomorrow. So, yes."

"Fine. I'll be there in thirty minutes."

Before he can speak another word, I end the call. A truck drives by and I jump back at the sound of it, hand to my chest. Steady, Nadine. Steady.

"You all right?"

A man's voice. This time it's Teddy. He's on his porch, hands in his pocket. Dear God. How much of that did he hear?

"I'm fine." I muster a smile. "Lots on the go."

"Shoot. I was going to trouble you for a favor, but I probably shouldn't. It would be obnoxious to ask."

"What favor?"

"Never mind. You're clearly preoccupied."

Yes! I want to scream at him. *I am fucking preoccupied!* Instead, I look at my watch. Half an hour.

"What do you need?" I ask.

"This is embarrassing, but I can't seem to figure out the washing."

The washing? I frown, unable to compute what he means.

"The washing *machine*," he adds, chuckling. "Laundry."

"Oh. Is it broken?"

"I don't think so. I have a cleaner. She comes once a week and does the wash, but she's flown off to visit family. So I've been left to my own very poor devices."

"So you . . . you just don't know how to use it?"

At this Teddy releases a roaring laugh. I stare at him, my feet glued in place. Finally, he shrugs, sheepish.

"I know," he says. "It's terrible."

"Well. I suppose I could show you."

He waves a hand. "I can ask Paul instead if he's around. I'm sure a modern man like him knows—"

"No, no," I say, my voice singsong. "It's fine."

Throughout our marriage, Paul has often remarked on my uncanny ability to continue with quotidian tasks in the face of deep stress. Folding laundry before a funeral, arranging playdates before heading in for minor surgery. Or, showing a useless man like Teddy how to work the washer on a day full of growing upheaval. What can I say? You do what you must do.

In a daze I pick my way through the shared front garden and around his sports car. I climb the porch steps until I am face-to-face with our tenant. His aftershave tickles my nose. It always strikes me how tall Teddy Rosen is; I have to crane my face upward to maintain eye contact. He opens his front door then waves a hand to allow me in first. We stand for a moment in the foyer.

"Shall we?" I say.

This house is the perfect Victorian reflection of ours, its attached neighbor. When we bought it, I took care to paint and furnish it in a style that feels both uniquely tasteful and widely appealing. It's always disorienting to walk through a home that is a mirror of your own, everything laid out the same but backward—a parallel universe. I haven't been in here since Teddy moved in six months ago, and I'm glad to see that, aside from the dishes piled in the sink, he's been keeping it clean.

As I follow Teddy down the hall to the basement stairs, I think of

Margot's story. *He closed his hand around my bare arm.* Really? This man? He seems sort of meek. And clearly hapless, unable to manage the basic workings of a washing machine. Hardly the makings of a degenerate Romeo. Margot might well have gotten it wrong.

The basement on this side is unfinished, the floor still cement, the plumbing for a bathroom only roughed in. Along our adjoining shared wall, I see the door. The Sister Doors. Teddy tracks my gaze.

"I've been meaning to ask you about that door," he says.

I tell him the story about the two sisters.

"What a remarkable thing," he says. "I love to think of their children passing through here freely. Who needs a front door?"

"Paul wanted to seal them off. At least on our side."

"We have so little whimsy in our lives. And what's a little portal if not whimsical?"

He's exactly right. It's always bothered me that Paul doesn't see the beauty in it. These doors installed for no other reason but to create some magic in the toil of two women's lives—an homage to their sisterhood, their bond. Without thinking I take hold of the door's knob. I'm surprised to note that his side is unlocked.

"Well," Teddy says, pointing to the machines in the corner, a large pile of man clothes on the floor. "Without further ado."

I approach, nudging the pile of clothes with my toe.

"Are you going to separate them?" I ask.

"Separate?"

For the love of God.

"I'm embarrassing myself here, aren't I?" he says.

I laugh. "Well. You'll want to separate the pile into dark clothes and light. So the colors don't bleed. Only fill the machine halfway. This pile should make roughly two loads."

"Got it."

He follows my instructions, selecting the dark clothes from the pile and tossing them into the machine. I clear my throat and hover at the largest distance I can muster.

"Next?"

I scratch my head. "Do you have soap?"

"I assume so," Teddy answers.

I find the laundry pods on a shelf and remove one from the packet.

"Don't eat them," I say.

He frowns, missing the joke.

I guide him through the painfully simple steps of turning on the machine and selecting the cycle. Once the machine begins its work, I explain the transfer to the dryer. Then we stand there, facing each other.

"You think you have a handle on it now?"

"Yes," he says. "I'm a better person than I was five minutes ago. Thanks to you, Nadine."

"You're welcome."

He steps away first. On our passage back to the stairs, I peer into the storage room. There's a desk and computer set up, a daybed and a bookshelf in the otherwise unfinished space. The safe we'd provided in the bedroom closet upstairs has been moved.

"You keep your office down here?"

"Yes," Teddy says, pulling its door closed. "Odd, I know. I'm a product of the dreariness of London. I found the sunlight in the up-stairs rooms overwhelming."

"My office is in the basement too. Just on the other side of the door, actually."

"Aren't we just two peas in a pod?" he says.

"Are you still working?" I ask. "I thought you took early retirement."

"I dabble," he says, patting at his chest. "Stock trading is stressful stuff. I developed a bit of angina. My doctor wanted me to slow down. So I did. Turns out, the slow life suits me."

"Why did you leave the UK?"

He shrugs. "I'm a bit of a nomad. Without work to keep me occupied, it didn't feel like home anymore. Does that make sense?"

"It does."

Awkwardness fills the prolonged silence.

"Did we ever meet?" I ask him. "In our youth?"

"I don't think so. I'm a fair bit older than you."

"Did you ever go to Terriville? You knew Seymour. And Paul's older brother."

"That little town where they had summer farms? Once or twice, I think." He nods, thoughtful. "Funny. When your mother's first book hit the bestseller list, Seymour sent me a few clippings. Mentioned that she was from Terriville. And then, what? A decade later? The younger of the infamous Walsh brothers married you, her daughter! Seymour loved to keep me abreast. I only knew of your mom's family because Seymour had a real thing for her little sister way back when. Used to make all kinds of excuses to go visit her."

I feel it like a blow to the chest. "Colleen," I say.

"Yes. That's right. He was quite in love with her, actually. I was very sorry to hear about her death. I know it devastated Seymour. It must have been devastating for your family."

"I was only ten," I say. "I found her body."

Teddy appears shaken. "My God. What a trauma."

Trauma. How odd is it that this man is the first person in my life to actually use that word. Not even my mother has ever called it what it is.

"I don't remember much, to be honest," I say.

"That happens with trauma," he says.

"I guess it does."

I look to the ceiling, to the pipes and wires that weave through it, blinking hard.

"Can I say?" he continues. "I've always found it a little strange the way you all reconnected later on. That you ended up at the same college. That Paul Walsh ended up marrying you. Seymour and Lionel moved in on the same street as you two. And now me. Sometimes the world feels really small." He pauses in thought. "It's miraculous, really. The tentacles of fate and coincidence."

Yes. How can it be that this man, virtually a stranger, has articulated it perfectly? *The tentacles of fate and coincidence.* Behind us, the washing machine churns noisily through the first stages of its cycle. With a jolt, I look at my watch.

"I have to go," I say. "I need to be somewhere in a few minutes. I've lost track of time."

"You've lots to do," Teddy says. "I'm sorry to keep you."

Upstairs, Teddy and I face each other in the foyer. Some part of me wants to give him a hug, to hold him close. Jesus. I am such a fool. He extends his hand to me with a mock formality. We shake.

"Thank you, Nadine. Things will get brighter from here."

"Yes. They will."

I exit and descend to the lawn. When Teddy's door clicks shut behind me, I raise a hand to my heart and breathe deeply. I need a cigarette. How stupid was I to douse my pack in the sink? I have just enough time to stop at Marvin's on my way to the library.

WHEN I ARRIVE AT MARVIN'S STORE, I stop outside for a moment to gather myself. I need to engage my autopilot here, to carry on despite the roiling in my chest. One last deep breath before pressing open the door. Inside, I find Marvin behind the counter, not Lacey. He looks up from his book and offers a warm smile.

"Nadine!"

"I was here this morning just after seven," I say. "You, apparently, were still in bed."

"First time I've slept in in over a decade."

"Surely that's not true."

"It definitely is. I feel like a new man."

"Well, you look great. Rested. Ready for a party?"

"We'll see. Let's just say I'm amenable to the possibility. I bought a fancy shirt the other day. I just might show up."

Might? I point to the book he's reading. My mother's latest. "You call yourself her biggest fan but you're going to skip her birthday party?"

"You've read this one, I assume?"

"I got an advanced copy. The perks of being Marilyn Millay's only daughter."

"Do you know how much you could get for an early copy on eBay?"

"I'll keep that in mind should we fall on hard times."

"You could give it to me and let me sell it."

I laugh. Is he joking?

"I'm here for cigarettes," I say.

"Not your second pack of the day, I hope?"

"God. Did Lacey tell you?"

"No. But why else would you be here at seven in the morning?"

"Maybe to say hello to you?" I say.

It's funny how you share little secrets with certain people in your life. Zachary, the cheese maker, the only person who knows of my affair. And then Marvin, the one person, my mother aside, with any real insight into the depths of this secret smoking habit.

"Do you like the book?" I ask.

"This is actually my second time through it. No offense, but the main character actually reminds me of you."

I bend to collect a pack of gum from the lower shelves. He's studying me. I look away.

"Sorry," he says. "She's a great character. Sly, protective. Smart. It really was a compliment. Maybe you're your mother's muse."

"Unlikely."

There's an awkward pause.

"We never really did address things, did we?" Marvin says. "You know. What happened between Lacey and Damien. I wanted to apologize."

"For what?" I ask.

"For Lacey. The way she behaved."

I meet his gaze directly. "Well. It wasn't the first time a hapless mom walked in on her kid fooling around. It's fine. A fairly normal trajectory for a pair of fifteen-year-olds, wouldn't you say?"

"I guess so. But fifteen-year-olds can be sneaky."

Is Marvin alluding to something specific? He has one of those faces that feels impossible to gauge. Normally I'm good at calibrating conversations, directing them to where I want them to go. But my mind is haywire. All I want is cigarettes and gum. The party isn't far off. I'm supposed to meet Julian Simone at the library in a few minutes. What the fuck is happening? Marvin must sense my anxiety, because he turns his back to collect the cigarettes from the enclosed shelf behind him. He doesn't need to ask what brand. He tosses them on the counter in front of me.

"Are you always this worried?" he asks.

I straighten. "I'm hosting a party in a few hours. Is that not reason to worry?"

A thickness hangs in the air now. Painful, awkward. I reach into my tote for my wallet then hand him a twenty. He knows to drop the five and change into the charity box next to the cash. The bell jingles to mark another's entry to the store. Both Marvin and I turn to see Lionel standing there, hands in the pockets of his khaki shorts. He looks at me like a puppy dog, forlorn and helpless, his shirt wrinkled and half untucked.

"I need to talk to you," Lionel says to me.

I look back to Marvin, whose expression remains chillingly neutral.

"I'll see you at the party tonight, Lionel," I say, working to keep my voice steady. "We can chat then."

Before I can react, Lionel strides forward and grasps my arm, guiding me to the back of the store where rows of dairy and soda are lined neatly in the glass-doored refrigerators. I hear a faint *"Hey!"* in protest. I toss a glance back to Marvin.

"It's fine," I call. "He's a friend."

A friend. Ha! I want to scream bloody murder, claw at Lionel's eyes, and then run. Instead, I allow myself to be dragged to the back of Marvin's store like a fool.

"What the hell are you doing?" I say to Lionel once we're safely out of Marvin's earshot.

"You're not answering my messages."

"Fuck you," I say. "Are you following me?"

"I saw you pass by our house. So, yeah, I followed you here."

"Jesus. Now you're a stalker? You need to leave me alone."

I can feel Marvin's eyes heavy on us, only our heads visible to him over the rows of cereal and toilet paper, our whispers low and sharp.

"There's something I need to tell you," Lionel says.

"I'm not talking to you here."

His hand reaches for my shoulder, brushing the tip of my breast. To my horror, my body reacts right to my knees. I swat his hand away, crossing my arms over my chest.

"Do you want me to make a scene?" I ask. "Because I will. I'll yell."

"Nadine," he says, exasperated. "Jesus Christ. This isn't about . . . us. You and me."

I shake my head, eyes to the floor.

"It's about Isobel."

"What?"

Lionel brings his fingers to his temples.

"Lionel? What the fuck are you talking about?"

"Listen. I had drinks with Seymour a few weeks ago. He got really hammered. I had to drag him back to his condo and put him to bed. He started crying and . . . confessed something to me."

"What?" I ask, my voice low.

"A week before her overdose, River was taken in by the police. I don't think she was officially arrested. But she was questioned. Something to do with . . ."

"With *what*?"

"Escorting. That was the word Seymour used."

My stomach lurches. "What does this have to do with Isobel?"

He raises his hands defensively. "I promise you, her name never came up. But I know how close they are. Isobel and River, I mean. The closest of friends. They remind me of"—he pauses, his eyes sad—"of me and Paul, actually."

"What the fucking hell? Why didn't you tell me this before?"

Lionel scoffs then, remarkably, appears to wipe a tear from under his eye. "Are you kidding me, Nadine? I've been trying! Texting you every goddamn day. Stalking you to the fucking corner store. I figured maybe you knew, but then . . . I don't know. I thought about telling Paul instead. Since I couldn't pin you down. But I just"—Lionel looks to the floor—"I needed to make sure you knew."

"Jesus Christ. Is there anything else?"

"No. I don't think so."

We both startle when my phone rings in my tote. I scramble for it. *Paul*, the caller ID reads. I swipe to answer.

"Hi," I say into the phone. "I'm at the corner store. A few more quick errands. Just ran into Lionel."

"Hey," Paul says. "Say hello."

I lock eyes with Lionel. "Paul says hi."

"Hi, Paulie," Lionel says, leaning in.

"I'm on my way home," Paul says. "I wanted to check if you need anything else while I'm out."

"No," I say. "I'm good. Thank you."

"Okay. Love you."

I hang up and step closer to Lionel. "You need to tell me everything you know," I say.

"I'm telling you everything I know. I swear, Nadine."

My chest is tight, aching. What do I do? Everything swirls.

"Can you leave me alone now?" I say. "Please?"

"Do you need anything? Can I do anything?"

"I need you to leave. Now."

He does. Marvin's boring glare follows Lionel as he exits. I hang back, leaning against the refrigerators. I close my eyes.

Breathe, Nadine. Do I say that out loud? *Breathe.*

"You okay?"

My eyes spring open. Marvin stands a small distance away.

"I'm fine," I say. "Thank you, Marvin. Just a lot going on right now."

I skirt past him to the front of the store. Have I paid for my cigarettes? What time is it? I'm late to meet Julian Simone. Marvin resumes his perch behind the counter. I've never before seen the expression he wears. Tense. Angry, even.

"My wife had an affair," he says. "Took off with my good friend, actually. Moved west and started a whole new family. When Lacey was a baby. You probably didn't know that."

"You've alluded to it," I say.

"It's a pretty terrible thing to endure."

"It would be," I say. "But that's not what you just saw, Marvin.

Between me and that man. In case you're making an assumption that—"

"I assume nothing," he says. "I know you guys are all friends. I know Lionel—that's his name, right?—I know he and Paul have been friends forever. They come in together sometimes. It's all good."

"Right," I say. "All good. Did I pay you already?"

"You did."

The shift in energy between us is so seismic that I feel jolted. A deep waft of scorn emanates from Marvin. His jaw pulses. Normally I'd work desperately to smooth things over, cover my tracks. Instead, I find myself tamping down my rage. I'm ready to blow. Who does Marvin think he is? I scratch a stain off the counter's enamel with my fingernail, my hand hovering close to his, hammering my gaze into him until his eyes shift downward.

"Never mind all that," Marvin says. "There's a party to think of."

"Yes," I say, turning to leave.

"Tell your husband I'll see him tonight."

Marvin utters those last words when I'm almost out the door.

It can't be. Is he threatening me?

Surely no. He wouldn't dare.

T HE ROUTE TO THE LIBRARY CUTS through residential streets to the other arterial road that marks the south end of Winngrove. I'm smoking as I walk. I'm dehydrated, so each inhale comes with a trace of nausea that has the strange effect of grounding me. I'm five minutes late.

My phone pings.

Come home! Isobel has written in my group text with her, Margot, and my mother. **Girls**, she's labeled the chat.

A few more errands, I write. **Dad will be home soon.**

He's already home.

I will be too, I write. **Soon.**

Don't make us stalk you, Margot writes.

All I offer in response is a heart emoji. I feel almost in a trance, as if I'm watching myself from above. I pass through the library's revolving door then duck by the distracted librarian and into the dark rows of stacks. There he is: Julian Simone, leaning into a shelf of travel hard-covers, a large book fanned open. He's slimmer than I perceived him in the hospital. Maybe even handsome in this more forgiving light. He wears a dress shirt and khaki pants. Business casual. He looks up.

"Mrs. Walsh," he says. "Only a few minutes behind schedule."

"You're lucky I'm here at all."

He slams the book closed. *Journey Through Maldives.*

"What do you want, Julian?"

"I was thinking about tonight," he says. "You. Throwing a big party."

"It's my mother's birthday. That's what you do on people's birthdays. You throw them a party."

"I hope you'll be spared any major drama this time."

"Excuse me?"

"It's exactly thirty years ago since the last big Marilyn Millay birthday party, isn't it?"

I say nothing. My jaw pulses.

"The death of Colleen Fitzgerald," he says. "That would make an excellent book title, actually."

"What do you want?" I repeat.

"Don't worry. I'm not here to renegotiate the terms of our deal."

"Good. Because that would end really badly for you."

He smiles. "That sounds vaguely like a threat."

"Not vaguely. It *is* a threat."

"We shouldn't stoop to threats."

I step so close that I pick up his scent, some kind of piney cologne.

"Listen to me," I say. "There is no *we*. Do you understand? There will never be a *we*. You and I reached an agreement. We signed an iron-clad nondisclosure. Let me be clear: the terms of our deal stand, and you'd be reckless to disregard them."

A steadiness overtakes me as I speak. For nearly three months, I've held this card to my chest. When Julian Simone came to see me in the hospital, I learned in short order that he'd indeed done his homework. His trips to Terriville had proven dangerously fruitful, and he was armed with devastating facts. Imagine how bewildering it felt to learn secrets about my own family from a hack journalist. Secrets my mother opted to keep from me. Truths she denied me. And yet, instead of confronting my mother, instead of raging at her for the betrayal, I opted to handle it as one does when they have the means: by throwing money at it. I paid off this nosy journalist to stand down, to give me veto power over everything he writes about my mother, my family. Then I kept his secrets—and our deal—from everyone.

Julian reaches again for the stacks, this time withdrawing a book on cathedral architecture in Europe. I remember this about him from the hospital. He uses long pauses to control the pace of conversation. It was frustrating enough when I had nowhere to be. Now, here, I want to kill him.

"I'm going to leave," I say.

"I was giving you a minute to calm down, Nadine."

"What the fuck do you want?"

"Something's come up. Something . . . new."

I cross my arms, silent.

"I was contacted by a loved one of yours claiming they had some new information about your family. Something I might be interested in."

"Who?"

"You paid me to bury stories, Nadine. Not to reveal my sources."

"Julian? I will destroy you. Do you understand? You owe me full disclosure."

He frowns. "I'm not actually sure I do. But I was thinking, what if we . . . formed a partnership of sorts? You've already let me write a few mildly salacious articles about Marilyn. That piece about her work as a men's club hostess got a lot of traction."

"She's not ashamed of that. She was putting food on the table."

"Good for her," Julian says. "But you must have enjoyed taking her down a peg. You've lived your entire life in the shadow of Marilyn Millay. Just look at you today. Running around planning her birthday party like you're the mother and she's the child."

I loathe him. I loathe him because he's right. Julian Simone is right. I *do* resent Marilyn. I always believed we were a team, but then this man, this grotesque rat of a journalist, uncovered what my mother had done. What she'd kept from me. And those secrets have now become my burden—a burden I've carried for months on her behalf. She's my mother, yet I'm the one protecting her. And to what end? Would the world stop spinning if the truth emerged?

"Look at you. You're shaking, Nadine. Don't you see? You owe your mother nothing."

Tears spring to my eyes. Fuck. I look down at the stained carpet.

"You need to stop," I say. "The deal was, I pay you and you stop combing her past."

"I *did* stop. But I have this guy at the police department. He fills me in on anything of note. I give him names of people I'm curious about and he'll cross-reference them for me in the system. He's especially amenable now that—thanks to you—my pockets are a bit deeper. So I asked him about you. Mrs. Nadine Walsh, nee Millay. And two cases popped up! One, an archive. A police interview from thirty years ago with a little girl named Nadine. You."

My elbow lifts to rest on the stacks of books.

"And the second time your name came up? This one was from six weeks ago. Well after we cut out deal. An overdose case, and your name was in the file. Mother of the girl's best friend, present when her daughter was interviewed by the police. And then, boom! Not a week later, a loved one of yours reaches out too, with information on the same case. I mean, my God. To be gifted one source is lucky, but two? Sometimes a journalist catches a break. I certainly did in the case of this River Dunphy."

I gather a fistful of his shirt at the chest and move to within inches of his face.

"Don't ever speak of her," I say. "Do you understand me? She's a child. She has nothing to do with my mother."

"That's not true, Nadine. They're connected. By you. You're the connection."

"Listen to me. Listen to every fucking word I'm about to say. I paid you seven fucking figures to stop prying. We signed a binding contract. And you seem to be willing to disregard it, but I won't allow that. Do you understand? If I hear you utter River's name again, if you go down this path, I will end you."

"These threats are quite aggressive," he says.

"I want the name of your source and everything you have, emailed my way in the next hour. If you don't, well . . . I don't even know what to tell you. You'll find yourself treading in very dangerous waters."

"Come on," he says. "Do you really think these secrets won't emerge anyway?"

This is the sort of thing that renders a person murderous. A veritable stranger waltzes into your life and threatens to upend it, to tear apart all you've worked to protect. I release my grip on Julian's shirt and use my flat hand to smooth out the wrinkles I've made. Is he afraid? We stand so close. I can feel the patter of his heart on my palm.

"Can we back up?" he asks. "Literally?"

"What do you actually want?" I ask. "More money? Is that it?"

"As I said, I'd prefer a partnership. But . . . money never hurts."

This. This is the risk. You take steps to cover tracks, to protect the people you love. To bury secrets. But then you've opened a Pandora's box. There might be no end to it. No point where it stops.

"For now? What I'd really love is to be invited to the party tonight."

I close my eyes. At once I'm struck by the vision of Colleen. She's in the kitchen at my grandparents' farm, sitting across from me, smiling. My eyes pop open again.

"Send me what you have from this so-called source," I say. "And from your corrupt little cop friend. Send me that, and you can come to the party."

Julian's eyes widen. I've surprised him. He smiles. "See? Now that's a partnership."

"Now. Send it now."

"Yes!" he says. "It's all encrypted on my laptop, so I'll need a few—"

He stops short when my phone pings in quick succession. I extract it to read the messages.

We're stalking you, Margot texts in the group chat.

I've just tracked her on my phone, Isobel adds. **She's at the effing library!**

Uh-oh, Marilyn writes. **Do we go fetch her?**

Fuck. No. I need to get out of here.

Actually, Margot adds. **Nadine, can you stop at your mom's house on your way home and pick up her juice press? We need it for the punch.**

Sure, I write. **Will do. See you soon.**

My fingers tremble. I toss my phone back in my tote and back away, waving a hand at the laptop bag at Julian's feet.

"Everything. Now. Do you understand me?"

"I think we understand each other, Nadine."

"Fuck you, Julian."

I hold his gaze as I back down the tall row of books toward the library exit. I can posture all I want, threaten him, lord our agreement over him, but nothing changes the fact that he is the holder of our secrets. I cast him a final glance over my shoulder. He offers a playful wave.

See you tonight, he mouths.

I COVER THE HALF MILE TO Marilyn's house in a near trot then let myself in using the keypad on her back door. Her kitchen is bright, the air-conditioning spiked to frigid levels. I turn on the sink tap and lean forward to chug directly from the flow.

Gather yourself, Nadine. Get a grip.

I locate the juice press on the counter then stand still at the center of the kitchen, catching my breath. There's an analog clock above the fridge. It ticks and ticks. I remove my phone and refresh my email a handful of times, waiting for Julian's name to appear.

My ears ring in the silence. I fill a large glass with water then wander to the wall of photographs by the breakfast nook. Most of these pictures are of Damien and Isobel, one of my wedding to Paul. There's no evidence anywhere in this house of my mother's life in Terriville. Her childhood, her parents, her sister.

After Colleen died, Marilyn and I never returned to the farm together. But I did, alone, the summer I turned sixteen. My grandparents had both just died, and the farm was to be sold at auction. My mother was handling it all from afar through lawyers, intermediaries. I begged her to go, but she refused. So one day after I'd gotten my driver's license, while my mother was busy with media interviews, I took the car and drove myself to Terriville.

The end of the farm's driveway was marked by a NOTICE OF AUCTION sign. I drove up the lane and parked, turning in slow circles on the lawn as the memories jumbled together. The house was in disrepair. From the porch, the barn appeared so much smaller and dilapidated, farther back from the house than I remembered it. That threw me. The details didn't quite align. Still, as I stood there alone, the jolt of nostalgia was overwhelming, a glitch in time and space, as if I were standing again at my mother's party six years earlier, searching the crowd for Colleen.

My mother's party. That night, my grandfather locked the barn doors to prevent people from bothering the horses. But the small door around the barn's back was open. Sometime around dusk, I went in search of Colleen at the place I always seemed to find her. But I found the barn empty. I checked the small storage room. Nothing. Finally, I heard a creak and looked up. The loft.

I climbed the ladder in my party dress, my sandals slipping off the wooden rungs. In the highest loft, I found Colleen sitting cross-legged, alone. Her eyes again looked glassy.

'What are you doing up here?' I asked her.

'Holy fuck, Nadine. You're everywhere. You just appear.' Her red lipstick was smeared. 'Get out!'

'I don't want to leave you alone. Are you okay?'

Colleen shifted to all fours and crawled to where I stood on the ladder.

'Nadine,' she said, a whisper. 'A friend is coming to see me. It's a secret. You can keep a secret, right?'

I'm snapped back to my mother's kitchen by the beeping code on the back door. Panic overtakes me. I tuck into the living room, my back against the wall, hiding like a fugitive. Someone enters.

"Nadine?"

Paul. I return to the kitchen to find him standing in the open doorway.

"I came to find you," he says. "The girls texted me. They're worried about you."

"You scared me."

"Are you okay?"

He strides my way and wraps me in a hug.

"I don't know," I say. "I'm a little stressed out."

"I was hoping our little romp would've helped that."

I love Paul. I do. But sometimes, he's on a different planet. He slept like a log last night. Tonight, he will drink and mingle, like everyone else, not a care in the world. He is relaxed after our *romp*. He is never haunted by nostalgia, by memories. To him, the past is the past. Gone. Eyes forward.

"Hey," Paul says. "Your mom reminded me that today is the anniversary. Of that other party."

"Yes. I was just thinking about that, actually."

"If I had half a brain, I'd have remembered that on my own." He presses his nose into my hair. "I'm sorry I didn't put it together. You have so much on your plate. So much on your mind. I'm worried about you."

Perhaps I don't give Paul enough credit. Something breaks open in me. The sobs rise before I can quash them. Paul strokes my back and coos at me. By the time my tears relent, the breast of his shirt is soaked through. Paul guides me to the living room and we sit on the couch, knee to knee, facing each other. I wipe my eyes, sniffling.

"Are you mad at me?" he asks.

"No," I say. "Why would I be?"

"Because I'm not helpful enough?"

"I'm overwhelmed. It's not about you."

He nods, frowning.

"Truthfully, I've been a little overwhelmed ever since I left the hospital. My brain feels glitchy. I can't straighten out what I should be focusing on and what I should be letting go."

"It was a bad accident. You need more time to heal. We can cancel the party, you know. People would understand."

I glare at him. "It starts in a few hours."

"So?"

I shake my head. No. We aren't canceling Marilyn's birthday party. How naive, the notion that canceling would make my troubles go away.

Paul and I sit in silence for a moment. He worries my hands in his, playing with my wedding ring. It occurs to me that I could just tell him. Let him in on the secrets. Not *all* the secrets. Just one. I sit tall and look directly at him.

"I've kept something from you," I say. "Something big."

Paul's eyes narrow, wary. "Okay?"

"I feel like there's a hurricane building up around me and it's about to hit shore."

"What? Nadine. You're scaring me."

I swallow and wipe at a falling tear. "You know that journalist? Julian Simone?"

"The slimeball stalking your mom?"

"Yeah. He and I have been . . . interacting."

"What do you mean?"

"He reached out when I was in the hospital," I say. "I let him come see me. It was the painkillers, maybe. I was whacked out from the infection. Bored. And angry, to be honest. You and the kids weren't exactly visiting me for hours at a time. I felt a little abandoned."

Paul sighs. "I was trying to keep things going at—"

"I know. But I was left to my own devices and my brain was jumbled. And Julian claimed to know things that no one else knew about my mother. So I asked him to come see me. And it turns out he had some pretty . . . some pretty big dirt on my mom. He wanted me to corroborate it."

"Did you?"

"No." I scratch my head. "I couldn't."

"What were these bombshells?" he asks.

"I can't get into it. Not now."

"For fuck's sake. Are you kidding me?"

"Paul? Please. Can you trust me? I'll tell you everything. But I can't right now. I need to get through tonight."

"Okay," he says. "Is that it?"

"Not quite."

I reach out to stroke Paul's cheek. He wears an expression of deep worry, sadness.

"When Isobel was born, I opened a bank account. For myself. I didn't have a job. No money of my own, and I found that deeply stressful. When you grow up with nothing, money can be stressful. You know how my mother set up that system years ago where I get a slice of her annual royalties?"

"The tax dodge?" Paul offers.

"Yeah. I don't even think my mom knew how much I was getting. The size of the cut. It was only a slice, but a slice of a huge pie is still . . . a lot of money. So I put half of it in our joint account, and I'd take half of it and squirrel it away into my secret account. You know, in case of . . ." I trail off and look to the floor. "You're a lawyer, Paul. You know how these things work. Divorce, death. I needed a safety net. I was protecting myself."

He considers this. "Okay. So you have some secret stash. What does this have to do with Julian Simone?"

In the throes of our more passionate arguments, Paul's lawyerly steadiness can be downright infuriating. But in moments like this, I'm grateful for it.

"I used my stash money to pay Julian Simone to go away."

"How much?" Paul asks.

"A million."

"Are you fucking kidding me?"

I can't meet his gaze.

"Did you get an agreement in writing?"

"There was a lawyer," I say. "A nondisclosure contract. But he's been circling again. Claiming there's new information. He's found more dirt. He even mentioned River today and some worm he's got in the police department. My name was on the file because I sat in on Isobel's interview."

"Christ, Nadine. You have a cease and desist, right? Beyond the nondisclosure?"

I shrug. At this Paul stands and paces the length of the room, fuming. "So let me get this straight. You paid him off, which means he won't print whatever dirt he had. But you didn't paper anything firm to stop him from digging for more? That's what I mean by cease and desist."

"The deal was that he'd stop. That it would all stop. All of it."

"But he's not stopping. He's writing about your mom. That story, the one about her working—"

"I approve or veto anything he prints. That's part of the deal."

Paul laughs in disbelief. "So you're working with him?"

"No! I'm managing him."

I see it, the flush in his cheeks. But Paul isn't mad because Julian Simone has threatened us, threatened our family, my mother, possibly even River and by extension Isobel, me. He's mad because he's a lawyer and my husband, and I've left him out.

I stand and straighten my shoulders. "We can talk about this tomorrow," I say. "I'm not getting into it now."

"You brought it up, Nadine."

His acerbic tone sets me alight. I step around the coffee table and march over to him, jabbing a finger into his chest and pushing him until his back is against the living room wall. This shocks him. He laughs and grips me hard by the wrist.

"You lied to me," he says.

"You don't get it, do you?"

"Are there other things? Something else you'd like to share?"

I push up against him, pressing my hip bone in. He jolts slightly.

"Did Seymour ever tell you anything about River?" I ask. "About the trouble she was in?"

Paul frowns. "No."

"You'd tell me, wouldn't you?"

"Of course I'd tell you. What's gotten into you?"

"I need you to understand something, Paul. I'm the one who holds everything together. I'm the one who fixes things when they fall apart. Sometimes you know nothing about it. That's not me lying to you; that's a luxury I'm affording you. You are spared the grind in so many ways. There's an entire ocean under the surface that you never have to contend with. You understand that, right?"

He nods almost imperceptibly. I press against him even harder, my lips to his ear.

"Right?"

"Right. Jesus, Nadine."

He lifts a hand to my hip, sweeping the underside of my breast with his thumb. When I kiss him, I feel his body sink into mine. He untucks my shirt and tugs me in by the waist. But then his phone rings. We both jump. Paul withdraws his phone from his back pocket and checks the caller ID.

"Isobel," he says.

"Answer it."

He swipes to accept the call then puts it on speaker. "Hi, Izzy."

"What are you doing?" she says.

Paul is flushed, breathless.

"You've both been at Nana's for, like, an hour. I'm tracking you."

"Not an hour. Ten minutes, tops," Paul says.

"I'm getting Nana's juicer," I say. "Like Margot asked."

"Whatever. The band is here and the caterer keeps asking Nana questions she can't answer. She shouldn't be answering questions about her own party."

"It's okay, Isobel," I say, tucking in my shirt, locking eyes firmly with Paul before turning back to the kitchen. "We're coming home."

WHEN PAUL AND I ARRIVE HOME, we are accosted at the door by Isobel and Damien, the two of them tugging at our sleeves as if they'd been waiting at the window like they used to do as toddlers.

"Everyone, stand down," Paul says. "Let us take our shoes off, at least."

"I need my allowance," Damien says.

"What the hell, Damien?" Isobel slaps his arm. "Allowance? Are you eight? Where are you going? Nana's party starts in, like, twenty minutes."

"Not twenty minutes." I look to my watch. It's six p.m. "We have two hours."

"I need to go to the store," Damien says.

"He needs to buy flowers for his girlfriend," Isobel whines, mocking him.

"Actually, I'm going to buy cyanide to lace your lemonade."

"Stop it," I say.

Paul extracts a twenty-dollar bill from his wallet and hands it to Damien.

"You are such a spoiled brat," Isobel says. "Everybody's favorite Little Prince."

"Screw off, Izzy."

With that, Damien edges past us and out the front door. Isobel, Paul, and I stand in silence for a moment. Up close I am always struck by how smooth Isobel's skin is, how flawless, even when she's grimacing. Margot appears from the kitchen and sidles up to Isobel, linking arms with her. They are the same height, the same build. Isobel drops her head to rest it on her cousin's shoulder.

"The caterer had lots of questions," Margot says to me.

"So I hear."

"You disappeared," Isobel says. "What were you doing at the library?"

"You track me a little too closely," I say.

Margot laughs. "It is a little stalker-ish."

"I ran into a neighbor outside the library. Followed her in to catch up in the air-conditioning."

I can feel Paul watching me, noting how quickly I've regained my poise from only minutes ago. Even I amaze myself with how easily I can lie when it's required.

"She's always running into neighbors when she leaves the house." Isobel rolls her eyes to Margot. "I swear to God, I can actually feel myself decaying anytime I'm with her and she runs into someone. She could kill two hours chatting up the most random person alive."

"That's a mother's way," Margot says.

"Whatever," Isobel says. "I'm going to shower. No one else showers until I'm done."

Paul salutes her. "Aye aye, Captain."

In the kitchen I find my mother leaning against the counter, a cup of tea in hand, chatting with Gregory, the caterer. Margot assumes her position next to my mother at the kitchen island. I hand them the juice press. They are making the punch.

"Hi, Gregory," I say. "Isobel says you had some questions."

"Nope," he says. "All sorted. Just some details about setup, timing. Marilyn here got us squared away. We're good."

"Everything is coming together," my mother says. "You could even lie down for a bit if you want."

"You shouldn't be working so hard on your own birthday," I say.

"There's no greater gift to me than helping you," my mother responds.

"You're funny," I say. I don't mean for my words to carry an edge, but they do. Margot and my mother exchange a look, as if confirming some tidbit about me they'd agreed on earlier. I'm out of sorts, unhinged. When I spin to survey the yard, I nearly bump headfirst into a young server cutting his way through the kitchen. He carries a metal bucket the size of a laundry basket.

"For ice," he says. "Anywhere in particular you want me to put it?"

"Outside," I say. "Close to the door. In the shade."

If it were up to me, drinks would be served only at the bar. But Paul likes a bucket filled with cold beer. Even in a suit, even at a party of this kind, he prefers to drink directly from a bottle he's plucked himself from a vat of ice.

The caterers are all in T-shirts, not yet changed into the white, starched button-downs they'll wear tonight. My ears ring as I watch them.

"We don't actually put the ice in the buckets until the party has started," the young man is saying. When I turn to him, I realize he's been speaking to me this entire time, attempting small talk with his vacant hostess. I thank him before he nudges the patio door open with an elbow and disappears outside.

I pull my phone from my pocket and refresh my email again. The wheel spins longer than it normally does . . . *Checking for Mail* . . . and then a bar across the top indicates a sizeable download. I feel my heart flop in my chest.

"I'm going downstairs for a sec," I say. "Some last-minute RSVPs to attend to."

"Who RSVPs to a party the day of?" Margot asks.

"You'd be surprised," my mother replies.

I curl to the rear of the kitchen and take the back stairs to the basement. My office is dark. I flick on the light, close the door, and sit. Alone. The ceiling creaks with the many footsteps overhead. At my desk I open my laptop and call up the email from Julian Simone.

> It's all in one zip file. I'm extending an olive branch by sending you my Terriville file too. I hope you agree that we are on the same page, Mrs. Walsh. We want the same thing. See you tonight.
>
> JS

My hand hovers on the mouse before I finally click the file open. I don't need to do this now. I could go back upstairs. But I won't. I won't. Instead, I stand and pace, stopping in front of the Sister Door. I press my ear to it, its metal cold against my skin. If I strain, I'm certain I can hear the tumble of the clothes dryer on the other side. Since I left him this afternoon, Teddy has dutifully switched the first load to the dryer, a middle-aged man's first attempt at laundry. Is he down in the basement too? I feel a baffling urge to knock. I squeeze the dead bolt on the door and consider twisting it. Free will is a remarkable thing; the notion that I could just open this door and intrude upon Teddy, break the unspoken agreement of privacy that we all adhere to because those are the rules. But something tells me Teddy wouldn't be put off by it. He might not even see it as an intrusion. He might, I think, even be happy to see me.

My computer pings. The zip drive has downloaded.

I snatch my laptop and my notebook and sit on the floor, my back against the coolness of the metal Sister Door. Julian's folder is divided into two files. I click open the first, labeled *CIF*—Colleen Isabella Fitzgerald. What appears are crookedly scanned photographs of handwritten reports. Total pages: twelve. The first few pages are the initial police report. The handwriting is a messy combination of print and cursive. My eyes land on my own name halfway down the page.

Deceased located at approximately 4:45 a.m. by Nadine Millay (10), who is the daughter to deceased's sister Marilyn Millay (30). Child seemed in good spirits and able to answer basic questions at investigation site. Interview scheduled at Detachment for 10:45 a.m., report to be attached.

In good spirits. My God.

The next page is titled Coroner's Summary. I scan down. *Toxicology shows high levels of alcohol and . . .* the word is illegible but ends in -*tin*. Some kind of narcotic. *Deceased showed bruising on shoulder and wrist and hip, injury to the neck conducive to a fall from upper level of the barn. Evidence of recent sexual activity.*

At the bottom of the page: *Cause of death: Fall. Accidental.*

My stomach aches. Stop. I should stop.

Next is a list of the interviews conducted. My name is first. There
is no transcript of the interview, just a point form summary with remarkably little detail.

> *Child was cooperative.*
> *Note child using present tense to describe deceased. Child*
> *asked if deceased was asleep.*

My eyes blur with tears. I flip through the pages then stop suddenly.
There. I see it: Seymour. A paragraph.

> *Interview with Seymour Dunphy (16) conducted between*
> *4–5pm. Youth's mother was present. Youth claims deceased*
> *spent much of the evening in or around the barn. Claims he*
> *tried to stop deceased from drinking. Was uncertain who pro-*
> *vided narcotics. He left party at 9 p.m. and walked home with*
> *visiting friend. Alibi corroborated by mother and by friend.*

The "friend" name is scribbled, but I can make it out—*Lionel Rob-*
inson.

Seymour was interviewed by the police. I knew this. He told me
long ago. Many of the partygoers were interviewed. I scan for any more
familiar names but see none. There is no mention of Paul. Brief gloss-
ing of interviews with my grandparents, my mother, others. I need to
stand up. I need to shake this all off and go upstairs. I flip back to the
details of my interview.

> *Child unable to remember seeing deceased at party.*
> *Child indicates no signs of trouble leading up to the day.*

There. The omission. *My* omissions. I didn't tell the police what I'd seen. Any of it. The encounter in the days before the party. The Jeep with no doors. And then the night of the party, Colleen in the loft after dark, waiting for someone. Even after her death, I was so fearful of Colleen's reaction that I told the police nothing. I buried it all.

What difference might it have made if I'd been forthcoming? That's impossible to know. It certainly wouldn't have brought Colleen back to us.

Trauma, Teddy called it. If I allow this to wash over me now, I will not be able to gather myself before the party. I will snap open. Break apart.

I read the final line of my interview report: *Jewelry worn by deceased returned to family.*

Indeed. At the end of the interview, the detective produced a clear plastic zipper bag and handed it to me. 'Give this to your grandparents. I think they'd want to have it.'

The necklace with the flower pendant. The one I'd saved for so diligently and mailed to Colleen at the farm as a fifteenth birthday present. It never occurred to me that the detective was out of line to be handing the necklace to me and not to my grandfather who was sitting in the lobby just down the hall. I slipped the plastic evidence bag into the pocket of my dress, knowing full well that I'd forever keep that necklace for myself.

I hover the mouse over Julian's zip drive to shut it down. But then I click on the second file. The file about River. It's a series of emails collated into one file with some sections redacted, including names. Skimming my way down, it's clear that Julian has attempted to protect the identity of his source, my *loved one* as Julian said, but his efforts are so half-assed, that I know if I just keep scanning, I know I'll find . . .

"Nadine?"

Margot. Before I can stand, Margot has rounded my desk and gapes down at me, at this scene before her, wide-eyed.

"What are you doing on the floor?"

I understand how this looks. I'm hunched up, my back to the Sister Door, laptop on my legs, my notebook open. I am a crazy person. Unhinged.

"Nadine! What the hell?"

"I know. I know."

"Do you want me to get Paul? Or your mom?"

"God, no. I just needed a minute. To gather myself."

"Okay. But you're on the floor. With your computer. You need to stand up."

"I can't," I say. "I mean, I can. But I need a minute."

Margot lowers herself to her knees and plucks the laptop gently off my legs. She looks at the screen.

"What is this?" Her eyes narrow. "Why do you have an email from Julian Simone?"

I shake my head. "Because . . . I stopped him . . . I'm stopping him."

"From what?"

"He got ahold of River's police file. And he claims he has an inside source. Someone close to me."

I search Margot's face for a shift in expression. She clicks on the mouse, before catching me studying her. A wave of realization washes over her.

"Don't you dare say it, Nadine."

"I'm not. It's just . . . you're one of the only people who knows. About the video. Who has access to the . . . facts. Julian Simone said—"

Margot lifts a finger to silence me. "Listen. I'm going to forgive you for having that thought. I know you're bent out of shape, Nadine.

So I'll forgive you for thinking, even for a split second, that I'd be capable of betraying you like that. Betraying your family. *My* family."

I look to my hands. "I know you would never."

"Good."

She pats my leg and returns her focus to my computer. I'm grateful to Margot for being so forgiving, for stooping—literally joining me on the floor—to engage in this.

"Look," she says, edging closer to me, pointing to the screen. "This supposed snitch knows about the video that Isobel took. They've exchanged emails about it. Julian Fuckhead has blacked out the sender's name. See here? *Video filmed by Marilyn Millay's granddaughter.* Why would Julian Simone care about a video of River?"

"Because of me," I say. "It's something to lord over me. And my mother."

"Is he blackmailing you?"

"Something like that," I say.

She frowns. "Right. Okay. I get it."

"I wish I could see that damn video," I say. "There's definitely no way of gleaning the source?"

Margot scrolls through the pages of emails.

"All the names are redacted. It's just back and forth about the terms. About money. Holy shit. Wait. Wait."

She runs a finger along the screen to highlight a line of text in the middle of the page.

If you want it, come to my store.

Store.

"Marvin," I say.

"Or Lacey," Margot offers.

I shake my head. "It says '*my* store.' It's Marvin."

"That prick," Margot says.

Yes, I think. *That prick.* It all makes sense. The recent tension between Marvin and me, his hostility today. The ongoing comments about our different lots in life, my willingness to *fraternize with the unwashed.* A wife who abandoned him, a failed writing career buried somewhere. If there's to be a traitor in my midst, then I feel some modicum of relief that it's not someone I love. Marvin does not have enough standing in my life to dare threaten it.

"Lacey had the video," Margot says. "He must have gotten ahold of it."

"It seems he did."

"So what do we do now?" Margot asks.

"I'll take care of it. You don't need to worry."

I reach over her to close the zip drive. Then I take the laptop and place it in the drawer of my desk.

"I'll do whatever you need me to do," Margot says.

"I know you will," I say.

"But Nadine? We need to focus. On tonight. We will deal with this in the morning. Okay? You'll leave it alone until then, right?"

"Yes," I say, my gaze unfocused. "Okay."

Margot takes my hand and squeezes it, guiding me to the office door.

"Right now," she says. "I need you to get ready for the party."

I WILL SHOWER AGAIN, THIS TIME upstairs. In our en suite I go to turn on the water then realize I can hear a flow through the pipes. Isobel must still be in the shower. How long has it been? I exit our room and duck into hers.

Isobel is now seventeen, and yet her bedroom has remained mostly unchanged since she was a toddler. Last year we had a contractor add a walk-in closet, and I offered to modernize it in other ways too. Upgrade her bed, repaint the mauve walls. But Isobel balked. She loves her room, the string lights around the window, photographs of her friends taped everywhere, her stuffed animals still piled on the travel trunk in the corner. A little girl's room.

I sit on her bed.

In our basement apartment, my mother and I shared a room, my twin bed running perpendicular to her double. The only private space I knew as a kid was the bedroom reserved for me at my grandparents' farm. I squeeze my eyes shut now and try to summon it. An old dresser in the corner, the wooden window frame painted shut, lace curtains that did nothing to block the sharp morning light. A single bed. Colleen's room just down the hall.

I promised Margot no more ruminating. An impossible pledge, I know.

Note child using present tense to describe deceased, the report read.

For years, my mother accused me of the same.

'Colleen likes this song,' I'd say, fiddling with the radio dials in the car.

'Liked,' she'd correct me. 'She liked this song.'

I don't believe my mother meant to be cruel in these corrections. Just factual, honest. Surely she was worried about me, even if I never gave her much reason to be. After Colleen died, after we stopped visiting the farm, little changed outwardly with me. I kept up my grades, did well in school, made friends. I was liked by my teachers in high school. I mostly stayed away from drugs or alcohol. I played sports and joined clubs. In fact, Marilyn often marveled at my resilience.

But it wasn't that I'd bounced back from the grief, the trauma of losing Colleen. I'd simply buried it all. And six months ago, when I hit my head, everything shook loose. *Child indicates no signs of trouble leading up to the day.*

What lies I told to protect Colleen. So many omissions.

By the time Isobel emerges from the bathroom, I'm in a daze. She waves a hand in my face.

"Hello?" She sits beside me on the bed. "Are you in trance mode?"

"Hi." I rub her bare shoulder. "Sorry. I was daydreaming. You okay?"

"What are you doing in my room?"

"Waiting for your shower to finish. Maybe we can chat for a minute."

"Chat," she says dryly. "People chat about the weather. You don't chat."

"How's River?"

"I told you already. She's the same. Basically dead."

"Isobel. Don't."

"Whatever. Tell me again why you're in my room. I'm not trying to be a bitch, but I need to get dressed."

"Yes. Sorry. I'll leave."

She leans forward to towel her hair then flips it upward, spraying me with shampoo-scented droplets.

"You've been extra weird today, Mom. Your stress is stressing me out. So if you have something to say, why don't you just spit it out?"

I adjust so I'm facing my daughter.

"I saw Marvin at the store this afternoon. He mentioned something that . . . bothered me."

Isobel rolls her eyes. "Lacey and Damien's drama isn't my issue."

"He mentioned a video. One that you might have taken? Of River?"

This is a half-truth, a means of throwing Marvin to the lions while also protecting Margot as the original source of this revelation. I am building a house of cards today, pitting a series of untruths against each other. Isobel's eyes brim with tears. She stands and marches to the walk-in closet, closes it, then emerges not a minute later in track pants and a hoodie, her wet hair dripping.

"What the fuck?" she says. "I'm actually going to kill Damien. He promised me Lacey deleted it. And now her fucking dad knows about it?"

"Isobel. Listen to me. You need to tell me the truth."

"Why are we talking about this *right now*?"

"You just said we should—"

"Yeah, because I thought maybe you were going to scold me for not watering the houseplants or something. I swear to God, Mom. Lately, everything is so major with you."

I breathe and wait.

"I deleted it, okay," Isobel says. "No one saw it. Maybe two people. River saw it the day after I took it and freaked out, so I deleted it right away. Damien always takes my phone when he runs out of data and he saw it before I deleted it. He texted it to himself like a little pervert. I had no idea he'd done that. Then Lacey said something to me about it and I absolutely raged on them both. Like, I threatened them with a painful death. Not painful enough, I guess."

"What was on the video?"

"Nothing! It was nothing! It's not, like, evidence or related to . . . what she did. You can put away your useless criminology degree."

"You don't want to leave any tracks, Isobel."

"Tracks?" She throws her head back in a shrill laugh. "Oh my God. You think you're an amateur cop or something."

"You were interviewed by a police officer and didn't say anything about a video, Izzy. That's not great."

"You mean the cop who basically gave me PTSD by putting me in a room and berating me after I found my friend half dead?" She mimics a thoughtful pose. "Yeah, sure. Why wouldn't I sit there and willingly confess to a cop every dumb thing my friends and I have ever done? I'm not about to betray my best friend. That's why!"

"Let's not revise history, Isobel. He hardly berated you. He asked you a few simple questions."

"He never asked me about a video." Isobel paces the room. She picks up her phone from the bedside table, glances at it then throws it on the bed. "It was nothing. The video was nothing! Maybe, like, two weeks before she took those pills, we were over at her house. And we were, whatever. Drinking. Okay? We stole some vodka from her mom. And we went downstairs to raid the fridge. Sherry was away for the weekend, so Seymour was at the house, and he was in the kitchen with that guy who lives next door. The fake British guy."

"Theodore. Teddy."

"Whatever. Yeah. Teddy. Anyway, we said hello because we're polite. We have manners. And River does this thing when she tries to pretend she's sober. She stands up all straight like a soldier and gets super formal and weird. It's funny. So when we got back to her bedroom I was filming her doing that, like, making fun of herself. And then she was imitating the neighbor guy, his accent or whatever, and the gross way guys talk to us."

I sit up, my hands tingling. "Guys?" I repeat.

"You know, Mom. Men."

"What do you mean exactly?"

Isobel throws her hands in the air then points at me. Her anger is heavy, palpable.

"Every man is gross with us, Mom! Every man except for our dads, maybe. They just ask us these stupid questions, and they're always trying really hard not to look at us—at our *parts*—which is way worse than just ogling, or maybe they do ogle when they think we won't notice, and it's just gross. Do you know what I mean?"

"Yes," I say. "I do."

I think of Margot's words earlier this afternoon: *'Girls just have that built-in sense.'*

"We do this thing where we imitate them," Isobel says. "We call it Dirty Old Man. It's a dumb routine. And River was doing that, but then she got stupid about it, and started taking off her clothes, like doing this striptease in a British accent, and talking about that guy, Teddy, like 'Oh, come here, Dirty Old Man, Teddy Bear' and I was filming because—I don't know?—because it was hilarious? But the next afternoon she asked me about it and we watched it and River freaked on me. Watching it sober, you could see that it was . . . not great. Not actually that funny at all. Like, weird. She was mad about it. She kept freaking out that her dad might see it. Why would I show it to her dad? So I deleted it. Then Damien, sneaky shit! Takes my phone and sends it to himself to show his girlfriend. I threatened him and Lacey with torture if they didn't wipe it. So it's gone. Forever. If that cop, Officer Dumbfuck, wants to come charge me with child porn or whatever, he can't even try, because the evidence is erased."

"Isobel," I say. "You're not in any trouble."

"That's not how you're making it sound!"

By now she's almost wheezing, she's so upset. I rise and take hold of her by the shoulders. She collapses forward into my arms. Lately, Isobel has felt unreachable to me, as though we are occupying the same space but separated by a thick partition of glass. I know it's partly that recent events have stirred up more in me than I can bear—more than she can bear too. How do you temper your child's grief when it unexpectedly triggers your own?

"Will the cop find out about the video?" Isobel asks through her tears.

"No. I don't think so. He doesn't need to know."

"So you won't tell him?"

"No. But, Isobel? I need to ask you something else. Was River in any trouble? Was she doing anything else that might have been getting her into trouble? Apparently, the police spoke to her at some point before she overdosed. Something to do with . . . escorting."

"I can't believe this. That was all bullshit!" Isobel says. "Like, River was a call girl? So fucking stupid. Some sophomore told her mom that River came up to her in the bathroom and asked her if she liked older guys. If she wanted to make some money. It was a *joke*. The mom called the cops! The police talked to River for like ten seconds then realized it was all so dumb."

"So she didn't?"

"Didn't what, Mom? Say it."

I pause, lowering my gaze. "She didn't sleep with older men for money."

Isobel's laugh is a trill. "You're unbelievable."

"It's just, Izzy, with the video. And the police—"

Isobel shakes her head vehemently. "No! Jesus, Mom."

But her voice wavers. The tears come. I hug Isobel tightly. She is afraid. Of what? Of losing everything? Of secrets shaking loose? I'm angry too. Not at Isobel. I'm angry at Marvin, the traitor. And even more than him, for reasons I can't fully understand, I'm angry at my mother. The heat of Isobel's breath moistens my shirt. Her cry has shifted to a whimper.

"Shhh," I say. "It's okay, darling. You've had such a difficult few weeks."

"You know what kills me?" she whispers.

"What?"

"One day you wake up with no idea that your entire life is about to change. Everything is just . . . normal. Boring. You're this robot, showering and getting ready for school like any other day. And then, boom. Shit goes down. Everything is worse. Your whole world is different. Like, the lights have gone out."

"Life can be unfair," I say. "Tragedies surprise us. But things do get better eventually. Like you said, there are signs of hope with River. She could still wake up."

"Or not. She could pull through and never be the same. You're proof of that."

Never the same? Is that how my daughter sees me since my fall? My own tears threaten.

"Do you want me to cancel the party?" I ask.

She pulls back. "Now? Are you kidding?"

"We can call it all off. Nana won't care."

"Don't you dare. Don't put that on me," she says, wiping a tear. "I'm fine. Are *you* fine?"

"I'm fine. Everything is okay."

This too is a lie. I'm not sure why I even bother with it. Isobel doesn't believe me. We don't believe each other.

"I'll leave you alone now," I say, standing. "Do you need anything?"

She shakes her head and lies down on her bed. I leave the room, clicking her door gently closed behind me.

In the hallway, I'm at a loss for what to do next.

Shower. That was the plan. But my feet are cemented to the floor. The hullabaloo grows louder downstairs. I'll check in once more before showering. This godforsaken party. Marilyn would have been perfectly content with a family dinner and a handmade card from her grandchildren. But I couldn't cancel it. I can't. I will honor this day even if it kills me.

THE KITCHEN IS ABUZZ. IT'S ALMOST seven o'clock. Nearly one hour until our guests arrive. There must be ten catering staff here now. Out the window the band members chitchat among themselves as they tune their instruments. They're set up on the patio, a rectangle of special tiles laid on the grass in front of them to create a makeshift dance floor. The dining table is lined with trays. I see the cheese platters; Zachary must have dropped them off. In the living room I find my mother and Margot cross-legged on the sofa, drinking lemonade. Their chatter is light. They look to be in perfect tandem.

"The cake was just delivered," Margot says. "I put it downstairs in your office."

"Good. Thank you."

I wonder if Margot's told my mother about the state she found me in barely an hour ago, tangling with my laptop in a fit on my office floor. They both watch me as if it's my turn to speak.

"The band is ready to go," Marilyn finally says. "I've asked them to keep things a bit quieter until the guests start arriving."

"Yes. Great."

"This is a little embarrassing," my mother says. "Old lady parties should be confined to the local diner."

"You're a star, Marilyn," Margot says. "And stars should shine bright."

"Indeed," I say. "On that note, I should probably go shower."

"We were thinking," Margot says. "Maybe I should go home with your mom and get ready at her house. To avoid too many people trying to shower at once here. If we leave now, we'll make it back before eight."

Something in the *we* she employs irks me. They've been a pair today, Marilyn and Margot, the two of them merging their lists and sidling up to each other like a couple of schoolgirls.

"Where's Paul?" I ask.

"Um." Margot tosses Marilyn a glance. "I think he's outside."

"Helping the band set up?" I ask. "I didn't see him out there."

"No."

"What's he doing, then?"

Margot's face strains. "Having a pre-party cocktail? I think Seymour and Teddy are over."

"Marvin too," my mother adds.

"Marvin from the store?" I ask, incredulous.

"I know." Margot looks at me wide-eyed. Marvin, of all people. "Don't ask me. I went outside and he was just . . . there. I don't know why or how."

"What the hell?" I look to the ceiling, blinking hard. "Okay. Thank you."

"I can go collect Paul," Marilyn offers. "Shoo the rest of them away until start time."

"No. I will. It's fine."

"Are you sure, Nadine?" Margot asks.

Her question is loaded. She knows there's a risk to this: I could explode on Marvin. Or Paul. I'm on tenterhooks.

"I'll behave," I say. "I promise. You two head out. You'll be back before eight, right?"

"You got it," Margot says. "Dressed and ready for action."

They stand up in unison. I feel a sudden jolt of wrath directed at my mother.

"By the way," I say to her. "I invited Julian Simone tonight. He emailed me. So I invited him."

Margot's mouth drops open. "You did what?"

"He might have shown up anyway," I say. "So I took control."

Marilyn's studying me. She knows me too well. I'm throwing wild jabs at her. I'm up to something.

"I trust you," my mother says, ever poised. "You're taking control. Whatever you think is best."

"Right," I say, shooing them away. "Off you go."

Once they're gone, I check myself in the hallway mirror before marching through the kitchen and out to the yard. Indeed, there they are, the four of them fanned around one of the rear tables with cold beers in hand. Paul has dutifully set the centerpiece aside and removed the tablecloth. Marvin faces my direction but hasn't noticed me yet. He is sitting too erect, his expression locked in a weird smile. Even from here, I can tell he's uncomfortable. Good. Screw him.

What I'd like to do is a grab one of the centerpieces from another table and whip it at Marvin's head. Instead, I greet the band leader, engaging in small talk until I can be certain that the drinking foursome have taken notice of my presence in the yard. When I glance their way again, all eyes are on me. I approach.

"You're in trouble," Seymour says to Paul.

"Not at all," I say, smiling, avoiding Paul's gaze. "Nothing wrong with an early drink to loosen up. As long as you don't make a mess."

"Paul's way ahead of you," Seymour says, pointing to the folded tablecloth.

"Marvin here was just telling us about life at the store," Teddy says.

"It's quite the gig," Seymour says. "Real bird's-eye view of the neighborhood."

Marvin shakes his head almost imperceptibly. "I actually just dropped in because Paul bought candles for the cake then forgot them on the counter." He lifts his beer. "They forced me into joining them."

Tell your husband I'll see him tonight, Marvin said as I left his store this afternoon. I want to bore my gaze into him, glare at him until he melts. It's funny how you dread the prospect of betrayal at the hands of your closest friends, your family. That's what we all fear. But when betrayal comes from someone on your periphery, someone like Marvin, it feels almost preposterous. Like a bad joke.

Seymour kicks at an empty chair with his toe. "You join us too, Nadine. For a quick toast before the party starts."

I sit. Paul proffers a beer from a cooler under the table. I can't look at him. Instead, I look to Teddy, who smiles at me warmly.

"Seymour was telling me a minute ago that you've all known each other since you were kids," Marvin says.

"Not me," I say. "I met them all in college. I was younger than them. A sophomore."

"That's still a kid," Paul says.

"And I'm older than this bunch," Teddy adds. "Finished college before they'd even started."

"Teddy was friends with my older brother," Paul offers Marvin.

"Wow," Marvin says, shifting on his chair. "Talk about six degrees of separation."

"Yes," I say to Marvin. "You might want to take notes."

He smiles at me curiously, the dig going over his head.

"Teddy transferred to London partway through college," Seymour says. "Under a bit of a cloud, if I recall."

"Really?" Paul laughs.

"I'd developed a bit of a . . . tendency to party too hard. My parents sent me to a military college in the wilds of northern England."

"Sounds fun," Marvin says.

"I assure you," Teddy says. "It was not."

"You recovered from the experience well enough," Seymour says. "Got yourself a big job at the bank, traveled the world, bought yourself a few fancy cars."

"But never a wife," Paul says.

The joke lands with a thud. Paul coughs, aware of the depths of his backfire.

"Nope," Teddy says. "Never lucky enough to find a wife."

"You've all done pretty well for yourselves, I'd say," Marvin offers.

I watch them banter, sipping my beer. Only minutes ago, I promised Margot I'd behave myself out here. Not cause any scenes. Say anything out of line. But I can't stop myself. I can't.

"Well," I say. "To what should we toast?"

"How about we toast you, Nadine?" Teddy says. "Our lovely hostess?"

"No, no. Not me. If you don't mind, I might drag things down for a minute. Maybe we could toast my aunt Colleen. She died thirty years ago today, after all."

Paul reaches for my arm and squeezes. "We could, if you'd like."

"Seymour," I say. "It occurred to me recently that River and Isobel are older now than Colleen was when she died. Isn't that remarkable? They're still just girls. That struck me."

"It is remarkable," he said. "She was so young."

"You remember her, don't you?"

"I do," Seymour says. "A bit."

"Come on, Seymour," Teddy says. "You were in love with her."

"In love with her?" Seymour says, shaking his head. "We were children."

Marvin appears bewildered. I've made their little gathering awkward.

"To Colleen Fitzgerald," Paul says, lifting his drink. "A toast to honor her."

We all raise our beers, clink, and then sip. The silence that follows is awful. When my eyes meet Seymour's, he looks sad. Stricken.

"Well," I say, handing Paul my still-full beer. "Thank you for obliging me. But I really need to go get ready."

"You do!" Teddy exclaims, tapping his watch. "The party's in an hour."

Before I can retreat, Seymour reaches for my hand.

"She really was a lovely girl, Nadine," he says. "I know we never really talked about her much. But Teddy's not far off. Colleen was my first crush. We were so young, you're right about that. She was so young. I never got to see her much, but I was always happy when I did. It was a terrible loss. If I've never said so before, I'm really sorry."

Oh. I'm stuck by his sincerity, the kindness in his gaze. What is happening?

"Thank you, Seymour," I say. "I appreciate that."

216

Another long silence follows. Finally, Marvin stands.

"I should get back," he says. "Lacey's manning the store."

"Thanks for slumming with us, Marvin," Teddy says. "See you to-night."

I am careful to ignore Marvin as he takes his leave.

"I should get home too," Teddy says. "Leave our hosts to their final preparations. I can't wait to celebrate the esteemed Marilyn Millay."

"Yes," I say, pasting on a smile. "Neither can I."

EVENING

THE CURTAINS IN OUR BEDROOM ARE drawn. I'm in a T-shirt and leggings, my hair wet, sitting on our bed, my legs stretched out before me.

"Mom?"

Damien has appeared in the doorway. He looks worried.

"Are you okay?" he asks.

"Fine," I say, smiling. "Just meditating. I'm about to get dressed. People will be here in thirty minutes."

"Okay," he says. "Seriously, though. Are you all right?"

There is such sadness in his expression, in his question, that I gesture for him to come closer. He crawls onto bed next to me so that our shoulders align. There was a time, not so long ago, that this very boy fit handily into the nook of my lap. Now his legs stretch a good four inches longer than mine. I am still brimming with this fierce and protective motherly love—these days more than ever—with so few opportunities to let it show.

"I'm all right," I say, patting his hand. "Perfectly fine."

A moment of quiet passes between us. I reach out to tuck a strand of his long curls behind his ear. Something is wrong. If Damien were satisfied by my answer, he'd get up and leave. There's more to this visit.

"Are *you* okay?" I ask him.

"Yeah," he says. "But I'm worried about you."

"I'm fine, dear boy. You don't need to worry."

He nods, but then his face purses and he begins to cry. How long has it been since I've seen tears from this boy? Months? No. Years. I gather him and pull him into a hug. He attempts to muffle his cries by pressing his face into my shoulder.

"Damien," I say. "What's wrong?"

"Isobel came into my room and said I might get arrested."

I pull away from him to study his face. "Jesus," I say. "Because of the video?"

"Yeah. She said you found out about it. That it counts as child porn. That I could get tried as an adult and go to jail."

"Listen to me, Damien Walsh. Are you listening to me?"

Damien's sniffles, rubbing at his nose.

"I haven't seen the video," I continue. "But from what I under-stand, it isn't like that. Your sister is just being dramatic. She's sad and scared. You all made a mistake, but no one is getting arrested. Got it?"

I bunch the bottom of my shirt and lift it to wipe his tears.

"Lacey said her dad knows about it," Damien says. "That he trans-ferred it to his own phone."

Of course he did, I think. And now he's dangling it in Julian Simone's face.

"It's not like Marvin is going to share it. But I'll talk to him about that. He probably just wanted to make sure whatever was going on had nothing to do with Lacey. And it doesn't, right?"

"What?"

"The video. It doesn't have to do with you. Or Lacey. And you don't have it on your phone anymore. Right?"

"Yes. Right."

There's a hint of hesitation in his voice.

"Tell me the truth, Damien. Did you delete it?"

"I did!" Damien says. "But I didn't realize your phone keeps the shit you delete for thirty days. And I just, now I feel like it's evidence."

"Evidence of what?"

"I don't know!" His voice cracks again. "There was this rumor going around that River was, like, hooking up with older guys. Maybe trying to gather other girls. I don't want to get in trouble. I wasn't the one who filmed it. But if you delete it, are you, like, tampering or whatever? I don't know what to do."

"Is the video still on your phone? Tell me the truth."

He nods.

"Okay," I say. "Give it to me. Your phone. Give it to me."

Damien obeys, leaning to pluck his phone from the pocket of his shorts. He unlocks it and hands it to me. I open the photo app and scroll to the folder of recently deleted items until I find it, a grainy video. I hold it up and Damien nods.

"Please don't watch it," he says. "I'll die."

"I won't. I'm deleting it."

I *do* delete it. But first, I angle the phone away from Damien and airdrop it to myself. Then I delete it. I set his phone on the bed and hug him again.

"It's time to get ready," I say. "Promise me you won't worry about this. I'm not happy with you or Isobel, and we'll deal with that. But no one is going to jail. Because no one committed a crime. Okay?"

"Okay."

"Hey." I pat his leg before standing up. "Do you think Lacey might come tonight?"

He shrugs. "I don't know. I don't really want to talk about it."

"Got it."

Damien hovers at the door without leaving. I'm making the bed when Paul walks in wearing nothing but a towel around his waist, having showered in the basement. He retreats to the walk-in closet and throws on a T-shirt and boxer shorts. Isobel must hear the commotion, because soon she's at the threshold of our room too. She's wearing a pink strapless summer dress, her hair pulled back in a loose bun, her feet still bare. I'm stunned by her, how gorgeous and poised she is, how womanly.

"Wow, Izzy," Paul says. "You look absolutely stunning."

"You actually kind of do," Damien says.

Isobel curtsies for us. "It's Margot's dress. She let me borrow it."

"Well," I say. "It's truly something."

She holds a toiletry bag up.

"Can I do your makeup?" Isobel asks me. "I brought my supplies."

"Sure," I say. "I'd love that, actually. But we only have a few minutes."

"Not too much makeup," Paul says.

Isobel rolls her eyes. "Typical. You want Mom to be hot but also take less time primping than you do."

"Do I primp?" he asks.

Our eyes meet. I've been angry at Paul today, but standing here, the four of us in our master bedroom, watching him wrap an arm around our son and squeeze him affectionately? The anger seems to melt away.

"You two are going to be friends tonight, right?" Paul says to the kids. "No fights, okay? No public scenes."

"I'll be nice to him. Least I can do before he heads to jail."

"Shut up, Izzy." There's a small crack in Damien's voice.

"What'd I miss?" Paul asks, baffled.

"Nothing," I say.

"Yeah," Isobel adds. "It's nothing, Dad. If we need a lawyer, we'll let you know."

"Alrighty," Paul says. "Damien, why don't us lads get ready in your room?"

Paul collects his outfit from the closet then the two of them disappear down the hall.

I look at my watch. Seven forty.

Isobel lays out her makeup tools on the dressing table in the closet. I open the jewelry drawer to search for the necklace I planned to wear tonight—Colleen's silver chain with the ornate flower pendant. My gift to her all those years ago. I hold it on my flat palm, measuring its feather weight.

"Aren't you wearing that silk jumpsuit tonight?" Isobel asks.

"Yes. A black one. Spaghetti straps."

"Then you need earrings. Not a necklace. Especially not that one."

Isobel takes the necklace from me and holds it to her own neck. Its flower matches the pink in her dress, the pendant resting perfectly in the recess of her jugular notch.

"I've never seen this before," Isobel says, fingering it.

"Yeah. I've had it forever. It's sentimental."

"Can I wear it?" Isobel asks.

"You definitely can."

I step behind Isobel. I won't tell her where it came from, why I've

225

kept it hidden for so many years. I squint to clasp the fastener and click it in place. We stand there for a moment, looking into the full-length mirror, me peering over her shoulder. Isobel is so beautiful. It still stuns me to look at her, tall and shapely, the way a human can straddle the line between childhood and adulthood, this hybrid creature part woman, part girl. I squeeze her shoulders and smile. The surge of love I feel for her is almost feral. I would do anything to protect her. I hope she knows that.

"Okay!" Isobel says, snapping us out of it, guiding me to the chair. "We could do a bit of a smoky eye, nothing too sharp, just some liner and mascara, a bit of shimmer on your lids. We'll find you some droopy earrings. I know Margot has some good ones if you don't. Messy bob for the hair. Then a bright red lip? It'll pop against the black."

"It will," I say. "You have five minutes."

"Got it. A red lip isn't very summery, but you're the hostess. We want you to stand out."

"Yes, we do."

I close my eyes to allow Isobel to pencil my lids.

Thirty years ago this very night, Colleen allowed me to watch as she applied makeup before the party. How I'd gaped at her in that green dress with its spaghetti straps, its tight hold on her young body. The lipstick she applied was a deep shade of red. When she turned to me, I was shocked by its effect. It warped her features into those of a woman much older than fifteen.

'Sexy, right?' she said. 'Open your mouth. Like this.'

I obeyed. She used a finger to dab me with lipstick.

'Look at you,' she said. 'Pretty little girl. The boys will love you.'

When I bounded into the hallway to check myself in the mirror, I was intercepted by my mother. She crouched and used the back of her hand to wipe the lipstick off. Then she marched into Colleen's room.

'Don't you dare,' she said, a fury in her voice. 'She's only ten years old.'

Now, I open my eyes. Isobel leans in close, dabbing at the skin around my eyes with a bare finger.

"This mascara is waterproof," she says. "In case you cry. Not that you ever cry."

"I do too," I say. "I cry."

"Even before this whole shit with River," Isobel says, "I've probably seen Sherry cry like ten or twenty times. You? You never do."

"I got that from Nana, I guess. Poise, above all."

"I'm not sure that's a good thing. At least Sherry lets it all out. You just bury it."

Bury it. Indeed I do.

Isobel bites at her lip as she works. When she's done with my makeup, she starts on my hair, spritzing it, tousling it, dragging over the hair dryer. All the while I sit in the chair, thinking back to this morning when I stood at the kitchen sink, poring over my to-do list, plotting out my day. Just over twelve hours ago, and yet it feels like an entire lifetime has unfolded. Time is funny that way, as Isobel pointed out earlier; most of our days are entirely unmemorable. Others, like today, feel almost too momentous.

"Okay," Isobel says. "Don't look in the mirror yet."

She collects the jumpsuit from the back of the door and fetches my wedge sandals as I slip it on. She plays with my hair until she's satisfied that it all falls as it should. Then she takes me by the shoulders and rotates me to the full-length mirror for the reveal.

Wow, I think. *Wow*.

"You look really good," Isobel says. "Like, really hot."

"Ha. I don't know about that."

"No, seriously. You look really fucking good, Mom."

I smile. "Thank you, baby girl."

"All we need is earrings. Margot has the perfect pair. I'll be right back."

Isobel exits the closet. She is right. The jumpsuit is an elegant cut, and her makeup job is both subtle and sharp. I see bits of my mother in my reflection, and Colleen too.

My heart is racing. I can't have it racing at the party. I collect my tote from the bedroom and find the pill bottle in the lining pocket. Tranquilizers. Tonight might be overwhelming. I shake one out, break it in half, then drop it in my jumpsuit pocket. A security blanket, that's all. I return to the closet and wait for Isobel to come back with earrings.

On the makeup table, my phone buzzes. The alarm I'd set this morning.

Eight p.m. Let the party begin.

M Y MOTHER AND I STAND IN the front hall, a receiving line of two. It's eight fifteen. The patio doors are open. Outside, the band plays a jazzy medley.

"You look gorgeous, by the way," Marilyn says. "A perfect outfit."

"So do you, Marilyn. I'd expect no less."

It's true. My mother is gorgeous at sixty. She wears a silk camisole with a light blazer overtop, loose white pants that cinch high on her waist. Black heels. So stylish and elegant. A true beauty. Normally, we'd stand close, chitchat and gossip in between greeting guests. But I'm angry with her. I am. So angry. Surely she can sense it.

I had a wooden sign handmade for the front door—COME IN!— so it opens at regular intervals. The earliest arrivals are mostly from Paul's law firm. Some friends of my mother's from yoga, book club. Marilyn greets each new arrival with an air-kiss and a breathy thank-you for their birthday wishes.

"Talk about gorgeous!" she declares when her book editor enters in a flowing floor-length summer dress. Everyone is buoyant, thrilled to be here. A breeze sifts through the hall from the patio doors. Paul has already set up camp in the living room with a small cluster of colleagues, his ability to hold a crowd not waning one bit with age.

It's a perfect night.

"God," my mother says. "Look at these outfits. I'm flattered by the effort."

"Your birthday is an event," I say.

"And look at Paul," Marilyn says. "What a showman you married. He could have been a movie star, the way he enthrals."

"Don't tell him that. I'll never hear the end of it. He'll quit law and move us to Vegas."

Damien bounds down the stairs, beelining directly into my mother's arms.

"You look gorgeous, Damien," my mother says.

"Thanks, Nana. So do you."

He's watching the door. And then it opens, and Marvin and Lacey enter. Lacey must have texted Damien to alert him of their impending arrival. She's in a tube dress patterned with bright flowers. Damien's face reveals his awe. He blushes when she steps forward and links her arm into his. Marvin, right behind her, wears a tan linen suit. He's shaven. He nods at me then extends an awkward hand to my mother.

"Happy Birthday, Marilyn."

"Thank you, Marvin. I brought a pen. Did you bring me any books to sign?"

He laughs. "I left them at my store. Where you're welcome anytime."

Fucking traitor.

"Control yourself, Dad," Lacey says. "Hi, Marilyn. You look beautiful. Happy birthday."

"Why, thank you, dear."

With that, Lacey and Damien set off for the kitchen. But before he's out of reach, I pull Damien back by the arm.

"Stay in the yard," I whisper. "Or the kitchen. Those are your boundaries tonight. That's as far as you go. Do not breach the perimeter. Got it?"

"Got it, Mom. Jeez."

"And watch yourself, okay? Keep track of your sugars."

He rolls his eyes. "I've got two doses in my pocket."

"Good boy. Why don't I hold one for you?"

Damien reaches into his pants then covertly slides the syringe into my open palm, the safety cap locked in place. I drop it into my pocket.

"Can I go now?" Damien asks.

I blow him a kiss. "You can. Be good."

"I should mingle too," Marvin says. "Leave you both to greet your guests."

"We can catch up later," I say. "I'd love to introduce you to a few people. Julian Simone is coming. You know, the journalist? I'm sure you'd love to meet him."

Marvin's face falls. He coughs and laughs at the same time. "Right," he says. "Sure."

I elbow my mother. "Marvin here calls himself your number one fan, Marilyn. Quite presumptuous, isn't it?"

My mother laughs. "I'm thrilled to have any fans at all."

I watch as Marvin flushes from his neck up. He smiles tensely then sneaks past us down the hall.

"What was that all about?" Marilyn asks.

"Nothing," I say.

Two young caterers appear before us, one with flutes of prosecco and the other with trays of appetizers. I take a drink and a selection of the bites. Stupidly, I skipped dinner. I'll need more in my stomach to get through the night.

"You've got that look," my mother says. "That existential look."

"I do not." I sip my drink. "It's just nerves."

"Are you angry with me?"

I glance sidelong at her. "I don't know, Marilyn. Maybe I'm just tired of keeping your secrets."

"What's that supposed to mean?"

I won't answer. I can't answer. Not now. The door opens again as I pop an appetizer into my mouth.

No. For weeks I've imagined how this scene might unfold: Daphne and Lionel arrive at the party just as I've fallen into conversation with one of my husband's handsome junior law partners. I've got a drink in hand, my lipstick is perfect. Lionel notices me before I notice him. But that's not what's happening. Instead, as Daphne and Lionel approach to greet me, I'm pressing a napkin to my lips, my cheeks chipmunked by the effort to chew through the crudités. Shit.

"Are we late?" Daphne asks.

"Not at all," Marilyn replies.

Lionel leans forward and kisses my mother's, then my cheek.

"You look wonderful, Nadine," Daphne says. "That jumpsuit is fantastic. And, Marilyn? You're a revelation. If I look half as good as you at sixty, I'll be thrilled."

"Stop. Where is that baby of yours? I thought she was coming."

"We found a sitter," Lionel says. "It's our first time out without her."

"Now that's cause for celebration," Marilyn replies.

"I'm sorry, Nadine," Daphne says. "I brought my breast pump. Can I put it somewhere?"

"Of course. Why don't you put it in the den off the kitchen? It locks, so you'll have some privacy if you need it later." I look to Lionel. "We were blown away by Daphne's generous gift. The wine."

"So thoughtful," Marilyn adds.

"I know you'll be in high demand tonight, Nadine," Daphne says. "But I'd love a word when you have a minute."

Lionel watches me. A word?

The door opens again, and suddenly the foyer is full. Marilyn and I are surrounded, mired in well-wishes and small talk. Daphne squeezes my hand before wandering into the kitchen, her diaper bag over her shoulder. When the crowd finally thins, Seymour and Teddy find their way to us.

"You've cleaned up beautifully, Nadine," Teddy says. "In under an hour, at that."

I feel myself blush. What an odd thing to say. "Teddy, this is my mother, Marilyn Millay."

He extends a hand. "Theodore Rosen. Teddy. I'm a huge fan, Ms. Millay."

"Teddy?" my mother says. "That's a nickname a man should probably shed before his eighteenth birthday."

Teddy roars with laughter, but my mother's smile is ice cold.

Meanwhile, Seymour appears distracted. He pulls his phone from his pocket.

"Is everything okay?" I ask him.

"They're, um, running another test tonight. At the hospital. I'm awaiting word from Sherry."

"Right," my mother says. "We'll keep our fingers crossed."

"Thank you," Seymour says.

"Plenty of drinks in the kitchen," I say.

"Condo Man," my mother says, once they're out of earshot. "Here at this party while his comatose daughter is undergoing tests at the hospital."

"We can't always be there for our kids," I say.

My mother raises her eyebrows. "Well. That's a direct hit. I actually felt it land."

"I'm just saying. Your venom toward Seymour serves no one."

"It serves me," she says. "He's always been a brat. Even as a boy."

"You said you don't remember him as a boy."

"I said I don't remember Paul. But Seymour was around at bit. Mostly I remember that his father was a total asshole. Terrible to my dad. A tyrant about the land. This smug, sports-car-driving asshole. And Seymour was just tagging along, spinelessly."

"He was a kid," I say.

"I'm not getting into this right now, Nadine. I know where you'll take it. I'm surprised you're defending him."

"Rumor has it he was in love with Colleen."

My mother shoots me a look. "See? You can't help yourself. He was a kid back then. And now he's a grown man mingling at my party while his wife holds vigil over his daughter at the hospital."

"Ex-wife."

"Whatever. He should suffer for it a little bit, shouldn't he? Let it be at my hands."

Again a tray is presented to us, and Marilyn swaps out her empty flute for a fresh drink.

"How many of those have you had?" I ask her.

"Three," she says. "So?"

"The night is young, Mom. You might want to pace yourself."

"Whatever." She chugs at the drink to spite me. "Do you think it's time to free ourselves from the shackles of the front door? I'd say most people are here."

"I think so," I say.

But before we can step away, the door opens again. And here he is, in my front hall: Julian Simone.

"Well, well, well," my mother says.

"Ms. Millay," he says, stepping forward. "Marilyn. It's been a long time."

"Since we saw each other in person? Years. I think it was that day-time interview. The one making the rounds again, ten years later."

"Much to my chagrin," he says. "The internet is ruining us, isn't it?"

"Well. We can't all be perfect all the time." My mother leans in, feigning a whisper. "I'd avoid my editor tonight if I were you, Julian. Or my lawyer. They might drag you into a dark corner and assault you."

"We wouldn't want that," he says.

"Have you met my daughter, Nadine?"

I extend a hand. "Mr. Simone. We're so glad you're here."

"I'm not certain that's true," he says. "But I'm glad to be here none-theless."

To my surprise, my mother links arms with Julian, guiding him into the kitchen, tossing me a smile over her shoulder as she does. After a moment, I head outside too.

The air is less soupy than it was an hour ago. The sun is low. Soon the sky will be pink with dusk. We'll turn on the string lights. I stand at the threshold of the patio doors. There's a short line at the bar, and the tables are nearly full of laughing guests. What a dreamy scene this party is already. And the night has only begun.

SOMETIMES, AS I MOVE THROUGH A crowd like this one, I imagine a camera tracking me overhead, as though the party is a scene from a film and I, an actor playing a role. Tonight, especially. I *am* an actor playing a role: the happy and gracious hostess, ever calm and poised.

All the guests are here. In the house, I sweep from room to room, running my fingers along the sleeves of various partygoers as I pass, offering double kisses to friends and coworkers, to neighbors and their partners old and new. I laugh at jokes, collect empty glasses from tables and hand them off to caterers. I shimmy when the beat of the music picks up. I might just be putting on airs, but I'm doing a good job of it. Whatever roils beneath, whatever anger has built up in me over the course of this wild and fateful day, no one here is the wiser.

The good hostess. Yes. I play the part well. It doesn't help that I've had two glasses of prosecco already. In the kitchen, I sample some of Zachary's cheese platter then angle my way past a group of catering staff.

Outside, the band plays instrumental mingling music. I spot Isobel in a corner standing under our tall dogwood shrub. She is speaking to two girls and one boy in a hushed tone, whispering, fingering the necklace. Colleen's necklace.

River, I hear. She is talking about River. Her audience leans in, hanging on her every word. Isobel catches my gaze and offers me a wave. Her friends turn and wave at me too, and then whisper something to her. She nods and smiles at me. What did they say?

"Nadine!" Paul calls. "Come here!"

He stands on the dance floor space with an assortment of friends. Along with a few of his junior colleagues, there's Seymour, Marvin, Teddy, Daphne. Paul is holding court. He's in storytelling mode.

"Does everyone have a drink?" I ask on approach.

"I'm on my third," Seymour says.

"I was trying to tell them the story of your mother's rise to fame," Paul says to me. "But you tell it better."

"It was meteoric, wasn't it?" Daphne asks.

"It wasn't, actually," I say. "It was a slog for a lot of years."

"But look at what good fortune befell her after that," Teddy says.

"Ah, yes," Daphne pipes in. "A woman's success is usually about luck, isn't it?"

The group falls into an awkward laugh. Daphne sips her wine. I'm impressed.

"Marvin remembers when her first novel became a bestseller," I say. "Don't you?"

"I do," Marvin says. "She was on the cover of *People* magazine."

"He's her number one fan," I say. "Basically, a stalker."

Paul looks at me quizzically.

"But Marvin's right. She *was* on the cover of *People* magazine," I continue. "Eventually. But that was actually a year after her first novel was published. When it came out, it didn't sell. At all. Less than five hundred copies. They terminated her contract and the book ended up in remainder bins."

The group draws closer, thrilled to be privy to gossip about the famous birthday girl.

"The *New Yorker* profile skipped all of this," Daphne says. "Someone should find Julian Simone. He loves a juicy Marilyn Millay story."

Again, laughter.

"Well," I say. "After the book flopped, Marilyn went back to working as a waitress. Then one day, months later, a famous actress was photographed reading my mother's book on a beach holiday with her controversial new beau."

"Eek!" Daphne squeals. "Can we guess whom?"

"Google it," I say. "There are tons of paparazzi pictures. A few days later, someone asked the actress about the book in an interview, and she gushed. She absolutely gushed and declared that she'd already told her agent to find out about the film rights, and hey, didn't anyone happen to know where to find this Marilyn Millay writer anyway? We got a call from her publisher that night."

"We," Teddy says. "I love the plural pronoun. Are you a writer too?"

"Marilyn and Nadine are a *we*," Daphne says.

"They certainly are," Paul adds.

Marilyn approaches. Soon Isobel and Margot join too.

"We were just talking about you, Marilyn," Daphne says.

"Good. After all, aren't I the guest of honor?"

The group nods in unison.

"Isobel," Daphne says. "I absolutely love your necklace."

"It's my mom's actually. She let me wear it tonight."

Daphne approaches and, with Isobel's permission, lifts the pendant to study it.

"My sister collects necklaces like this one," Daphne says. "The flower is an amulet."

"What's an amulet?" Isobel asks.

"Something meant to protect its wearer," Daphne says. "This style was really popular once. All the rage."

"Vintage," Isobel says, beaming my way.

"Well!" Paul exclaims, clasping his hands together. "Seems to me that almost everyone is here. Perhaps a toast is in order?"

"Please, no," my mother says.

"Don't worry, Marilyn. I'll be charming. And brief."

Before I can protest, Paul strides up to the band, catching them at the end of a song and positioning himself in front of the microphone. Isobel nudges my shoulder.

"Did Dad run this speech by you?" she asks.

"He did not."

"Pray he doesn't make an ass of himself," Margot says.

"He won't," my mother says, a slur in her voice. "Not our Paul. He won't."

"How much have you had to drink?" I ask her.

"I've seen her guzzle at least four proseccos already," Margot quips.

"Snitch!" my mother declares.

Everyone quiets when Paul taps his glass to signal a toast. He clears his throat, making a show of it, sweeping a hand toward my mother and me standing off to the side.

"We're gathered here tonight to celebrate a famous lady's milestone birthday. But first, indulge me as I honor our hostess. My gorgeous wife, Nadine."

Someone calls out my name.

"As most of you know," Paul continues. "Nadine's had a difficult year so far. I'm not sure how many among us could shatter a hip and come out of it not only stronger, but more beautiful."

"Groan," Isobel whispers.

"And so, I just wanted to take a moment to toast our formidable hostess. My wife, as gorgeous as the day I met her, she who throws the best parties. And with little help from her hopeless but very grateful husband."

This elicits the roar from the guests that Paul was clearly vying for.

"I love you, Nadine. We all do. We're so happy you're well again. And so, a toast. To you, Nadine!"

Everyone lifts their glasses in unison.

"Thank you, darling," I say. "Perhaps we can channel some of that affection into help cleaning tomorrow's mess."

This too incites a roar. We are quite the tag team. I turn to the yard, and the first face I see is Marvin's, now detached from our little clique where he'd stood mostly silent while we discussed my mom's career. I lift my glass to him, holding the stare until he looks away. Marilyn lists into me, her weight against my shoulder.

"And now, let's toast our guest of honor," Paul says. "Ms. Marilyn Millay."

"Marilyn!" someone echoes joyfully.

"Look at the two of you," Paul says to my mother and me. "Mother and daughter. One thing that's been exceedingly obvious to me since the day I met Nadine is the lengths these two women will go to protect each other."

There's a hush in reaction to Paul's more serious tone.

"Two fierce women who've endured so much. When I first met Nadine, I . . ."

"You do protect me," Marilyn whispers to me as Paul's speech continues. "He's right, isn't he?"

"I don't know what you mean."

"You protect me, Nadine. From, say, a certain journalist in our company tonight. Whom you paid off. That's why you're angry. Admit it."

While I absorb her words, Marilyn trains her focus on Paul as he speaks.

"How did you know—"

"Come on, Nadine. Julian Simone was the book editor at the *Times* for twenty years. We have a lot of people in common. People whose loyalties default to me. I heard a rumor that he was paid off to bury stories. A tidy sum too. Who would do that but you?"

"Mom. You're drunk."

"Not that drunk. Am I wrong?"

"You're not wrong," I say.

"So let's be clear," Paul is saying. "I know where I stand when it comes to the formidable and glorious Millay women. I am the third wheel. They will always be each other's true love!"

My mother raises her glass. "You're a close second, darling Paul," she calls out to him.

"To Marilyn!"

Glasses clink all around us. I lean into my mother and whisper, "Why didn't you say anything?"

"I knew you'd tell me eventually, darling. Most secrets emerge eventually."

Now Paul is holding the microphone out to us.

"Speech!" he calls. "Marilyn? We want to hear from you."

"Don't go up there," I say. "You're drunk."

"I'm going up," Marilyn says. "I have a few things to say."

My mother kisses my cheek and pauses for a moment, resting her hand on my face, just as she used to do when I was a little girl. Then she steps forward to the stage and takes the microphone from my husband.

T AP, TAP, TAP.

"Is this thing on?" my mother says. "Yes, it is!"

Marilyn Millay looks around, absorbing the attention. Her beauty is effortless and elegant. But she's unsteady. Paul joins me and then Isobel and Margot are next to us too, the four of us front row for whatever spectacle is about to unfold.

"I think she's kind of hammered," Margot whispers to me.

"She'll be fine," I say. "She knows how to work an audience better than any of us."

"What a lovely lot of people you are," my mother begins, her voice a sultry drawl. "Coming here to celebrate an old lady's birthday. So, a speech, is it? That's what we want?"

Everyone hoots.

"Perfect! Then let me follow my darling Paul's lead and begin with my daughter, Nadine. Paul just told you our whole history. Nadine and I were dirt poor for many years. We lived in a tiny little basement apartment. The sort of place where sweaty pipes cut across the ceiling and water collected in the corners when it rained. And Nadine never complained about that life. She never did. Even as a toddler, she had this sort of"—my mother pauses, choosing her words carefully—"this industrious nature. She could identify problems and simply fix them. And that hasn't changed, has it, darling?"

"Nope!" Margot shouts.

"I want to say thank you to Nadine, for our . . . partnership. I know that's a bizarre word for a mother to use. But we are partners, soldiers in the same wars, if you'll forgive the hyperbole. On my sixtieth birthday, I feel gratitude for many things. All of you, for one. And my darling grandkids. Paul, even."

"I love you too, Marilyn!" he calls.

Again, the crowd laughs.

I hug myself closer to Paul and his warmth jolts through my body. I focus on the expressions of the band members seated behind my mother, the guitarist frowning, the drummer's face frozen in a dumbfounded smile.

"I'm among friends," Marilyn says, waving the drink she holds limply. "Am I not?'"

"You are!" someone yells.

"Was this a mistake?" Paul whispers. "I didn't realize she was so—"

"She's fine."

My mother lifts the microphone again. "I'm grateful for you, Nadine. For all the ways you've endured. Survived. Thrived. Today isn't just my birthday. It marks another anniversary too. A tragic one."

Now Marilyn pauses again. She's letting the tension build. We lock eyes. Her head drops ever so slightly to one side. A deep hush has fallen over the yard. They understand what's happening, the tectonic shift that's coming. If they retain this silence, Marilyn will keep talking.

"There's a photograph in my daughter's dining room. Some of you have probably seen it. It's a black-and-white picture of a girl who looks much like our Damien. Those gorgeous curls. You!" She points to a young caterer. "Can you go get it? The black-and-white photo. A girl."

The caterer nods and disappears through the patio doors. Isobel tugs the back of my jumpsuit.

"Mom! What the fuck is she doing?"

"I don't know, Izzy," I say.

"Stop her!"

"I can't."

"She's about to make a total ass of herself."

"No, she won't," I say.

In under thirty seconds the caterer returns, breathless, the frame hugged to his chest like a prized possession. My mother thanks him, then turns the photograph outward for all to see. "Some of you knew Colleen Fitzgerald." She points. "You, Seymour Dunphy. I believe you knew her."

Seymour smiles awkwardly, hands in his pockets. "I did," he calls to the stage. "As a kid. She was a lovely girl."

"Wasn't she?" my mother says, emphatic, her voice popping in the microphone. "Paul knew her! Nadine and Paul realized this remarkable fact on their second or third date, if I'm not wrong. Paul?"

"That's accurate," Paul says.

"See? As a writer, you'd worry that this kind of coincidence might strain all credulity. My editor would call it preposterous. Wouldn't you?" Everyone laughs uncomfortably. "Where is she? My darling editor? Anyway. Real life is always full of surprises. I believe this from the bottom of my heart."

"Hammered," Margot says under her breath.

"But!" My mother punches the air with a fist. "Our Colleen died. Tragically. Thirty years ago today. She was found dead, actually. By Nadine. The morning after my thirtieth birthday party. And some of *you* were there. Talk about fate."

A nervous titter passes through the guests.

"Stop her, Mom. For fuck's sake," Isobel pleads.

"I had a long bath this morning," Marilyn continues. "And I got to thinking about how your life can change in a single day. You know? Those days when there's a before, and then an after. Where everything shifts in an instant. The truth is, my whole life has been dictated by one little secret." She holds a single finger aloft. "One."

"Nadine?" Paul says, tugging at my arm, worried.

"It's okay," I say.

"Where is Mr. Julian Simone?" Everyone twists and turns until Julian is spit out right in front of my mother, his face flushed. "You love a good secret, don't you, Mr. Simone?"

"Don't we all?" he replies.

My mother laughs. "Well. Any writer worth their salt will tell you that the best way to kill a story is to spoil the plot twist. And you know what?" Marilyn pauses, the words catching in her throat. "It doesn't even matter. The secret itself is nothing. The only thing that matters is one's fear of it. So allow me this confessional. A little birthday gift to myself."

The silence is so remarkable, so surreal, that I can hear the clatter of cutlery through the open kitchen window as clearly as if I were standing at the sink washing it myself.

"We told the world that this young woman, Colleen, was my sister," Marilyn says, holding up the photograph. "But she wasn't. The truth is, I got pregnant when I was fourteen. The father was scandalously older than me. I was a little girl, pregnant. Absolutely no one could ever know. My mother would be certain of that. So, after months of baggy sweatshirts and a summer confined to the farm, I gave secret birth to a beautiful baby girl, then handed that baby girl over to my mother. She was christened Colleen, and the world was told she was my sister. And then? She just *was*. She was my sister. Did anyone ever suspect? No doubt. But my parents demanded respect. Obedience. And they got it." She pauses, choking briefly on her words. "Once she was my mother's child, we never spoke of it again. Colleen was my sister. End of story."

This deathly hush. I should be stepping forward, taking the microphone gently from my mother's hands, guiding her to the safety of our family huddle. But I can't. I won't. To think of all the trouble I went through protecting this secret since learning about it months ago, paying off Julian Simone to bury it, circling my mother from every angle in an effort to coax a confession, just so Marilyn could stand up here and spill it all in one fell swoop.

I hate her. I love her.

"What the fuck, Mom?" Isobel says.

"What is she talking about?" Paul asks.

"She'll never live this down," Margot says.

"Yes, she will," I say. "She's Marilyn Millay."

My mother locks eyes with me, smiling with a tenderness that tightens my chest.

"You are my second child, Nadine. Yes! I got pregnant again five years later when that same terrible man came circling again. What a little harlot I was. Incorrigible." This elicits a small burst of tense laughter from the audience. "This time I was not going to hand my baby over, so what did I do? I left. We left, didn't we, Nadine? We became our own little family. We survived and now look at us." She sweeps a hand over the scene. "You in this home with your gorgeous husband and your magnificent children, Isobel and Damien. We are incredibly lucky, are we not?"

"We are," I call to her.

"My firstborn died at fifteen. And all along, she believed that I was her sister. But let's not dwell on secrets. Or tragedies. At least not tonight." She lifts her flute of champagne high. "Let's instead raise a glass to Colleen, who deserves to be celebrated. To Colleen. To friendship, to family, to celebrations. To the magic of fate. To us. All of us!"

At this she lifts the microphone and taps it against her glass, then drinks. The crowd turns to each other to clink glasses, baffled, stunned. I ping my own glass against Paul's. My mother steps off the stage and brushes shoulders with Julian Simone on her way past.

I can't hear her, but I can read her lips perfectly.

"Fuck you," she says to him, smiling.

Then she joins us, accepting Isobel's hug gratefully.

"Nana! What did you just do?"

"I made a scene, didn't I?" my mother says, stroking Isobel's hair.

"It's fine," Paul says. "Hey, gossip is the best, right? You made everyone's night."

"Except for Julian Simone's," I reply.

"Indeed," my mother says. "Except for his."

"I have to say, this is quite the party," Margot says. "It's not even ten o'clock. Where can it possibly go from here?"

T HE GUESTS HAVE DISPERSED IN A stupor, a series of cliques formed in the yard and in pockets of the house to debrief the scene they just witnessed. My mother remains with Margot and Isobel, Damien joins them too. A moment ago, I watched as Julian Simone skulked through the kitchen, head down, and out the front door. Gone. Coward.

Me? I'll need to mingle. That's my job, isn't it? To ensure a touch point with every single guest? Especially now.

"Nadine!" A woman, an associate at Paul's firm, pulls me into her circle as I pass through the kitchen to the dining room. "Are you *okay*?"

"I'm absolutely fine," I say, waving a hand.

For the life of me, I can't remember this woman's name.

"Did you know . . . all of that?" another asks.

"Indeed I did," I say.

I did know, but not because my mother told me as she should have done long ago. This is the lie we'll now tell, Marilyn and me. My beloved aunt was, in fact, my full-blooded sister. Our father was a molester preying on a girl far too young to consent. I knew because a smarmy journalist found me in the hospital as a blood infection coursed through my veins and presented sealed records he'd uncovered in Terriville, records that included the birthing doctor's affidavit. These guests will never know that my mother deceived me. Better that they think me in on the secret.

I head into living room. Questions. Stares. *Did you know? How did someone as famous as Marilyn Millay bury this for so long?* I make my way through, nodding—*I know, I know, quite the confession!*—then cut across the kitchen to head back outside.

"Nadine?"

My name in a whisper.

I peer into the den. There stands Lionel, alone. I step into the room and close the door behind me.

"You have thirty seconds," I say.

"Have you spoken to Daphne?" he asks.

"No. Why?"

Behind the door, the caterers are calling out orders. *More plates! Clear the flutes!* Lionel is close enough now that I could reach out and touch him.

"I think she knows, Nadine."

"About what?"

"About us!"

"There is no us, Lionel. It's been over for a long time."

"Maybe, but it would still bother her. And since the baby came, things have been . . . challenging. She keeps saying she wants to get to know you. It feels a bit like a threat."

"Or maybe she actually does," I say. "Want to get to know me, I mean."

There's a knock at the door. Lionel and I both freeze.

"Lionel? Nadine?"

It's Daphne. I open the door and she steps in. Lionel greets her with a peck on the cheek, much as one would a distant relative.

"I saw you both come in . . ." she says. "I hope I'm not interrupting."

"Of course you're not," I say.

"I need to pump. I'm a little full."

"Goodness," I say. "Here. Sit on the chaise."

I collect the diaper bag she'd left in here and set it next to her. When Daphne looks to me, her eyes are glassy.

"Lionel," I say without looking at him. "Get your wife a glass of water. A towel too. To protect her dress while she pumps."

He obeys. I close the door behind him and face Daphne head on.

"Let's get you organized."

"I'm just going to say that I really don't like coming in here and finding you and my husband . . ." She trails off, wincing. "Can we just be truthful with each other, Nadine? Please?"

I nod. Through the door, I can hear the muffled sounds of the band starting up again.

"Lionel and I had an affair," I say. "Before he met you, obviously. It was short. I regret it, and I believe Lionel does too."

"Maybe he does," she says. "Maybe he doesn't."

"Listen. It was obvious as soon as Lionel met you that he was smitten, deeply in love. Lionel and I are old friends. We strayed from that briefly, but that's what we are. What we were always meant to be. Old friends. I swear on my life."

"Right," Daphne says. "Sure. Okay."

On the chaise Daphne prepares the breast pump. What a strange and vulnerable thing to be doing in this moment.

"I need to get back to the party, Daphne. Is there something else you'd like to say?"

"You know what, Nadine? I don't care about the fucking affair. All I wanted—all I want—is a way in. I feel like I'm decent company. But this bloody clique of yours can feel impossible to penetrate. You've all been friends since you were kids. It's a shitty feeling, to be honest. To feel left out all the time."

All I can do is stare at the floor. "You're right, Daphne. I've been unkind to you."

"Well, not unkind. Not exactly."

"Yes, exactly. And I'm sorry. You deserve better. You actually *are* decent company."

Daphne shimmies one shoulder out of her dress and lifts the pump to her chest.

"Maybe not at this very moment," she says.

"Paul doesn't know," I say.

"And I won't tell him," she replies. "What's done is done."

The door opens before either of us can say more. Lionel reenters, a towel and glass of ice water in hand. He kneels in front of Daphne and lifts the water to her mouth so she can sip. A profound sense of relief overtakes me when Margot appears in the den's doorway too.

"Everything okay in here?" she asks.

"Yes," I say. "We were just getting Daphne sorted to pump."

"Lovely," Margot says. "How bovine."

Remarkably, the four of us laugh.

"Can I steal our hostess for a minute?" Margot asks.

I smile, grateful. "You can."

I exit the den, closing the door behind me. Margot pulls me by the arm to the back stairs and down to the basement, along the hallway into my shadowy office. Then she turns to face me dead on.

"Listen. Isobel just told me that you grilled her earlier about escorting? Are you okay?"

"I have the video," I say.

"What? How?"

"Margot? I ..."

"Holy shit. We can talk about this tomorrow, okay? I'll dig in deep with you, I promise. But right now, we're at a party. *Your* party."

"Damien didn't delete the video. I sent it to my phone."

"Oh my God." Margot buries her face in her hands and groans. "Did you watch it?"

"Not yet."

"Okay. I'm not even going to try to redirect you here." She waves a hand at me, impatient. "Where's your phone?"

I extract it from my pocket and key in my passcode. The airdropped file from Damien's phone is right there. It takes about thirty seconds for the video to download. Margot and I huddle together. I press play. The screen is shadowy, unfocused.

What do you want to say? Isobel's voice, off-screen.

The camera points at River. She's on her own phone, pressing buttons until a song comes on. She's wearing a green dress, talking, drunk. River's eyes fall to Isobel's camera. She begins to dance.

Dirty old man, she says. *Are you my Teddy Bear?*

It gets sultry. It's hard to watch.

You love it when I wear this dress.

"Jesus Christ," Margot says. "That poor little girl."

River lifts the dress over her head then twirls and tosses it to the camera. She's in a bra and underwear now.

Don't be a slut, Isobel says, laughing. *You're so weird!*

He loves me, River says.

Gross! says my daughter. *Who loves you?*

You love me, right, Teddy Bear?

I'm turning this off, Isobel says.

No. River crawls toward the camera. *Don't. I'm not finished yet.*

The video ends. My breath is caught in my throat. The dress. The green dress. It's not exactly the same as the one Colleen was wearing when she died. But it's close.

"Are you okay?" Margot asks.

I shake my head.

"I don't get it," Margot says. "Is this Teddy guy a pimp?"

"We should go upstairs," I say, quiet, trembling. "I've been away from the party for too long. People will think something's wrong."

Margot takes me by the shoulders. "Answer me. Are you okay?"

"I don't know. No. Yes. I have to be, don't I? I have no choice."

"Take a deep breath."

I do. One deep breath, then two. Three.

"What do you want to do?" she asks me.

"I want to go back upstairs," I say.

"Okay."

Margot guides me by the hand out of the office and up the stairs, through the kitchen and the patio doors. The first person we encounter is Marilyn. Aside from some smudged mascara, she appears positively joyful, another drink in hand.

"Darlings! My God, there you are, Nadine. I've been searching for you."

"I was tending to guests," I say.

Margot still holds my arm. When I smile at her, she releases it and allows herself to be pulled to the bar by my mother.

It's well after ten. Any remnants of daylight have left the sky. The makeshift dance floor is now exactly that—a dance floor. The band has transitioned to upbeat songs.

Smile, I think. *Look around at your guests and smile.*

I do.

For thirty years, I've buried the past. And more recently, I've replayed it over and over again, searching for the missing pieces. I scan the crowd. Where is he, Teddy Rosen? The tentacles of fate and coincidence. Past and present, Colleen and me. The connection.

It's you, Julian Simone said to me today. *You're the connection.*

A SLOW SONG COMES ON. MY ears buzz, but I'm steady. I spot Seymour weaving through the tables to where Margot now sits with Isobel and a few of her friends. Their laughter stops when he pulls up and extends a hand. Isobel takes it, standing and allowing Seymour to guide her to the dance floor. I watch as his arm curls around her back.

I don't even notice Paul next to me. He hands me a cold glass of water.

"You need to hydrate."

I don't answer him. I don't even move.

"Do you want to dance?" he asks.

"Not now."

He tracks what I'm focused on.

"Nice to see Isobel in a good mood," he says.

"Would you dance with someone's seventeen-year-old daughter?" I ask him.

"I don't know. Wouldn't I?" he asks, scratching his head.

"Do you think Isobel wants to be dancing with Seymour?"

"She could have said no," Paul says.

"Really?" I pause. "I don't think you would. Dance with a teenage girl, I mean. Unless she's your own daughter."

"Well, then. Why don't I go cut in?"

"Please do," I say, craning to kiss Paul's cheek. "Thank you."

Paul sets his beer on the edge of the garden box behind us and strides to the dance floor. He takes Seymour by the shoulders, a gesture of manly joviality to offset the awkwardness of his intrusion. Isobel's face is blank. She allows her father to cut in, then Seymour retreats from the dance floor and returns to the table full of lawyers near the back of the yard. I watch Isobel and Paul closely, trying to lip-read their conversation. I'm relieved when Isobel laughs, her posture relaxing into her father's. He spins her in a full circle.

Where is Teddy Rosen? I don't see him. Lionel and Daphne are on the dance floor now too, Isobel and Paul, and then Damien and Lacey.

I reach into my pocket and feel its contents. My lipstick. Damien's syringe. The half a pill I dropped in earlier seems to have turned to powder that coats the tips of my fingers. Before I fully register what I'm doing, I've ducked inside the house. I'm upstairs in search of my tote. I find it in our master closet. I locate the pill bottle in its lining and shake four loose into my hand and then into my pocket. I wash my hands in the powder room, reapply my lipstick, then make my way back downstairs.

The song hasn't ended yet. For a long moment, I watch Paul and Isobel on the dance floor. They enchant me, the two of them, their faces carving the same profile.

Then suddenly, I'm no longer alone. Marvin has snuck up beside me.

"You were in la-la land just there," he says.

"I've had a few drinks," I say. "I was just watching Paul and Isobel dance."

"This is quite the party, Nadine. It's magical. Something right out of *The Great Gatsby*."

"I hated that book in high school."

He laughs. "You might have been a bit young for its complicated themes."

"Not that complicated," I say. "Money and greed. You know that's all it's about."

Marvin laughs again, tensely this time.

"I brought you a gift," Marvin says. "But you'll need to hide it away."

Marvin reaches for my hand then places something into it and folds my fingers closed. I uncurl my fist to find a silver vintage lighter engraved in cursive with my initials: *N.W.*

"This is not an endorsement of your bad habits," he says. "More an acknowledgment of friendship. A hostess gift."

"Come on, Marvin. Let's not do this. We're not friends."

"Excuse me?"

"How's Julian Simone? I hear you two know each other."

Marvin clears his throat. "I don't know what—"

I touch his arm. "Let me stop you before you make things worse for yourself. You see Paul out there? On the dance floor? He's a nice guy, isn't he?"

"Your husband? I don't know. I guess so."

"He's a corporate litigator. Nice guy. But in legal settings? He's got a reputation for being a predator. He takes pleasure in ripping people to shreds."

"Nadine. Please."

"Where's Lacey?" I ask.

"I don't know."

"Probably with my son. Those two really seem to like each other."
Marvin is silent.

"Listen to me," I continue. "We all have plenty to lose, Marvin.
I'm not sure you realize just how high the stakes are for you at this
moment. I'm going to tell you to delete that video of River and you're
going to swear on everything you love and cherish that you will. Because if you don't, if I ever hear of any of this again, if I so much as
catch a whiff of you talking to anyone about my family, about River
or my daughter or my mother, I'll declare war. And I promise you, I
bring a much bigger arsenal to the battle than you ever could. You get
what I mean, right?"

I watch his Adam's apple throb in his throat. "Yes," he says.

"Good." I hold the lighter aloft before dropping it into my pocket.
"A very thoughtful gift, Marvin. You're the only person who knows the
depths of my dirty habit. Thank you."

And then I walk away.

When the song ends, Isobel and Paul hug, then go their separate
ways. I edge across the dance floor. I need to find him. Him. A server
cuts into my path and proffers a tray. I select a glass of pink-hued prosecco. Finally, inside the kitchen, I see him. He's chatting with one of
the young servers. He must sense my gaze because he looks my way.
Teddy.

I smile and point to the floor. *A dance?*

Teddy excuses himself and saunters over.

"Do I really get a moment alone with the hostess?"

"You do," I say.

"How delightful."

Another slow song. I set my prosecco down on a table and accept his hand. On the dance floor, Teddy pulls me in tight, too much, too quickly. The fabric of my jumpsuit is thin enough that I can feel the heat of his hand through it. I feel my stomach begin to turn so I hold my breath against it. Poise. I need poise.

"You've outdone yourself tonight, Nadine. I've been to some great parties, but this one takes the cake."

"We've had a little bit of everything, haven't we? Comedy. Drama."

"That was some revelation by your mother."

"She'll say anything to hold an audience."

He throws his head back in laughter. "Indeed."

"Can I ask you something?" I say.

"Anything you'd like."

"Why did you leave the UK?"

"You asked me that earlier."

"I'm not sure you answered."

"I wanted to come home. This has always felt like home."

Teddy is an expert dancer. I need not even think of where to step. His firm grip guides me.

"One more question," I say. "What's the first car you ever owned?"

Teddy pulls me closer. "That's a random question."

"I think the answer says a lot about a person. Seymour's first car, for example, was a Corvette."

"Ha! Why does that feel sad? Poor Seymour. What was yours?"

"A Volkswagen Beetle. My mother bought it for me when I left for college. She let me pick the color. I chose green."

"Green. Perfect."

"And you?"

"I'm embarrassed to say that I didn't own a car until I was nearly forty."

"Dear me."

"My parents didn't trust me enough to buy me a car. I was lucky, though. My cousin used to lend me his old Jeep. A Wrangler."

There. There it is. A perfect drop of fate. I close my eyes and inhale deeply. "A Wrangler. The kind with no doors."

"Exactly," he says. "What does that tell you about me?"

My mouth is painfully dry. I put my lips to his ears. "That you're lucky," I say.

"Really?" he says, his cheek brushing mine. "I suppose I am."

When the song ends, Teddy steps back and offers me a mock bow.

"Thank you, Nadine. It's been an honor."

I say nothing. All I can do is smile.

T HE GUESTS ARE UPSTAIRS AND OUTSIDE, but I am back in the basement, staring at the wall. The Sister Doors. Before I can stop myself, I've turned the dead bolt and opened our side. The second door, the door to Teddy's basement, is still unlocked. I knew it would be.

Two steps and I am in an alternate universe, a mirror of my home. I close both doors behind me. If I strain, I can still hear the faint sounds of the party next door. My party. The bass of the band. The laughter.

I stand perfectly still. The air down here feels staler than on our side. The light in the laundry area is still on, a pile of clothes folded poorly on top of the dryer.

I glide across the hall and enter the makeshift office space, flicking on the light. When we set up the house for renters, Paul and I lined the back of this room with wire shelving. To most people, this would function as a storage space. But not for Teddy.

The desk is neat. Aside from his open laptop, I spot a couple of local real estate brochures, some books on business, a cell phone bill, a medical requisition with his full name across the top: Matthew

Theodore Rosen. I use a pencil to hit a key on the laptop. The screen is locked. I slide the pencil into my pocket and step back. What am I doing?

Wait.

The safe. I saw it earlier. When Paul and I bought this house, I furnished it with shorter term renters in mind, including a fireproof safe in the bedroom closet as some website on rentals had advised me to do. Teddy must have had it hauled down here.

I close my eyes. This is my safe. Mine. I know the code. How could I ever forget? My mother's birthday: day, month, year.

I punch it in. The safe jolts open.

I know I am trespassing, breaking the law. Teddy could arrive home at any minute. But this what any mother would do. Search for answers.

I open the safe door completely. On the top shelf is a cigar humidor. Wait. I shouldn't touch anything, should I? I scurry to the laundry room in search of a rag to wipe things down.

On the bottom shelf is a stack of unsealed manila envelopes. I remove them and peer in each one by one. Stock and bond certificates, insurance documents, an old deed to some land in the UK, a copy of a will. One envelope is heavy when I lift it. I shake it and look inside—a mix of loose Polaroid photos.

My pulse is a fast thump between my ears. Twice in my life I've felt this same sense of premonition. Once, at the age of ten, approaching the open section of my grandparents' barn early on a Sunday morning. And again, six weeks ago, climbing the stairs to River Dunphy's bedroom, tracking the sounds of Isobel's panicked wails. This feeling? It's the certainty that you're about to come across something terrible. That what comes next will change everything. So you take a deep breath and step forward.

I press the envelope open and overturn it to dump its contents to the floor. About thirty photos in total.

Girls. Young girls. How old? Fourteen? Sixteen? It's hard to tell.

I use the rag to sift through and pick up each one. The settings of the photos are all different. Some look like hotel rooms. A few appear to be taken in the same home. The girls aren't smiling. They look disoriented. Drugged, perhaps. Some stare right at the camera, others cast their eyes down. Some don't appear conscious. Many of the pictures are older, some newer. The girls are not naked, but they aren't fully dressed either. Most of them wear dresses that have been pulled up above their waists. Tight. Summery. Green.

My stomach twists when I find the photograph of River. Dear God. She has a hand draped over her eyes, but it's her, partially clothed. I want to vomit. I place the photograph in my pocket and sift through the remaining.

And then I find it. The one I'm looking for. Every detail returns to me at once. Colleen seated so strangely in the hay, unmoving, the strap of her faded green sundress fallen off her shoulder. That dress. I'd watched her try it on. My head throbs now. My fingers feel numb.

Except in this photo I'm holding, Colleen is alive. She sits, a hand lifted to shield her from the camera's sharp flash. Aside from a circle of space lit up by the flash, the background is darkened. I can barely make out the low beams of the barn loft. This photo was taken at night. I pull it close to my face. Colleen's eyes look hazy. She is pale, out of sorts. She's in the loft.

'A friend is coming to see me,' Colleen said to me that night. 'It's a secret. You can keep a secret, right?'

'Why is it a secret?' I asked.

'Because he wasn't invited to the party.'

That's what she said.

I put the photo of Colleen in my pocket. In all my rage, my sadness, I feel overwhelming relief too. There is no photograph of Isobel.

On autopilot, I pinch the rag to return the pictures to the envelope, and the envelope to the safe. I click it closed, then engage the lock before rubbing the buttons and handle with the rag.

I stand and retrace my steps across the basement to the doors. I open one, then the other, peeking first to make sure my office on the other side is empty. Blessedly, it is. Just like that, I'm back on my side, returned to my home, to tonight, to this party, to what will come next.

I T'S TIME FOR CAKE.

The party scene before me is dreamy, triumphantly fun. It is nearly eleven o'clock. The band plays a faster song now, the dance floor is full of moving bodies. A full moon is high in the sky, bright. Why do I feel so calm?

I see him. Teddy. He's at a table with Seymour and Lionel. I begin to weave my way through the crowd, taking my time, engaging my guests. All smiles.

In the kitchen of our basement apartment, all those years ago, my mother hung a framed, handwritten version of a poem by her beloved namesake, Edna St. Vincent Millay. "The Dream," it was called. The line that stuck with me, that still sticks with me, is the first: *If I weep, it will not matter*. Even as a girl, I understood that sentiment perfectly: sadness alone accomplishes nothing.

Halfway to the table, I stop a caterer as she passes by.

"Do you mind?" I say, pointing to her tray of flutes.

"The whole tray?" she says.

"Please."

There are six flutes spread in a perfect circle. I hold it with one hand, my finger fanned open under it for balance. I reach into my pocket and feel for the pills I'd placed there earlier. I pinch one hard to crush it, then, with a swoop, drop the powder into the flute closest to me. It's all so fast, a sleight of hand. A trick. I repeat it with a second pill in the same flute. Third. Fourth. I don't even stop walking. No one takes notice of me. It's magic.

When I reach the table, Seymour sees me first.

"Look at you," he says. "Talk about service."

"I figured a toast is in order," I say. "To neighbors, maybe? Old friends."

"A toast!" Lionel says. "What a splendid idea."

I am careful, meticulous, in passing them out. One to Lionel, one to Seymour. The flute closest to me goes to Teddy. I offer two more glasses to nearby guests then take the final one and set down the tray. Everyone at the table is watching me. I feel Teddy's eyes boring through me. My stomach twists at the look of him. I can't close my eyes; if I do, I'll see nothing but Colleen. Those girls. Instead, I look to Lionel.

"To old friends," I say. "The ones bearing witness to our lives."

"Indeed," Seymour says. "Indeed!"

"To old friends," Lionel says.

"To us!" Teddy adds.

We all raise our glasses and drink. When both Teddy and Lionel pull back at only half-empty, I make a joke about reaching out to tilt their flutes. All of us, bottoms up.

"You are a magical hostess," Teddy says, slamming his empty glass to the table. "Truly, Nadine."

"A hostess with many guests to tend to. So off I go. Be good!"

And then I spin on the heel of my wedge sandal to cut back across the yard. I find Paul next to the band.

"Go get Marilyn," I say. "It's time to blow out the candles. Set her up at the table closest to the door."

He kisses me again. "On it."

I take Isobel and Damien each by the hand and pull them off the dance floor and up the patio stairs into the kitchen. The sheet cake is on the island. It holds sixty candles that Margot is lighting.

"That's a fire hazard," Damien jokes.

But he and Isobel line up dutifully, each grasping a side of the cake. Margot takes a photograph then switches to video, following them as they balance the large cake between them. Isobel and Damien adjust their posture to match the other, to balance out the weight they're carrying together. I feel a surge of love so intense that it nearly knocks me over.

Paul and my mother wait outside at the table. As soon as the cake crosses the threshold, the band's drummer offers a beat and cues us to sing "Happy Birthday." My mother clasps her hands together, beaming. She is drunk but happy. It takes her several breaths to snuff out all the candles. Everyone cheers. My heart races.

Gregory the caterer swoops in to collect the cake so it can be divvied up. He stops in front of me before entering the house.

"We'll put out the cookies and coffee now," he says.

"Sounds perfect," I say. "But don't stop with the drinks."

Gregory laughs. "Never."

It's all about airs at this point. Appearances.

The music starts up again. And there's Teddy, pressing his way through the guests gathered on the dance floor. Does he look pale? By now the pills crushed into his drink would be taking effect. And too many drinks on top of that. I sidestep to greet him.

"Shall we dance again?" he asks.

"We could," I say as I take his arm. "Or we could go downstairs to my office. If you'd like."

He smiles, coy. "Nadine."

"Teddy."

"I'm a little woozy," he says. "You won't take advantage of me?"

"Well. I just might. Stairs are off the back of the kitchen. Just like at your place."

His eyes widen. "Vixen. My God."

My stomach churns. Once he's in the house, I watch him turn the corner to the basement stairs. I go to the foyer and reapply my lipstick in the mirror. I can hear giggling outside, so I peer out the door window. Damien and Lacey are walking up the street toward Marvin's store. Lacey's head is on his shoulder. I think to open the door and call to them, but I can't. I let them go.

Let's do the math on murder, my mother said at the New Year's Eve party. Teddy was there. He brought the good wine. Did he laugh at her musings? Perhaps he did. He knows firsthand just how right she was: it's too easy to get away with even the worst of crimes. I'm going downstairs to find him.

T HE BASEMENT IS DARK BUT FOR the sliver of light underneath the bathroom door. I knock quietly.

"Teddy?"

"Yes?" he answers, garbled.

I twist the knob. Locked.

"It's Nadine."

I hear the lock turn. The door opens. Teddy leans against the sink, his head hanging over it.

"I'm sorry, Nadine," he says. "This is embarrassing. I'm a little out of sorts."

I step in, then close and lock the door behind me. "Uh-oh. You do look pale."

"Might I have a glass of water?"

"Of course."

I fetch a glass from under the sink and let the tap run cold before filling it. Teddy accepts it and sips.

"You came down," he says.

"I did. You're supposed to be in the office."

"You were flirting with me."

"Was I?" I ask.

He sets the glass down and closes the small space between us with a stumble, resting a hand on the door behind me.

"You're gorgeous, you know."

Bile climbs my throat. His breath is rotten. He winces and presses a hand to his chest.

"My oh my. You're really unwell."

"Heartburn," he replies, backing away. "And a trace of angina."

"Why don't we sit you down?" I suggest.

Teddy allows me to guide him to a seated position on the edge of the bathtub. I wet a cloth from under the sink and press it to his forehead, standing over him. It comes down to this: four pills crushed into one of the many drinks he gulped down. A weak heart. Teddy is vulnerable. I kneel so our faces are level.

"You're a good one, Nadine. A good girl."

"I'm not a girl at all."

"Paul is a lucky man."

When I dab his forehead again, he takes a light hold of my wrist. I don't shake it loose.

"You know what?" I say. "Since we're alone, why don't you tell me about the night Colleen died."

He frowns. "Excuse me?"

"Colleen. My aunt."

"Your sister."

I smile. "Right. You were with her the night she died, Teddy. In the barn."

He laughs. "What gives you that idea? I wasn't even invited to that party."

"True. You showed up later, though."

Teddy shakes his head and grimaces. "Nadine. I'm not well."

"I think it was you in the barn with Colleen," I say matter-of-factly. "I know it was you." This might work. I might guide him to it, prompt the truth. "You killed her," I say.

"What? I've never killed anyone in my life."

"Then what happened?"

"This is madness, Nadine."

But Teddy makes no attempt to leave. He's sweating, dizzy. Trapped. I extract the photographs of Colleen and River from my pocket and hold them up to his face.

"Quite the collection you have," I say. "There are dozens of these."

"You broke into my house? My safe? You're fucking crazy."

"Technically it's my house. *My* safe, but whatever. Why don't you just tell me what happened."

He laughs. "Fuck you."

"River confessed, you know. Before the overdose. She told Isobel everything. I've only learned this today. She named you."

A big lie, a gamble that dangles my own daughter. My heart races.

"Whatever it is you do, Teddy," I continue. "Assaulting girls? Pimping them out? It ends here. It's over. I'm on to you."

Teddy slides from the edge of the bathtub to the floor.

"You should just confess," I say. "Before things get a lot worse for you."

"There's nothing to confess."

"They're girls." I hold the photo of Colleen up again. "Colleen was just a girl."

"You call them girls, but sometimes . . ." He trails off, wiping the sweat from his forehead. "Nadine? I might throw up."

I move the garbage can next to him.

"I need you to tell me what happened, Teddy. She was innocent."

"Jesus," he says. "You think Colleen was innocent? You don't know a thing about her. She was a piece of work. A junkie. Always asking for freebies."

"Freebies?"

"For drugs. For money. She loved a good shakedown."

"She was fifteen," I say.

"Do you know how many boys she fucked for money?"

"Boys. Including you?"

He cocks his head but doesn't speak.

I blink hard. "You were with her when she died. I saw you. I remember now. I could admit that I withheld the truth all those years ago because I was ten. I was a scared little girl. And with all these photos, it's all quite damning, isn't it? The photos jogged my memory."

I lower myself and brush a sweaty strand of hair from his forehead. This show of tenderness might break me. What choice do I have but to coax him?

"Teddy? You can tell me."

"Your fucking sister, she attacked me!" He waves a weak hand. "We were up in that fucking loft. She was pushing me. Scratching at me. She wanted more money. She was accusing me of withholding. She was crazed. On a bad trip."

"On drugs that you gave her?"

"You can paint it whatever way you want, but I had to defend myself. And she stumbled backward and fell thirty feet through the trapdoor. The hay had been baled. She landed on the hard floor. I got down there and she wasn't moving. I dragged her over to the bales, but I couldn't wake her up."

"Or you pushed her."

"I didn't push her."

"She was lying on the bales when I found her. You arranged her like that?"

"What?" Teddy's skin is clammy, ashen, his lips tinged blue. "I need an ambulance. I need help."

"Did you call an ambulance for Colleen?" I ask. "When *she* needed help?"

His face twists. "Please."

I stand and refill his water glass, placing it next to him.

"I've figured you out, Teddy. I know what you do. To young girls. Maybe it started all those years ago. Maybe Colleen was your first. But River will be your last. Were you pimping her out too? Getting her to recruit more girls for you?"

"Jesus Christ. Would you just call an—"

"We're talking about children."

There's a sudden shift in his expression. Rage. He grabs my wrist again, this time harder. "Fuck you, Nadine."

"Did you try to recruit my daughter, Teddy? Did you try to recruit Isobel?"

He laughs bitterly, locking eyes. "No. Too much of a prude, just like her mom. Nothing like her aunt Colleen."

A hot wrath overtakes me. I grab his neck and squeeze his jugular. But then Teddy lunges forward and he's on top of me, pressing my body into the cold floor tiles. He jams his mouth into my neck.

Then I remember—in the pocket of my jumpsuit. Damien's syringe. I squirm to extract it. Why do I feel so calm? Teddy's weight grows heavy. He's weak. Tired.

He's whispering, but the words are impossible to make out.

I reach around him, squeezing him tight to me while I feel behind his back for the safety on the syringe. I don't need to see it. I unlock it blindly, expertly, springing the needle free. How many times have I done this? Thousands? But always in Damien's arm or leg. I aim for the muscle just under Teddy's skull, the one closest to his carotid artery. There. A direct hit. One quick press of my thumb and the syringe is empty. The needle retracts into the safety.

He yelps, rolling off me, batting at his neck. "What the fuck?"

I sit up and crawl backward toward the toilet. Teddy stares at me from against the bathtub as he rubs at his neck, his skin so pale it looks gray.

"What did you . . ." He trails off, dizzy.

The tiny puncture made by the child-size needles we still use for Damien will be masked by Teddy's hairline. Four crushed pills. Too many drinks. A bad heart. Insulin. Teddy's eyes open again. This time, they are pleading. "I need an ambulance. Jesus Christ."

"Yes! It seems you do. I should get back to the party, though. I've been gone too long. I'll just slip out and call one for you."

"Water," he says.

His head begins to bobble. The insulin is seeping into his bloodstream. I can see the life draining from him. His breath comes in hiccups now. He slides down the tub until he's lying on the floor.

It's safe now. I can stand. I catch a glimpse of myself in the mirror. My lipstick isn't even smudged. If someone were to come downstairs and find us now, what would they see? A hostess helping a drunk guest. Nothing more.

Teddy's lost consciousness. I could try to save his life. But I won't.

"I think you're going to die, Teddy."

His eyes flutter open. "You little bitch." He tries to roll onto his side but fails.

"Please," he says to me. "Please."

"They were all children," I say. "Children. You sick fucking man."

He can't even speak now. How long have I been down here? Ten minutes? Twelve? I step outside the bathroom. The music floats down the stairs. Now what? Do I walk away? Climb my way to the kitchen? No.

I turn into my office and place the two photographs and the used syringe at the rear of the bottom drawer to dispose of later. Then I re-enter the bathroom. Teddy makes strange sounds now—gurgling. He's repeating a sound, the letter *N*. Is he trying to say my name?

A well of tears rises in me. All those young girls. River. Colleen in her green sundress, lying on that hay bale where I found her the next morning, dead. Did she understand, as Teddy took her picture in the loft, that she was soon to fall to her death? Pushed or not, he let her die. He could have been the one to save her.

Teddy isn't moving. What have I done?

I could take out my phone now. Call 911. I could. Should I? I won't.

I bend and touch my fingers to his neck. It takes some digging to locate a pulse.

T O NADINE WALSH," OUR GUEST SAYS. "To an unforgettable party. What a night!"

"Yes," I say. "What a night, indeed."

A server approaches and holds his tray aloft so I can swap out my empty champagne flute. On perfect cue, the band starts on a familiar song. My position near the door offers me an excellent vantage of the party. All the guests. More than a hundred of them. It's midnight, and it seems that few have left.

I smile at no one in particular. My throat hurts. All I need is the appearance of calm. Of poise. I need Paul. I scan and find him at the far end of the dance floor, laughing in chatter with one of his younger colleagues. His gaze falls my way. At once he sees me, registers my face, excuses himself, and walks over.

"Is everything okay?" he asks.

"I don't know where Damien has gone," I say, a partial lie. "I really don't want to make a scene."

"Do you want me to do a sweep?"

"Would you?"

"I'm on it."

My mouth is dry, my face surely flushed, my hands still shaking. But Paul detects nothing. He assumes only concern for my son. He kisses my cheek and disappears into the house. I take a deep breath then cut between the tables laid out on the lawn. The flowers Margot and I picked for the centerpieces this afternoon are wilting in their vases. The white tablecloths are stained with spilled drinks.

"Nadine!"

Daphne calls me to the table where she and Lionel sit. "We just heard from the sitter," she says. "Baby's awake. I think we have to go."

I look to my watch. "You almost made it to midnight. That's quite the feat."

"It feels like it," she says.

"Why don't I collect the supplies in the den?" Lionel offers. "You two can say your goodbyes."

I nod and return Lionel's smile. Daphne taps under her eyes.

"Run a finger under yours," she says. "You've got a touch of wayward mascara."

I do.

"Thank you," I say.

With a wave goodbye to Daphne, I set off. The guests have removed their jackets and high heels, loosened their ties. Some are drunk. A few still dance. Everyone I pass smiles at me, offers me a raised glass or reaches for my arm to squeeze and comment on the loveliness of the night. I laugh at a few jokes. I make a few myself. I'm barely listening to one woman rattle on about the catering when I notice Isobel and Margot standing among the climbing hydrangeas at the back of the garden, absorbed by something on Isobel's phone.

I feel a stab in my chest. A deep, deep stab. It comes down to her, doesn't it? To Isobel? To Damien. To Margot. To my mother and Paul. To the people I love.

Inside, Paul is surely making his way through our house, top to bottom. He'll follow the trajectory he always does when searching for something: go to the obvious place first. I know he'll start upstairs in Damien's room. He'll open every door and closet, peer behind every corner as if he were looking for a lost shoe. He won't find Damien—I know he won't—and eventually, he'll take the back stairs to the basement. He'll check my office and the TV room. He'll peer into the bathroom. Maybe he'll spot the feet first. Dress shoes, toes up. He'll pause, flummoxed. Why is someone lying down on our basement bathroom floor?

Then he'll realize it's him. Teddy. Dead.

Paul, ever steady, will check for a pulse and note the coolness of the skin. He'll stand in the bathroom for a moment, breathing to stem the tide of panic, debating his next move with a lawyer's eye to outcome. He won't call 911 right away. He'll find me first, check his gut with his wife. Then, we'll call together.

The police and paramedics will arrive. Possibly the coroner too. The basement will be sealed off, the body carted out via the side door to an ambulance waiting on the street.

I don't notice my mother approaching until she flanks me. She's smiling. Drunk.

"Did I ruin your party?" she asks me with a hint of slur. "With my little speech?"

"It's *your* party," I say. "And no, you didn't."

I nudge her. She's gathering herself, working to avoid tears.

"I wanted to tell you everything," she says finally, a crack in her voice. "For years. There was just . . . a lot of shame. I just, I didn't—"

"Mom," I say. "It's okay. I understand. You held on to a secret for so long that it started to feel like the truth."

My mother looks to the sky and releases a long breath. "That's exactly it. Why are you so smart?"

"We can talk about it tomorrow," I say. "Or the next day. But not now, okay?"

"But will you forgive me?"

"I already have."

Marilyn rests her head on my shoulder. It takes all my might not to turn back to the house, to watch for Paul. But every sliver of body language matters now. I need to appear normal, just a hostess comforting her drunk mother and saying goodbye to her guests. I lock eyes with a random guest and smile, lift my empty glass in cheers. My mother pulls away from me first.

"So many people," she says. "Who the fuck are all these people?"

"Do me a favor." I hand her my glass. "Fetch me another drink?"

"My pleasure. I'll be right back."

I watch as my mother meanders around the tables, leaning into guests and air-kissing the cheeks presented to her. She points back to me and makes a drinking gesture. I laugh and wave at the woman she's speaking to, a friend from her yoga circle. My eyes fall to the patio doors. No sign of Paul. Yet.

How much time has passed since I came upstairs from the basement, since Paul left in search? The band still plays. The caterers are busy clearing glasses. Any minute now, Paul will appear. Later, murmurs will sweep through the crowd. *An ambulance has been called!* Someone is hurt! No. *Dead.* Someone is dead! The guests will be both aghast and thrilled, absorbing every detail they can. My mother will try to soothe anyone who appears rattled. Seymour will be the one most shocked when the identity of the dead man is revealed.

The odds of getting away with it? I have no choice but to take them.

Eventually, the guests will go home. Eventually, they'll rule his death an accident. What else could it have been? There's no trauma to the body, no injury or wound. They'll find a common sedative in his system, an overload of alcohol. Never a good mix. The insulin absorbed into the throb of his carotid artery will have vanished into his bloodstream, undetectable. Even if Teddy's secrets are eventually uncovered, even if Margot or anyone else asks me some pointed questions, the facts of his death will remain. A sickly heart, overloaded, stopped beating.

To the guests, these specifics won't even matter. They'll tell and retell the story, shaping it however they see fit. *Did you hear about the death at Marilyn Millay's birthday party? The neighbor's body was carted out of their basement on a gurney, covered in a sheet. It was the hostess's husband who found him. He'd been drinking all night. Dancing. I hear he had a bad heart.* Eventually, their versions will conflict in ways big and small. They'll contradict each other, argue over the details. No one will be sure of the truth. Of what really happened tonight. Not even me.

"Nadine!"

Margot calls me over. Isobel smiles widely next to her, but as I approach, I see that my daughter's eyes are brimmed with tears. She grips her phone.

"Why are you crying, my darling?" I say to Isobel.

"It's okay," Margot says. "She's happy!"

Isobel hands me her phone so I can read a text message. It's from Sherry.

Look who's awake, it reads.

There's a photograph attached to the message—River in her hospital bed. Her eyes are open and focused on the camera. She even appears to be smiling despite the tube jutting out of her mouth.

"My goodness," I say. "How incredible!"

I turn in search of Seymour. There he is, his face lit up as he stares at his own phone. He's laughing, wiping his eyes. He looks up and notices me. I lift my hands in prayer then give him a thumbs-up.

I have to go, he mouths.

Yes, yes. He does.

Thank you.

I nod in response.

"Is it a miracle?" Isobel asks, her voice almost pleading. "It feels like it's a miracle."

"It is," I say.

"It definitely is," Margot adds.

"What's a miracle?" Marilyn asks on approach. She hands me a fresh flute of champagne.

I tilt the phone so my mother can see the picture. She squints then gasps, immediately gathering Isobel and Margot into her arms. Their joy makes me want to cry. What a relief for my precious Isobel. I hear it in her laughter, a lightness that's been absent for too long. The three of them stumble and jump, their arms entwined. I want to join them, but I can't. Not yet. I feel stuck in place. Afraid. When I glance to the patio doors, there stands Paul. He's frowning and scanning the yard. Searching, no doubt, for me.

Time is so strange. Everything can change in an instant. One day

286

can carry the weight of a whole life. To think of those photos of River and Colleen now hidden in my office until I can properly dispose of them. The pain, the fear they must have felt.

In the photo on Isobel's phone, River's hand is laid across her chest, her pale and delicate fingers fanned open over her hospital gown. Ever since River and Isobel were girls, they've used a pat on the heart as their code. It marks their hellos and goodbyes, their shows of solidarity and reassurance. A hand to the heart. A simple signal of a love and devotion between two young friends. We should all be so lucky.

"Come," my mother says. "Come here!"

"Yeah, Mom. Give us a hug."

But I stand back. I can hear Paul now. He's calling my name. He's approaching.

It's not good, he'll whisper, ushering me away. *Something's happened.*

He'll need me to decide what to do. I'll feign shock, then take control. Fate has already intervened. From here, I'll do whatever needs to be done.

But before he reaches me, I set down my champagne on a nearby table. I put my hand to my chest to mimic River. Isobel does the same, then Margot. Then, noticing us all, my mother does too. What matters more than protecting those we love? Nothing. Isobel smiles at me and extends her hand. I step forward and disappear into their fold.

Acknowledgments

I love writing. Writing is hard. Harder still over the past three years with a pandemic and lots of other upheaval in place. I'm so grateful to the many people who've showed me so much care and support as I wrapped the Still series and started on this new adventure in *A Death at the Party*.

I begin with an enormous thank-you to the entire team at Transatlantic Agency for their incredible commitment to this novel, as well as their continued work to bring the Still books to the wider world. Samantha Haywood is the best of the best, both as an agent and advocate, and as a friendly and thoughtful ear for her writers. My gratitude also to Devon Halliday for her thoughtful notes on an early draft. Thank you also to Erin Haskett and her team at Lark Productions for their committed efforts to bringing my novels to life on-screen.

I'm so grateful to everyone at Simon & Schuster Canada for championing this very different book after the Still series closed. There is no better team than yours. Nita Pronovost, I marvel at your skills and your optimism, and I value our collaboration and friendship so much. Kevin Hanson has believed in me from the very beginning, and I've been so lucky to keep working with Adria Iwasutiak, Felicia Quon,

Natasha Tsakiris, Karen Silva, Melanie Pederson, Kaitlyn Lonnee, Mackenzie Croft, David Millar, Sarah St. Pierre, Janie Yoon, and the rest of the team.

To all booksellers who work so tirelessly to bring our novels to the world, but especially to Sarah Pietroski at my favorite local A Novel Spot Books, to Martha Sharpe at Flying Books, and to the wonderful staff at Bookmark in Charlottetown, PEI.

To my hockey family on the Eagles and the Sharks, especially to those who give us so (so, so!) many hours of their time to coach my sons . . . Anthony Gucciardi, John Germain, Natasha Hughes, Derek Allen, Chris Congram, Ted Eng, Scott Housken, and Brad Semotiuk. And to my fellow coaches, Riyaz Deshmukh, Patrick Dunphy, Julian Binavince, Patrick Zerebecki, and Caroline Godfrey . . . Years from now, I will think back to our laughs on the bench, our "meetings," our encyclopedia-length text threads, and our friendship as the best part of this whole coaching gig. I love you guys.

To the friends old and new, most of all Mariska Gatha, Kendall Anderson, Natasha Hughes (again!), Tamara Nedd-Roderique, my character namesake Nadine Gucciardi, Arja Pennanen-Lytle, Carmen Watkins, Sarah Faber, Claire Tacon, Christine Dovey, Doug Stewart, Angie Gucciardi, and Ida Bianchi. To Hollis Hopkins for being my other half, and to Jenna King, Aviva Armour-Ostroff, and Tara Samuel for holding me up always. To Elisa Schwarz, who's been my friend since we were babies and who amazes me every day with her humor and resilience.

To Steve Goldbloom, a former student from decades ago (I'm aging myself), now a peer and friend. Who knew? It's so fun to get to work with you and to suffer through the Toronto Maple Leafs fandom with you.

For my community and family on Prince Edward Island, where we've been so profoundly lucky to rebuild our roots in the past few years. To our dear friends and neighbors in Rustico, especially Mariska Gatha & Jeff Beer and Henry & Matilda, Janny Gatha, Blair & Andrea Trowbridge and Norah & Thea, Lise Buote, Pam and Allan Tierney, Katherine & Alan Morrow, Rowena & Mike Lawlor, Gerri & Joe Corcoran (and Lori and family!), Camren Chamberlain & Wren Eekma, Andrea Robinson & Patrick Kiely, Bill & Alana Coleman, and Freda Gallant.

I am forever thankful for my parents, Dick and Marilyn Flynn; my sisters, Bridget Flynn and Katie Flynn; and my in-laws, Beth Boyden, Jamie Boyden, Mark McQuillan, and Chris Van Dyke. To my nieces and nephews, Jack Boyden, Charlotte Boyden, Jed Van Dyke, Stuart Boyden, Peter McQuillan, Margot Van Dyke, Luke Boyden, Sean McQuillan, and Owen McQuillan—I am so proud of all the amazing things you are doing. To my extended family, including Marilyn and Ernie Boyden, Mary Flynn and all the Keefes, Carraghers, Flynns, MacDonalds, Shiels, McQuillans, Van Dykes, Bradleys, Manuels, with all my love. To Tim and Sue Stuart, we only wish you were here to marvel in it all alongside us.

For Millie, my sweetest puppy companion.

And finally, to Flynn, Joey, Leo, and Ian for everything. The four of you are my greatest loves.

About the Author

© JOEY STUART

Amy Stuart is the #1 bestselling author of three novels, *Still Mine*, *Still Water*, and *Still Here*. Shortlisted for the Arthur Ellis Best First Novel Award and winner of the 2011 Writers' Union of Canada Short Prose Competition, Amy is the founder of Writerscape, an online community for hopeful and emerging writers. Amy lives in Toronto with her husband and their three sons. Connect with her on her website AmyStuart.ca and on Twitter @AmyFStuart.